WHEN GHOSTS COME HOME

Wiley Cash is the prize-winning and *New York Times*-bestselling author of *A Land More Kind Than Home*, *This Dark Road to Mercy* and *The Last Ballad*. Writer-in-Residence at the University of North Carolina Asheville, he lives in North Carolina with his wife and two daughters.

'A fascinating, nuanced meditation on life – both the living of it and the taking of it – in the crucible of small-town America. Wiley Cash is our guide through this maze of old secrets and fresh hurts. Take his hand, follow his lead and face the truth.' S. A. Cosby, author of *Blacktop Wasteland*

'A treatise on race in America wrapped in a family drama wrapped in a mystery . . . Cash puts his whole heart on the page with these flawed, true characters, and the reward is ours.' Therese Anne Fowler, author of *A Good Neighbourhood*

'Both a gripping murder mystery and a thoughtful exploration of systemic racism in America. The perfect novel for our present moment.' Lauren Wilkinson, author of *American Spy*

'Taut, tense, and tender – this novel hits every note. I loved it and devoured it with fury, straight to its blazing end.' Lily King

'Cash reveals in such clear prose how family and history and the threads that connect us can contain such mystery. This is a masterful example of storytelling, told by one of the most open-hearted and clear-eyed writers.' Kevin Wilson

WHEN GHOSTS COME HOME

– A NOVEL –

WILEY CASH

faber

First published in the UK in 2021
by Faber & Faber Limited
Bloomsbury House, 74–77 Great Russell Street
London WC1B 3DA

First published in the United States in 2021
by William Morrow, an imprint of HarperCollins
195 Broadway, New York, NY 10007

This export edition published in 2021

Printed and bound by CPI Group (UK) Ltd, Croydon CR0 4YY

A CIP record for this book
is available from the British Library

ISBN 978–0–571–34522–9

2 4 6 8 10 9 7 5 3 1

For Mallory, again

WHEN GHOSTS COME HOME

TUESDAY,
OCTOBER 30, 1984

CHAPTER 1

Winston did not hear it so much as feel it as it passed over their house and into the trees across the waterway. He opened his eyes into the darkness of the bedroom. Had he been sleeping? He'd certainly been dreaming. If not dreaming, at least his mind had been seeing the same thing he'd seen over the course of so many nights. He blinked, rubbed his eyes. When he looked over at Marie, she was already sitting up in bed beside him, her sunken cheeks and wisps of graying hair tinged red by the glowing numbers of the alarm clock on her bedside table. *Her cancer and sadness are wasting her,* Winston thought, and then he knew the same was true for him. Just that morning Marie had forced him onto the scale after he pushed his eggs and sausage around on his plate. "One sixty-four?" she'd said. "Who's got cancer, you or me?"

Now, in bed, she looked at him as if terrified of what had woken them.

"Did you hear that?" she asked.

"I did," Winston said. He unfolded the covers off his body, and then he sat up and put his feet on the floor.

"It sounded like an airplane."

"It did," Winston said.

"But it's too late for a plane."

Winston turned and looked past Marie toward the alarm clock. It read 3:18 a.m. "It is late," he said.

"It sounded like it came in low," she said. "I haven't ever heard one come in like that before. And never this late."

Winston reached behind him and placed his palms flat against his back. His fingertips explored the knobbiness of his spine, and his thumbs closed around the soft skin on his sides that Marie liked to pinch when telling him he needed to gain weight. He stretched and sighed, curled his toes against the carpet. Then he stood and walked to the back window that looked out on the waterway. The county's tiny municipal airport sat through the trees on the other side of the water. He parted the aluminum blinds and peered out, half-expecting to find fiery wreckage blazing through the grass and disappearing in a gathering plume of smoke at the water's edge. But what he found when he looked out the window was what he always found: the dark, empty backyard; the inky black roll of the water; the thin, ghostly silhouettes of pine trees.

Marie clicked on her lamp. The window became a mirror, and Winston found himself staring into his own eyes.

"Do you see anything?" Marie asked.

"Not now I don't," he said.

"Sorry," she said. She turned off the light, but Winston had already let the blinds close. He reached for his pants where he had left them folded across the back of Marie's reading chair, and he stepped into them and tucked his T-shirt inside the waist.

"Where are you going?" Marie asked.

"Out there," he said. "To the airport."

"Why?"

"To have a look around. To figure out what we just heard."

"There's no sense in you going out there this late," she said. "Send somebody else."

"Nobody else this close," he said, which was true, meaning it was at least true enough to say. It was late October now. Beach season was over. Just about all the tourists had gone home. The county had slashed budgets back in July, and Winston had had to limit night shifts by assigning three officers to patrol the county while keeping someone on call at home and someone on dispatch at the office. Tonight was his night on call, even if dispatch hadn't called him yet.

"Send Glenn," Marie said.

"Glenn's not on call," he said. "And I don't think he's on patrol tonight. I *am* on call, and I'm right here."

"I don't want you to go. It's too late."

"Well, it's my job," Winston said. "At least it's my job until they vote me out next week." He smiled at Marie, then he turned toward the dresser and pulled a pair of socks from his top drawer.

"Keep talking all hangdog like that and they will vote you out," she said. "And if you keep going on these calls in the middle of the night, I'll start campaigning against you."

Winston lowered himself into her reading chair. He put his socks on. "You'd side with my political enemies out of spite?" he asked. "I didn't know you had it in you, Marie Barnes."

"Well, cancer can't take everything from a girl," she said. "Believe it or not."

"Now look who's talking hangdog," he said. He stood up and walked to her side of the bed. He bent toward her and cupped his hand under her chin, then he lifted her face to his and leaned in for a kiss. "I'll be right back," he said. "Go back to sleep, honey. You won't even know I'm gone."

"I always know when you're gone," Marie said. "Forty years now, and I always know when you're gone."

"Well, I won't be gone long," he said.

"You've been saying that for forty years."

"If you take care of yourself and go back to sleep then I'll be able to say it for forty more."

"I just don't want to be—" But she stopped and looked away

from him. The room fell into silence, and Winston would swear that he could hear the distant lap of the waterway outside their windows. Or maybe it was the sound of the ticking clock he sometimes heard in his mind. Marie looked back at him after a moment. "I just can't stop thinking about Colleen," she finally said. "I wish she'd call us back."

"I know, honey," he said. He fought the urge to break his gaze from hers, to drop his chin to his chest. He considered sitting down on the bed beside her, but he knew that doing so would delay his leaving even longer. "I know. Maybe she'll call tomorrow. If not, we'll call her. Maybe we can try getting ahold of Scott at work, ask him how she's doing." He'd said all of these things many times since he and Marie had come home from Texas, and he was tired of saying them, but he knew that, when it came to their daughter, Marie needed to hear certain things, and he knew that it was his job to say them.

For Winston, what had been a charming bedside scene—a scene of Marie worried over him in the middle of the night—had devolved into a kind of repulsion at Marie's mentioning their daughter's name. Winston's grief for Colleen was caustic, and he knew it had turned poisonous, infecting his heart and hardening it against Marie's own particular brand of grief and her need to share it with him. Unlike Marie, Winston's sadness was a thing he could bear only when he was alone.

He reached for her, held her fingers with the tips of his, gave her hand a little shake.

"We'll call the house again tomorrow," he said. "And then we'll get ahold of Scott at work if we need to."

Marie smiled a weak smile and lowered herself to her pillow. She closed her eyes, and Winston kissed her forehead again. He stood up straight and looked down at her. He watched her turn away from him and pull the covers up over her shoulders.

When the telephone rang on the dresser across the bedroom, Winston jumped like he'd heard a slammed door or a gunshot. Marie didn't even stir. "I bet that's Rudy," she said.

"I bet you're right," Winston said, trying to hide the breathless surprise in his voice. "There's my call." He left the bedroom for the hallway and took the stairs down to the kitchen, where the telephone was still ringing. He picked it up.

"Calls are coming in about some sort of noise out at the airport," Rudy said. "Sounds like it might be a plane crash."

"We heard it too," Winston said. "I was about to call in and tell you I'm headed out that way."

"You want backup?" Rudy asked, his voice as raspy and whispery as it always was. Winston knew Rudy smoked cigarettes and drank coffee in the dispatch room all night long during his shifts, but Rudy was the best they'd ever had, and he'd work the night shift when no one else wanted to, so Winston was willing to let Rudy's smoking slide.

"No," Winston said. "No sense in waking up somebody who's not already awake or pulling somebody else off patrol."

"All right, Sheriff," Rudy said. "Call if you need something."

Winston found his boots in the laundry room. He took his jacket from the hall closet and slipped it on, unlocked the safe in the back of the closet, and removed his pistol and holster. He lifted his walkie-talkie from the shelf above him and turned it on, its low white hiss breaking the silence of the quiet house.

Once he had his gear, Winston stood at the bottom of the stairs by the front door, listening for something, but for what he did not know.

"Marie," he said. His voice escaped his throat in a whisper. "Marie," he said again, "I'll be right back."

There was no sound from upstairs. The silence of the house encircled him, but Winston knew that Marie was awake, her eyes closed, her ears trying to do the same. He could almost feel her heart beating from where he stood at the front door, and for a moment he considered going back upstairs and touching her one last time, but he unlocked the front door, opened it, and stepped out into the night instead.

The black sky and its pinpricked canopy of stars pressed down on Winston as if he could reach up and push it away. The air was cool and heavy, and he could smell the trees—pines, yaupons, oaks—the moss that hung from them, the brackish air coming from the waterway behind him, the salty tang of the ocean on the other side of the island. The world was near silent, but he could hear the water moving.

Winston was halfway down the gravel walk when he looked up to find that Marie's burgundy Regal was parked behind the cruiser. Instead of taking the time to move it he climbed inside Marie's car and started the engine. The radio came on, a late-night talking head discussing Mondale's slim chances against Reagan. Winston clicked the radio off and turned to back Marie's car out of the driveway.

On the passenger's seat were the posters and flyers that Marie had picked up that afternoon in Southport, each one featuring a photograph of a younger version of Winston, the photograph accompanied by the phrase *Vote for a man you can trust*. He had been forty-eight years old the first time he had run for sheriff, and now he was sixty, almost twenty years older than his opponent. Something about seeing his young face and thinking about the even younger face of Bradley Frye—the man who would probably defeat him—embarrassed Winston.

Bradley Frye was the son of a local developer named Everett Frye, who'd spent decades building up this part of the North Carolina coast. Condominiums, shopping centers, expensive vacation houses. Now that the elder Frye was dead, his son seemed hell-bent on clear-cutting swaths of land and stamping out track homes and new developments on the sandy, swampy soil where forests and wetlands had sat just days before. Winston figured Bradley Frye was either making a fortune or driving himself into unimaginable debt. Regardless, he now had his sights set on local government, beginning with the sheriff's office. Although he'd gained some small amount of notoriety as a basketball player at Brunswick County High School in the late 1950s, Frye had never left the county after graduation. In his twenties he set about furthering his name by showing up drunk and looking for girls at high school parties, and when county schools integrated in the late 1960s and early '70s, Winston knew Frye as one of the local boys who'd load up in trucks to harass and beat up Black students protesting just up the road in Wilmington. In the years since, Frye had tried to soften the perception that people had of him—a good ol' boy with a rich daddy who could afford to play nationalist—by wearing golf shirts, khaki pants, and work boots while on job sites. And now forty-one-year-old Bradley Frye was the first challenger Winston had faced in nearly twelve years as sheriff, and something about seeing his own much younger face on the campaign posters in Marie's car told Winston that he was probably going to lose. Bradley Frye had used his inheritance to make a name for himself as a businessman, and over the summer he'd papered the county with billboards, yard signs, newspaper ads, and even a television commercial. The election was just a week away, and Winston knew it was all coming down to money; Bradley Frye had it, and Winston didn't, and that made him even more afraid of losing, especially when he considered what the loss of their income and health insurance would mean for Marie.

He'd been worried about her being too tired to pick up the posters and flyers after her treatment, and he'd asked her not to do it, but he wondered now if he'd only been afraid to continue involving her in what he had come to believe was a losing venture. He felt shame creep over him, and he tried his best to push it down and away from him in the same manner he'd learned to vanquish his grief and fear.

But those things—shame and grief and fear—still overtook him sometimes and fell upon him like a weight that wanted to remind him of its heaviness at the very moment he forgot to stoop beneath it. He found that the weight kept him hidden from people, certainly from Marie and Colleen. From the moment his daughter was born, Winston had wanted to make himself known to her in ways his father had never made himself known to Winston, but he knew he had failed because at that very moment he and Colleen were strangers to one another, all of them—Marie included—alone and lonely in their pain.

It seemed cruel and ironic, but over the past few years Winston had dreamed of himself as his father, a man who'd left this world when he was only seventy-two. If Winston's lifetime were to roll along the same track as his father's, that would mean he now had twelve years left, which on some days seemed like too much time, and on other days seemed like not nearly enough.

Winston had a habit, each year around his birthday, of trying to conjure his father's face at that same age. How old did that man seem in his mind's eye? Older than Winston, for certain. Probably wiser too.

Sometimes, in his quiet moments, Winston's mind would flash back to the last days at his father's bedside. His parents had lived their whole lives in the house he'd grown up in at the end of an unpaved, wooded road in a town called Gastonia on the other side of North Carolina. The house had sat at the base of Crowder's Mountain, and while his father was dying Winston and his younger brother had set up a hospital bed in his parents' bedroom by a picture window that looked out over the trees. It had been fall, an October very much like this one, in fact, and they had left the windows open to allow the scents of sweat and medicine and soiled clothes and bedding to leak from the sickroom out into the chilly world. But something else had happened: the comforting rot and waste and piney reek of the forest had found its way inside, so much so that for the rest of Winston's life, whenever he smelled pine, he was forced to confront the loss of his father with the clean, heavy nostalgia of a forest doing its work to live and die and live again.

But he still had that dream of being his father, and he'd had it again tonight before the sound he and Marie had heard had woken them both. In the dream, his father is in the hospital bed back in their house in Gastonia, his hands clenched around the sheet where it is pulled up to his chest. Winston is watching his father sleep and drift toward death, his dry tongue occasionally moving across his dry lips. Winston reaches for a cloth on the bedside table and dampens it with water. He passes the wet cloth over his father's mouth. In the dream, Winston looks down at his own hands and sees his father's, and then he realizes his hands are closed around the sheet, and he is lying in his father's sickbed, and he is dying alone.

Would Colleen sit at his bedside like he'd sat at his father's? Winston wondered if the old man had cared for him as much as Winston cared for his daughter. Surely he did, but it seemed impossible to Winston, impossible that his own father had been interested in or capable of feeling this love that could only be described as debilitating. It embarrassed him to think of his father loving him that much. And why was he thinking of it? What was he afraid of on these nights when he saw his father's hands as his own? Colleen sitting or not sitting by his bedside, swabbing or not swabbing his chapped lips with cool water? Was he afraid of the hole his passing might leave in her life?

Colleen was just twenty-six, but she had already lost a child, Winston and Marie landing in Dallas too late to even lay eyes on his body. What do they even do with a baby that never drew breath? They hadn't attended a funeral, and Colleen had never mentioned one. He'd been too afraid to ask her; he didn't know if Marie had asked her, and he was ashamed of that. He'd spent so many nights since lying in bed, hurting for Colleen and her lost child, his grandson. Now the thought of his or Marie's passing as compounding that hurt was too much for him, and for a moment he found himself wishing he and Marie had never had Colleen, had not created this life they would hurt for, this life that would hurt for them in return.

Jesus Christ, Winston, he thought, *why are you even thinking about this right now?* Was it Colleen's losing the baby? Was it Marie's being sick again, this time worse than before? Or was it the plane they'd heard—or at least the plane they thought they'd heard? The specter of a fiery crash flashed through Winston's mind with no sound, only the images of flames and the spinning down of huge engines. *But it was just an airplane coming in low,* he thought. *Or a dream.* Maybe he and Marie had dreamed the same thing, and he would arrive at the dark airport and find it just as quiet and empty as his side of the bed back home.

THE DAY BEFORE Halloween and not as cold as it would be, but cold enough to send the vacationers scrambling back to work and to school and to their lives somewhere outside Oak Island. Even the soft-spoken, unassuming Canadians—the ones who hadn't headed as far south as Myrtle Beach, whose wives had combed the autumn beaches in one-piece bathing suits while looking for sand dollars, and whose husbands had kept the municipal golf course open into the middle of the month—had all gone home.

The island, thirteen miles long and four miles wide at its widest and sparsely dotted with old single-family homes, fishing shacks, vacation houses, and trailers, was heavily wooded and quiet. It ran east to west off the southeastern elbow of North Carolina. To people who lived there, it felt like a place that had either gone undiscovered or had been forgotten by the rest of the state, that feeling growing so strong as to be nearly palpable as the island changed seasons and a blanket of unperturbed silence settled over it. As fall turned toward winter, the island always seemed to grow smaller, more remote, more insular.

There was no clock in Marie's car, and Winston had forgotten his watch where he usually left it beside his wallet and keys on the counter, but it was nearing 4:00 a.m. by the time he headed east down Oak Island Drive. Most of the businesses—a fudge shop, a T-shirt store, a pancake house, all the motels—had been shuttered for the off-season. The few places that had remained open for the winter had been closed for hours. After he and Marie had left Gastonia in 1963 and moved to Oak Island, they had joked that the island rolled up its sidewalks at 6:00 p.m., which was ironic only because there were no sidewalks. Winston thought then and he still thought now that the island would make an ideal place for someone to hide, and perhaps that's what he'd been doing all these years.

As he drove across the bridge above the waterway, Winston watched the light from the Caswell Beach lighthouse at the far eastern end of the island strafe the waterway in perfect increments. It flashed in his rearview mirror, and for a moment he could both see and feel its light in his eyes. When Marie's car climbed to the top of the bridge, the beacon light from the tiny airport appeared through the distant trees on his left. He had been at this exact spot on the bridge at night what must have been a million times over the years, and each time he felt like he was leaving the bright gleam of the lighthouse for the tiny spot of the beacon light, a light that was overwhelmed by the darkness of the mainland that waited for him in the woods across the water.

When Colleen was a little girl, both when they reached the apex of this bridge and the even taller and more magnificent drawbridge that spanned the Cape Fear River, her voice would come from the backseat, asking, "What would happen if we fell from here?" and Winston would consider what would cause someone to topple from such a height to the water below. Suicide? A vehicle fire? A bridge collapse? He pictured himself and Colleen holding hands and climbing over the guardrail before leaping into the still waters. No matter how many times she asked, he always answered her question with the same response: "I would save you."

But as she grew older her questions became more particular: "What would happen if we drove off the bridge?" or "What would happen if our car flipped over the side?" The more questions she asked, the more her fear became corporeal, and she began to construct detailed stories of the tragedies that would await them. Winston always knew the answers to the questions she had, because he had trained—made all his deputies train, as a matter of fact—for water rescues. The county was dotted with water: lakes, canals, creeks, and waterways disguised as rivers. They had encountered submerged vehicles before, and he'd pictured himself seat-belted into the driver's seat of a car upside down underwater, Colleen in the backseat. There would be about thirty seconds before the interior filled with water. He would remove his seat belt, reach back, and do the same to Colleen's. He would pull her into the front seat, and, as water poured into the car, he would use the spring-triggered pin on his key chain (he made Marie and all his deputies carry them) to break the window and climb out. He would remind himself to follow the bubbles to the surface, Colleen clutched in his arms, his eyes searching for the light above him while his lungs waited for air.

But he didn't explain all of this to Colleen when they passed over bridges during her childhood. Instead, he would look at her in the rearview mirror when she was young enough to sit in the backseat, or he would turn his head to look at her when she was old enough to sit beside him, the water through her window stretching out below them beneath the bridge, and he would always say the same thing: "Don't look down, don't look back. Just look where we're going."

WHEN WINSTON PULLED Marie's car into the otherwise empty gravel parking lot at the airport, the only thing he found waiting for him was a two-door white Datsun with North Carolina plates. It surprised him to find a car parked here this late, but he wasn't concerned. Perhaps it had broken down on Long Beach Road and someone had helped the driver push it into the lot before giving them a ride home. Perhaps someone had parked it here before piloting a private jet, although, given the make of the car, that seemed unlikely. Perhaps it was just abandoned.

He was not driving his cruiser so he did not have his standard-issue flashlight, but he cupped his hands around the Datsun's driver's-side window and peered into the car's interior. There was nothing to see aside from a crumpled pack of crackers on the passenger's seat, an open cassette case of Michael Jackson's *Thriller* on the center console, and an empty Styrofoam cup of what looked to have been coffee resting beside it. A child's seat was installed in the backseat, and an unzipped gym bag rested beside it, but from what Winston could see through the window it didn't hold anything interesting. This car could have belonged to Colleen or certainly to someone her age, and the contents revealed no great clues as to who owned it or why it was parked in an empty airport parking lot in the middle of the night.

Winston took his walkie-talkie from his belt and radioed Rudy.

"How's it look out there?" Rudy asked.

"Quiet," Winston said. "But there's a vehicle in the lot. If you'd run the plate for me."

"Of course," he said.

Winston stepped around to the back of the car and read out the license plate.

"Back in a second," Rudy said.

Winston slipped the walkie-talkie onto his belt and walked around to the front of the car. He folded his arms across his chest and leaned against the Datsun's fender. He looked toward the trees on the other side of the runway, his eyes searching for movement or a beam of light or whatever it was that could have made the sound that had woken him and Marie, but there didn't seem to be anything to see. His nose caught the cool, swampy scent of the waterway, just a mile or so to the south, and he thought of Marie on the other side of the water, lying awake in bed and waiting to hear the noise of his keys turning the lock on the front door. He thought of the sound they'd heard that had jolted them from sleep; the way it seemed to vibrate along the roof of the house, the deep hum it had sent through his body. He didn't know what else to do while he waited to hear back from Rudy, so he set off across the grass-covered field toward the runway.

THE LOT WHERE Winston waited sat closest to the south end of the runway, where two white lights marked either side of the landing strip, and Winston knew that if what they'd heard was an airplane then this was where it had touched down. The runway was made of grass—it would not be paved for a couple more years—and it was useless to search it for tracks that this potential airplane or any other may have left behind. The expanse of runway stretched ahead of him toward a stand of pine trees that rose out of the dark night a couple thousand feet ahead. Another set of lights marked the middle of the runway on either side, and a third set illuminated its northern end, but these lights were designed to be seen from the air, not from below. The sun would be up in a matter of hours, but

Winston didn't want to wait for the sun. He knew that if something was hiding from him there at the end of the runway he would have to go there to find it.

He nearly jumped when his walkie-talkie crackled to life with the sound of Rudy's voice.

"Got it," he said.

Winston slipped the radio from his belt and held it to his mouth. "Go ahead."

"It's a 1978 Datsun registered to a Rodney Edward Bellamy. Want his birth date and address?"

"Hang on to them. Won't do me any good out here," Winston said, not because he didn't need the information, but because he already knew it. Rodney Bellamy had gone to school with Colleen. He was the son of Ed Bellamy, one of the only Black teachers in Brunswick County, and one of the people who'd stood up against harassment and violence during school integration. Bellamy was a history teacher, but he was also a de facto civil rights leader, and he and Winston had worked together just as many times as they'd butted heads. A decade before, Ed had served as the face of integration in the county schools, and Winston had done everything he could to ensure that the county didn't have the kind of violence that Wilmington had experienced, but of course there was violence. Winston couldn't stop it all, especially when he knew that half his deputies hadn't wanted their own kids sitting alongside Black children, and they especially didn't want men like Ed Bellamy explaining the law to them.

Winston agreed with the stances Bellamy had taken over the years. But he also knew the importance, especially in a place like Brunswick County, of walking that fine line of legal authority and cultural memory. Ed Bellamy understood it too, meaning he understood that what people like Winston believed in private and what they were willing to say in public were not always the same thing.

Ed Bellamy was bold and outspoken because he believed he had to be to get things done. Winston was deliberate and careful for the exact same reason.

"Owner lives over in the Grove," Rudy said.

"Yep," Winston said. "Thanks, Rudy."

He slipped the walkie-talkie back onto his belt and then he set off toward the end of the runway, the sound of his footsteps falling silently on the ground beneath him.

Later, when he would think back on this moment, Winston would realize that he had been able to sense the enormity of the airplane before he even arrived and saw it for the first time. It sat sideways at the very end of the runway. Its silvery body was perhaps twenty yards long, and its wingspan easily thirty. Up close, it shimmered beneath the faint moonlight like a mirror, the two huge propellers on either wing stilled like closed eyes, as if the airplane had been sleeping when Winston found it, the cargo doors on its right side thrown open like a breathing mouth that sucked in air. Winston did not know much about airplanes aside from his brief brushes with them while serving in Korea, but he knew this airplane was old—perhaps a World War II relic—and that it had been too large for this runway, and that was why it sat in the position it did, a quarter of the way into a full turn that the pilot must have made to keep it from plunging into the trees just beyond the runway's end, the rear landing gear snapped in half and the tail resting awkwardly on the ground.

Winston unholstered his pistol and stood with it down by his side.

"Hello!" he called. He waited, but all he could hear was what seemed like the sharp, tinny silence of the airplane's presence. "Anybody in there?"

He only raised his gun when the bouncing beam of a flashlight caught his eye. Someone was coming across the grassy field from the parking lot on his right. Winston turned in that direction, and that's when his eyes fell on the body of a Black man lying on the grass alongside the runway. In the scattered beam of the approaching light, Winston saw that the front of the man's shirt had been blown wide open and his chest was dark and damp with blood. The man's eyes were open, but it was clear to Winston that he was dead.

He trained his pistol on the approaching flashlight, and he wondered who had shot the man on the ground in front of him, wondered if that same person was approaching him now. He was surprised by the night's turn of events, but in that moment nothing in him was scared. He was simply ready.

Behind the beam of the flashlight, Winston was able to make out the darkened face of thirty-four-year-old Captain Glenn Haste. He'd worked for the sheriff's department for almost thirteen years, and during that time Winston had never seen Glenn's face reveal an ounce of fear, but now his eyes were struck with panic. Winston lowered his pistol, allowed himself to exhale. He realized that his hands were shaking.

"Jesus, Glenn," he said. "I almost shot you."

"Well, Sheriff, I'm glad you didn't." Glenn lowered his eyes and his flashlight to the dead man on the ground between them, and Winston suddenly understood that the fear on Glenn's face had not come from a fear of his being shot, but from the shock of stumbling upon what appeared to be a shooting in the line of duty. Glenn kept his beam on the man's chest, the blood so fresh as to glisten in the light. He raised his eyes to Winston.

"Sheriff?" he said.

Winston, understanding the look on Glenn's face and the implied question in his voice, took an unconscious step away from the body. He looked down at the dead man, and a long-buried shame and terror washed over him.

"No," Winston said, nodding his head toward the body. "No, this wasn't me. I found him here. He was down when I got to him."

He tried to slip his pistol back into its holster, but he discovered that his hands were still shaking, and he had to reach across his body to hold the holster with his free hand so the pistol's barrel could find it. He looked down, saw that Glenn's flashlight gleamed in the dead man's open, unseeing eyes.

"No sign of a weapon," Glenn said. "Know who he is?"

"I think so," Winston said. "I had Rudy run the plates on that Datsun in the parking lot."

Winston knelt down beside the body and checked for a pulse. He didn't find one. He patted the man's pockets, and then he turned him slightly at the hips and felt his back pockets until he found his wallet. He slipped it out and removed the man's driver's license.

"Yep," he said. He looked up at Glenn. "Rodney Bellamy." He looked at the license again. "Twenty-six years old. Lives over in the Grove."

"Ed Bellamy's son," Glenn said.

"Yep," Winston said again. He looked inside the wallet, found a couple of twenties and a few smaller bills. Bellamy didn't seem to have been robbed. He slipped the driver's license back inside and stuffed it into Bellamy's front pocket.

He didn't know what it would mean to find Ed Bellamy's son shot dead on the runway in the middle of the night, but he knew it would mean something. Winston respected Ed Bellamy, and he feared him a little too. Both were reasons to dread making the phone call to tell him what had happened to his son.

"You okay, Sheriff?" Glenn asked.

Winston looked up at Glenn, and then he looked down at his hands. He clenched them into fists to hide their trembling. "Yeah," Winston said. "Yeah. You just surprised me coming up on me like that." He peered over Glenn's shoulder as if he were looking for anyone else who might be coming across the field. He looked back at Glenn. "What even made you come out here? Rudy get ahold of you?"

"Marie called," Glenn said.

"Marie called you? At home?"

"Yes."

"What did she say?"

"She said you thought a plane might've crashed." Glenn looked away as if what he was about to say next was going to embarrass both of them. "She said she didn't want you out here by yourself. I told her I'd come have a look around."

Winston sighed and shook his head. He wanted to be angry with Marie for calling Glenn, for overstepping and making Winston look like he couldn't handle his job on his own, but everything that had happened—the plane crash, almost shooting Glenn, finding Rodney Bellamy's body—crowded out his anger so that he had hardly conjured an ember of rage before it snuffed itself out.

Glenn smiled as if the embarrassment were behind them both. "I also wanted to come out because I've never seen a plane crash before."

Winston turned to his left and pointed at the end of the runway. "Well, it's your lucky night, I guess."

Glenn raised his flashlight and aimed the beam past Winston. "There it is," Glenn said.

Winston's eyes followed the beam of light where it shone on the plane's body, the open cargo doors, the frozen propellers. "Yep, there it is," he said. "Not much of a crash, but it's a whole lot of plane."

"Looks empty to me," Glenn said.

"We're still going to have to clear it," Winston said.

GUNS RAISED, THE two men made their way toward the plane. They stopped at the open cargo doors in the middle of the fuselage, and Glenn knocked on the exterior with his flashlight. There was an echo as if he had banged on the bottom of an enormous, upturned metal canoe. The nose of the airplane, propped up by the wheels beneath either wing, loomed above Winston on his right, but the fuselage narrowed greatly toward the end where it rested on its tail, the rear landing gear having completely collapsed.

The aircraft seemed simultaneously powerful and frail, and Winston could not believe that something so large could take to the sky nor that something so powerful could be grounded so easily. He reached out and placed his open hand on the airplane's body, nearly expecting to feel the rise of its breathing. He smacked it twice as if patting the belly of a horse before climbing into the saddle. "Hello," he called out. "Brunswick County Sheriff's Department." He nodded at Glenn, who raised his pistol, pointed his flashlight into the darkness of the aircraft's interior, and stepped up inside. Winston, his pistol also raised, stood by the door and listened to the creaking of the airplane's body as Glenn's footsteps shuffled around inside.

"It's empty," Glenn called out.

Winston holstered his pistol and stepped through the door.

The seats had all been removed inside the plane, and Winston stood in the middle of the fuselage and took in the scene: the pilots' chairs in the front; the long empty expanse as the floor stretched back toward him; the faint moonlight dusting the windows.

"It's empty now," Winston said, "but I'd be willing to bet it wasn't when it touched down." He moved his flashlight around the inside of the plane, its beam passing over every surface.

"What do you want to do?" Glenn asked.

"Get back in the bed and go to sleep."

Glenn laughed. "Me too."

"Let's go ahead and fingerprint everything up in the cockpit," Winston said. "And the doors inside and outside too. And then we'll call the morgue."

"You got it," Glenn said.

Winston stayed inside the aircraft and sent Glenn back to his patrol car for an extra flashlight and one of the crime scene kits they all kept in their trunks. While he was gone, Winston stood in the plane's open cargo doors and stared out at Rodney Bellamy's body. It was rarely the case, but everything that had happened that night had surprised Winston.

Once Glenn returned to the plane, he handed over the evidence kit, and Winston made his way toward the cockpit, moving uphill against the backward tilt of the plane. He dusted the cockpit controls carefully, paying special attention to the spots on the yokes where he knew thumbs and fingers would have been clenched tight as the plane came in over the trees not long ago. He moved to the instrument panel. Glenn held the flashlight while Winston worked. When he finished, he unspooled the tape and placed it over the spots where he believed good prints were most likely, but when he lifted the strips of tape and held them to Glenn's light, not a single fingerprint was revealed. He tried again, but there was nothing to see.

"Maybe a damn ghost flew it," Glenn said.

"Or they wore gloves and wiped everything down," Winston said. "But there's got be a fingerprint somewhere in this airplane."

If they found prints, Winston's office had no way of running them. He'd have to send them off to Wilmington, if not Raleigh. Even when the FBI stepped in—which Winston knew would happen no matter how long he put off calling them—it would be days before the fingerprints revealed anything. News of the airplane's appearance and Bellamy's murder would spread quickly, and Winston knew that everyone in the county would watch how the sheriff's office handled it, and then they would vote. Election day was just a week away, and Winston's chances to influence the opinion of his constituents were running out. But, for now, he had all the time he needed out here on the runway in the middle of the night, Glenn and him inside an airplane that was empty but for the sounds of their footsteps echoing against the metal walls. They worked slowly. There was no reason to rush. No one knew what had happened but them. The airplane had already landed, and whoever had landed it had disappeared. The only person who might have seen them was Rodney Bellamy, and he wasn't talking.

CHAPTER 2

She had not set the alarm clock because it was not hers; the alarm clock belonged to Scott, and it was already set for 5:00 a.m. Waking at that hour left him plenty of time to eat something at home, hit the gym at the health club he'd joined as soon as they'd moved to Dallas, shower, and make it to the courthouse by 7:00 a.m., which, he'd confided to Colleen, was almost half an hour earlier than any of the other first-year assistant attorneys were willing to arrive.

That morning, she'd been able to slip from bed at 3:00 a.m. with only a muttered "You okay?" from Scott where he lay, his back turned toward her. "Yes," she'd said. "I just can't sleep," but he had already tumbled back into a deep slumber.

They had not built the house they lived in, which was something she had dreamed of their doing together, but it was only twenty years old and new enough so that the oak floors did not squeak and the doors opened and closed securely and quietly, which was a far cry from the house she'd grown up in on the waterway in Oak Island, with its paper-thin walls, worn carpets, crooked staircase, and linoleum floors. She had been near silent as she walked across her and Scott's bedroom, opened the door, stepped into the hallway, and closed the door behind her.

The house had been dark and quiet, the only sound being the mechanical hum of the German grandfather clock that the previous owners had left behind. It now sat at the top of the stairs at the far end of the hallway. Their first night in the house, the clock had chimed with a series of deep, resonant melodies, and Colleen and Scott had been launched from their mattress as if they'd been electrocuted. Colleen had grown so used to being pregnant that her belly's unwieldiness was a feature of her new body that she never lost track of, but she had lost track of it that night. In her sleep and sudden waking confusion she had panicked at the heavy weight sitting atop her middle, and she had only calmed when Scott found her hand in the darkness and the two of them had lain together without speaking, listening to the slow, deep chimes of a song that seemed born in a distant era and a dark, forested continent that felt very far from their new lives in Texas.

The next morning, Scott had opened the glass cabinet and disabled the clock's chimes. In the bottom of the cabinet they had discovered a stack of old editions of the *Dallas Morning News,* each one marking a historic event: Pearl Harbor; the Armistice; the assassinations of Jack and Robert Kennedy and Martin Luther King; the moon landing; and every presidential election since World War II, ending with the November 4, 1980, headline "Gipper Cruises to Victory over Carter," along with a photo of Reagan and his wife waving from the stage on election night.

She and Scott had flipped through all the newspapers, wondering why someone had saved them, brought them to this house, and then left them abandoned in the bottom of the clock. Their talk turned to birth announcements, and they decided that, when the baby came in June, they would run announcements in Wilmington for Scott's parents, Oak Island for Colleen's, and here in Dallas for their own new family because this city would be the baby's home.

When they returned the newspapers to the bottom of the clock's

B 7eb-22

cabinet, they stacked them oldest to most recent, just as they'd found them. Now each time Colleen saw the grandfather clock, as she had on this dark morning, where it stood sentinel at the far end of the hallway, she thought vaguely but powerfully of time and change and tragedy and life and all the ways we hang on to these things, store them, and then take them out over the years to leaf through the memories in their pages.

To the right of their bedroom was the open door to what they called the office, a room full of boxes of their law school texts, a desk, and a few chairs. Across the hall was a guest room, the bed still made from when Colleen's mother and father had stayed just a few months before. They'd flown in for the birth, which was something she'd actually felt guilty about, given how expensive it was and how inexperienced her parents were with flying. Scott's parents had also flown in from North Carolina. They had stayed in a hotel, but none of them had stayed for very long.

The room beside the guest room was empty, but the last room on the right at the top of the stairs was home to the carefully and bliss-fully decorated nursery, a room whose door had remained closed since she and Scott had arrived home from the hospital. Colleen had stayed downstairs, leaning against the kitchen counter, while Scott had gone up and closed the nursery's door before Colleen followed behind him and headed for their bedroom. The next day, she bent in the hallway and stuffed a rolled towel beneath the nursery's door. She did not want to go in, but she also did not want whatever re-mained inside the room—memory, magic, hope, perhaps a spirit or a ghost—to escape.

In her bare feet and as quietly as she could, Colleen now padded down the curved staircase to the foyer below. They had not meant to buy a house this grand. Even with the new baby on the way, why did they need three thousand square feet, four bedrooms, and a "keeping room" in a house that already had a living room? But it was 1984 and Scott was an assistant U.S. attorney at the federal courthouse in Dallas, and money didn't seem to be a factor for them. It had never been a factor for Scott, and his father—who'd gotten Scott an interview for the job because he'd been college roommates at the University of North Carolina with the Texas attorney general and had kept in touch ever since—had talked so much about a first home as an investment. So, here they were, investors in a nearly empty home that was much too large for two people who rarely found themselves living in the house together unless lying in silence in bed at night.

Colleen turned on the dim, fluorescent light above the kitchen sink and opened the cabinet on her right. She took down the tin Maxwell House coffee canister, empty but for a wad of crumpled dollar bills. She selected five twenties and a range of fives and tens, and then she put the lid on the canister and lifted it back into the cabinet. This was their emergency money, and she didn't know if what she was doing qualified as an emergency. Her emergency, yes, but was it an emergency for both of them? She believed she could make the case that it was, but she didn't imagine that Scott would agree.

A jolt of nervous panic careened through her body, and she folded her arms across her chest and tucked her fists, one of them still hiding the wadded-up cash, beneath her armpits as if trying to warm herself. For a moment, she considered fleeing up the stairs and back into their bedroom, but then she remembered the money in her hand, and she felt that some invisible line of trust had already been crossed and she couldn't turn back. Then she considered opening the refrigerator and reaching for a beer to settle her nerves. The clock on the oven read 3:12 a.m., and Colleen tried to gauge the appropriateness of having that beer by calculating the hours from the previous night to the coming morning. She was closer to 2:00 a.m. than she was to dawn, and there had been times in law school, and certainly times in college, when she and her friends were still drinking when the sun came up, and although that was a few years ago, Colleen decided it wasn't so long ago as to feel unfamiliar, and, by now, nothing was more familiar to her than the taste of a beer when tasting it alone.

She opened the refrigerator and took out a Coors Lite, the chill of the glass bottle against her hand soothing her with its sharpness. The night and the house felt too dark and too quiet for such a sensation. After she popped the cap and took a long drink, she felt a calm settle over her that brought with it a clarity of action. She stood there, confident and barefoot in her pajamas, until she finished the beer, took another out of the refrigerator, and then left the kitchen and walked into the foyer.

A packed suitcase, shoes, and a change of clothes were hidden in the closet beneath the stairs. Colleen found the stash and stepped into the half bath off the foyer to change out of her pajamas. She left the light off in the bathroom, just as concerned about waking Scott as she was about seeing her face in the mirror in the midst of her escape. She feared that looking into her own eyes would shame her out of her bravery, and as she opened her second beer, she knew that she didn't need any more shame. She took a sip, set the bottle on the bathroom counter, and then got dressed.

Outside, the sky was still dark and the streetlights still shone, but something about the feel of the air and sounds of the neighborhood's birds told Colleen that morning was near. Before leaving the house, she had gone back into the kitchen for the beer bottle she'd left there, and now she walked to the side of the house by the driveway where they kept their trash can, and she lowered both bottles inside one at a time so as to make as little noise as possible. Her suitcase in hand, she walked around to the front of the house and followed the brick walk to the street, where she sat down on the curb and waited. The previous afternoon, she had scheduled a taxi pickup for 4:00 a.m. The prospect of leaving her car at the airport to accrue parking fees while she decided when and if to return seemed like a particularly selfish thing to do to Scott, and he didn't deserve her selfishness any more than she deserved his. They were two people constructed of pain and grief, and, in spite of that, the world would not be making allowances for them, so Colleen believed they had to make allowances for one another when they could. She hoped Scott felt the same.

The feel of the predawn neighborhood excited something in her, and Colleen remembered the first time she had ever felt this way. She had been in college back in Asheville, and she had been up late studying during the fall of her freshman year when she decided to leave her dorm room long after midnight to walk around the quiet, empty campus. What had thrilled her then thrilled her now: no one in the world knew exactly where she was. She had these predawn moments all to herself.

But she couldn't help wondering what the neighbors would think if someone were to peek through their blinds and see her sitting on the curb in the early morning with a suitcase beside her, her and Scott's front porch absent the carved, glowing jack-o'-lanterns, hay bales, and scarecrow decorations that dotted so many other lawns and doorsteps in the neighborhood. Even from the street, even at this time of night, it was clear that their home was a home without children.

During the spring and into the early summer, the neighbors had seen her coming and going, greatly pregnant. They would cock their heads and smile and wave, ask how she was doing, and ask her to remind them of when she was due. And then, one day, she had not been pregnant and she had not had a baby in her arms. Most of the neighbors had reacted like skittish animals, scurrying from their cars to their front doors in lieu of making eye contact. The few who did speak to her held their heads at the same cocked angle as before, but instead of excitement their faces portrayed embellished grief and sympathy, and she realized then that she preferred the cowardly neighbors to the bold ones.

The differences between the doctor and the nurses postdelivery had prepared her for the reactions of others. The doctor—a black-haired man she'd never met before—had rattled through a list of explanations that he acknowledged might not even be the correct explanations at all: perhaps her placenta had become detached; or maybe the cord had become constricting, "and the child—" He'd stopped there. The nurses, on the other hand, had lowered their voices and relaxed their faces, speaking—no, whispering—not with pity but with assurance, especially after the baby was delivered into a world completely silent except for the beeping of her own blood pressure monitor. It wasn't her fault, the nurses said. She'd done nothing wrong. Her son was beautiful. She was a mother. She always would be.

"Who knows?" the doctor had said. "These things happen."

These things did happen, and it had happened to her, and, a few months later, it felt like it was still happening.

She leaned back on her hands, stretched her legs into the street, and crossed her ankles. She closed her eyes and took a deep breath. She could feel the weight of the house behind her, Scott's presence in their bed pulling her toward him as if he were her life's centrifugal force. *How do you go home when you already have a home?* she wondered. And what would she do when she arrived? She could take another taxi from the airport to Oak Island, knock on her parents' door, and wait for them to answer. She could play it off like a surprise visit instead of an act of desperation. Or she could wait until they'd gone to bed, and then she could find the front door key where they kept it hidden beneath one of the old flower pots on the front porch. She could let herself in, stash her luggage beneath the bed in her old room, and then find a place to hide. She would be able to be at home without her presence being known, to hear her parents' voices without those voices asking her questions she didn't know how to answer. She wished she could go back into the house and open the refrigerator for another beer.

She kept her eyes closed, and although her fingertips pushed down into the dense grass of her front yard at her and Scott's home in Dallas, she felt herself tumbling backward into a memory.

She is hiding beneath the kitchen sink inside their old home in Gastonia, North Carolina. She is only four or five years old. It is dark and damp inside the cabinet. Whenever her mother turns on the faucet Colleen can hear water coursing up the pipes before trickling back down the drain. Her mother is preparing dinner. She knows Colleen is hiding there, but tonight she will forget.

Their house is small, and each night when her father comes home from work, she hears the front door creak open no matter where she is hiding. She always hunkers down in an attempt to make herself smaller, adrenaline coursing through her body like an electric current, and she listens as he tosses his keys on the table by the door and hangs up his belt and holster in the coat closet. He always closes the closet door and sighs out loud as if he is greatly disappointed.

"Where is everybody?" he asks the quiet house.

Her mother, who is always in the kitchen, waits a beat before replying.

"Well, I'm in the kitchen," she says, "but I don't know where Colleen is."

"Huh," her father says. "Well, I hope she hasn't run off."

He then begins moving through the house, opening closet doors, looking under beds, and pausing only to narrate his search to her mother, his voice rising and falling in mock curiosity, surprise, and disappointment.

"She's not in her bedroom. Surely she wouldn't leave us without taking her toys with her."

"I don't know," her mother says. "I'm telling you, honey, I haven't seen her."

If Colleen's body had been a glowing ember, the red-hot heat emanating from it would have given her position away. She always stifled laughs and repressed squeals of torturous anticipation, and each night she fought the urge to burst from her hiding place to surprise her father whenever she heard or felt him draw close to where she lay in wait. Sometimes he would surprise her by making noise as if leaving the room for another, and then returning to throw back a blanket or peek behind a door and scream, "Found you!" She would leap toward him, and he would scoop her up. She would throw her arms around his neck and close her eyes. She could smell him, the fading scent of his aftershave, the sweet cigarette smoke that clung to his clothes, a smell that she had only ever found comforting on him. He would squeeze her close, speak into her hair; she imagined that his eyes were closed. "I'm so happy I found you," he would say. "I was afraid that you'd left us."

But in this memory, he does not search for her when he comes in the door, though she is waiting for him nonetheless. The floor of the cabinet where she's hiding has been papered, and she runs her fingers over it, feeling its waxy film and the spots where the paper has begun to dimple and curl from moisture. Her back leans against one side of the cabinet; her knees are pulled to her chest. At her feet are boxes of Brillo pads and Ajax. It must be cold outside, because the smell of gas heat coming from the ducts lingers on the edge of her memory.

When the front door opens, her father does not call out, does not open the closet door to put his coat or belt and holster away. She hears his steps as he walks through the small foyer toward the living room. The springs give when he sits down on his chair. Outside the cabinet where she's hiding, she's aware that her mother has paused as if she too is listening and marking these alterations in her father's routine. Her mother goes back to her work.

"It's about time," her mother says. She waits, but there is no response. "I don't know where Colleen is."

Her father is silent. His chair creaks as if his weight has shifted, and Colleen wonders if he is settling himself or reclining or standing.

"Marie," he says. His voice is quiet, and Colleen recognizes it as a voice she has not heard before. "Come in here."

"Winston?" her mother says. She turns on the sink, and Colleen imagines that she is washing her hands before drying them on a dish towel. "What is it?"

"Come in here," her father says again.

She listens as her mother leaves the kitchen and crosses the small foyer to the living room. She can hear their voices, but she cannot make out what they're saying. She opens one of the cabinet's doors, but she can't hear them any more clearly, so she lets it close.

"What?" her mother says. Her voice is breathy, almost apologetic.

"Shhh," her father says. "Marie, come here."

She can hear her mother crying, and Colleen pictures her father holding her mother the same way he would hold her if he had found her during their hiding game. His eyes are closed. He is speaking something quietly into her mother's hair.

A few minutes later—it could have been longer because it is dark when she climbs out of the cabinet—she finds her parents sitting on the sofa together, hand in hand. Their faces are faces she has not seen before. Something bad has happened. A grandparent has died. Their dog has been run over like the neighbor's dog had been run over a few months earlier. Russia is going to bomb them.

"What happened?" she asks.

Her parents look at her, but neither of them says anything. Her father releases her mother's hand, and she pulls it back into her lap as if protecting it. Her father reaches his hand toward Colleen. His smile is an attempt at a smile.

"What happened?" she asks again. "Why didn't you come find me?"

He is still reaching for her. She offers her hand. He takes it, pulls her gently onto his lap.

"I was waiting for you," she says.

Her father wraps his arms around her. She can feel his breath on the top of her head, the sharp jut of his chin where it rests on her crown. Her mother rubs her hand up and down Colleen's back.

"I know," her father says, "I know you were hiding, but tonight I wanted you to find me."

Colleen would not know the story for years, and there was still a lot she did not know, but that day her father had responded to a call about a robbery in progress at a pharmacy near their neighborhood. A man was inside the pharmacy, holding the pharmacist, the cashier, and a few customers behind the counter. He had a pistol. Her father had entered the store with his gun drawn, and when the man pointed his gun at her father, her father shot him. He died at the scene.

No one had ever told Colleen that story. What she knew of it had been pieced together, and she believed that she had begun perceiving that story from her hiding place beneath the sink. She felt her parents' fear, uncertainty, and sadness. Sadness for the man her father had shot, sadness for his family, sadness for her father for having killed him, and sadness for her mother and for Colleen for having a husband and a father who had killed someone. Suddenly, she understood without ever having been told that the shooting was what had caused her parents to leave Gastonia and move 250 miles southeast to the coast. And she understood something else too: the great walling off of her parents' lives from hers. In many ways, she was forever beneath that kitchen sink in their old house, the one she still dreamed of often, listening to the voices of her mother and father in the next room, wondering at the mystery of their language, yearning for one of them to open the cabinet door and lift her out into the early evening dark so she could see their faces and know that she was home.

Colleen did not open her eyes when she heard the sound of a car coming up the street toward her, did not even open them when the car came to a stop just in front of her house. It wasn't until the driver's-side window rolled down and a man's voice said "Mrs. Banks?" that she opened her eyes.

"Yes," she said. She stood up and picked up her suitcase and walked toward the taxi without looking back. "I'm ready."

CHAPTER 3

By the time the sun had broken the horizon over the tree line, Winston and Glenn had given up trying to find fingerprints inside the airplane. All they'd managed to do was rouse two deputies from bed and call them out to the airport. Deputy Billy Englehart, a small, nervous man in his mid-thirties who'd been with the sheriff's office for just over a year, had arrived first, and he'd brought a tarp with him to cover Bellamy's body. When the other deputy arrived, a slightly older man named Isaac Kepler, who was tall and skinny and hardly ever said a word to anyone unless it was over the radio during his patrol, he and Englehart set up a perimeter using stakes and crime scene tape that encircled both the far end of the runway and the area around the body. In the weak morning light, Winston and Glenn and the two deputies had bent toward the earth in search of shell casings, and Winston had sent the two deputies down into the high grass alongside the runway, and he'd heard Englehart cursing and complaining the whole time.

Just before dawn, Winston and Glenn had found a set of tire tracks that ran from the parking lot out across the runway, right up to the end of it where they'd found the plane. With the morning light they'd been able to find where the tracks turned in a wide circle back toward the parking lot. It looked like whatever vehicle had driven out there had been pulling something behind it, probably a trailer.

"Somebody was waiting for this plane," Glenn said. He removed his hat and wiped his forearm across his forehead even though it wasn't warm enough for him to be sweating.

"And something got unloaded," Winston said. "The tracks heading out of here are deeper than the ones coming in. And Bellamy's car didn't leave these tracks. They're too far apart, the tires too wide. Somebody else was waiting for this plane when it got here. Figuring out what kind of tires left these tracks will tell us what kind of vehicle they belong to."

"I bet it was drugs," Englehart said.

Winston turned and looked at Englehart. He and Kepler had taken a break from searching the area. Now Englehart just stood there, slowly winding crime scene tape back onto the spool. He'd pushed his hat off his forehead so that Winston could see his straw-colored hair.

"Yep. Could've been drugs," Winston said.

Englehart adjusted his hat's brim, pulled it down to block the faint sunrise.

"Ain't no other reason to abandon an airplane and disappear," Englehart said. "If it wasn't drugs it was something else: illegals or guns, one."

"More money in drugs," Kepler said, the first words Winston had heard him utter since arriving.

Englehart looked down at the tarp that covered Bellamy's body, spoke to it as if the man beneath it could hear him. "That's the damn truth, ain't it, Rodney."

A call had gone out just before dawn that Rodney Bellamy's wife had contacted the sheriff's office to report him missing. According to her, he'd left home in the middle of the night for diapers and never returned. Winston had spent the hours since trying to figure out how Rodney had ended up here.

"Maybe 'diapers' is the coloreds' code word for 'cocaine,'" Englehart said. He laughed and looked around at the gathered group, but no one showed any sign of thinking his joke was funny.

"Knock off the jokes, Englehart," Winston said. He looked over at Kepler. "Y'all get back to processing this scene."

Englehart's face went flat as he finished winding the yellow tape. Winston had never liked the man, but he needed deputies, and he'd overlooked Englehart's laziness and off-color jokes for as long as he could. He wanted to snatch the tape from the man's hands and embarrass him by sending him home, but he knew that dark humor was how some men on the force dealt with death and uncertainty; they laughed at it because there was just no other way to make sense of its randomness, and this death felt particularly random, and there was a lot Winston had to make sense of. It was bad enough that Rodney Bellamy was Ed Bellamy's son, but now he'd also be breaking the news to a wife who'd be left behind with a baby. He knew Englehart could laugh about a thing like this only because he'd never get any closer to it than he was right now, but Winston would only grow closer. He dreaded it, dreaded calling Ed at the high school, dreaded breaking the news to him and asking him to meet him over at Rodney's house so his widow wouldn't be alone when Winston told her.

Winston looked past his three officers and saw two men walking down the runway toward them. "Shit," he said. It was Leonard Dorsey, chair of the county commission, and Hugh Sweetney, the airport manager.

He'd known Hugh Sweetney for several years. Sweetney had served as a pilot in World War II, and he'd come back to the North Carolina coast after the war was over and worked odd jobs until the county had built the municipal airport before deciding they needed someone to run it. Sweetney was quiet and reserved, but Leonard Dorsey was just the opposite: a loud, sweaty, nervous man from Raleigh who'd followed his elderly parents to the coast when he was in his thirties. He was past fifty now, and he'd made his money selling insurance and knowing everyone's business, and that money and knowledge had given him political power.

"Morning, Sheriff," Dorsey said. "Looks like somebody almost ran out of runway last night." He smiled an awkward smile, the kind of smile somebody smiles when they know they're interrupting something they shouldn't be interrupting. He walked past Winston and the other men and looked at the plane, and then he looked back at Sweetney. "What are we working with here, Hugh?"

As Sweetney passed, he nodded and smiled at Winston by way of *Good morning,* and then he stood beside Dorsey, crossed his arms, and looked at the plane, its mirrored body reflecting the early morning light. Sweetney freed one hand and rubbed at the gray stubble on his cheek.

"That's a DC-3," Sweetney finally said. "Been modified with those cargo doors. They stopped building them in 1950. It's a good aircraft." He looked behind them where the runway rolled toward the waterway. "Didn't have no business on a runway this short, though. Whoever flew it in knew it too, but it's a good landing, considering." He turned his head and stared at the place where the back wheel had collapsed. "It's a tail dragger, and they snapped the rear landing gear trying to turn it around here at the end. Lucky they didn't ground-loop it." He looked at Dorsey and then at Winston. "Plane seems okay, though, and that landing gear shouldn't be too hard to fix."

"Well, good," Dorsey said, as if something had been settled. He looked at Sweetney, spoke only to him. "We can get it out of here today, right?"

"Hell, no," Winston said. He stepped forward to stand in front of Dorsey. "We can't move this thing."

"Why not?" Dorsey said. He folded his arms and looked from Winston to the gathered group of officers.

"This is a crime scene," Winston said. He pointed to Bellamy's body beneath the tarp. "And you're standing right in the middle of it. That's a dead man right there, Dorsey. And who knows where this plane came from. We've got a lot of questions that need to be answered before we move it."

Dorsey turned and took a step toward Winston. He lowered his voice as if speaking to a child. "Look, Sheriff, you solve whatever mysteries you need solved. The only thing I know for sure is we got a plane stuck on the end of this runway and an airport that can't be used until it's gone." He looked over at Sweetney. "Right, Hugh?"

Sweetney lowered his eyes and looked at the plane. He sighed. "It needs to be gone before we can reopen the runway," he said. "That's for certain, but I'm not flying this aircraft from this airport. It needs at least thirteen hundred feet for takeoff roll. We barely got two thousand. It ain't near long enough if something goes wrong. A damn miracle somebody landed it like they did."

AFTER MAKING THEIR notes, Winston and Glenn walked across the grass toward the parking lot. Winston hadn't talked to Marie since he'd left in the middle of the night, and he figured she was awake and either scared or frustrated—maybe even angry—by now. But he was angry too. She had no business calling Glenn in the middle of the night and asking him to check on Winston, which was what Winston thought Glenn's trip out to the airport amounted to. Winston didn't need to be checked on. Most often, he just needed to be left alone.

They stopped at Glenn's patrol car. "I'd like to keep this under our jurisdiction for as long as we can," Winston said. He could've referenced the election and said, *We've got a lot riding on it,* but Glenn knew that, and he also could have said, *We need to look like we're in charge,* but Glenn already knew that too. Winston took off his jacket and opened the driver's-side door of Marie's Buick and tossed it onto the passenger's seat. "I'm going to step inside Hugh's office and call Marie, and then I'll ride out to Southport and see if I can talk to Bellamy's wife. Now ain't the time to ask her any questions, but I got to let her know. I'll call Ed too. See if he can meet me there."

"Good luck," Glenn said.

"Yeah, well," Winston said, "I appreciate that."

Winston asked Glenn to call the morgue to come get Bellamy's body, and then he told him to put a team together back at the office that would get busy checking on van rentals and storage facilities. He also wanted Polaroids of the tire tracks in the hopes they'd be able to match the tread to a vehicle or a trailer that had been rented. For now Winston had given up on finding any shell casings, and he sent Englehart out on patrol and assigned Kepler to guard the perimeter around Bellamy's body and to keep an eye on the airplane. Dorsey and Sweetney had remained out on the runway, and from where Winston and Glenn stood, they could take in the whole scene: the tarp covering Bellamy's body, Kepler positioned above it; Dorsey in his tan baggy suit and Sweetney in his polo and khakis standing out in the morning sun where the silvery body of the DC-3 sat, its tail collapsed on the ground just a few feet away.

Glenn turned and looked behind them. "Well, looky there," he said.

Winston turned too and saw a van from Channel 9 pull into the parking lot. He was surprised it had taken them this long, and he knew more news crews from Wilmington would soon follow.

He left Glenn where he stood and walked toward the news van, meeting the on-air reporter as she tried to make her way out to the runway, microphone already in hand, the cord wrapped around her forearm. "I'm sorry," Winston said, waving his hands in front of him to stop her from moving past him, "but this is a crime scene." He looked up as a cameraman hoisted his gear from the back of the van.

"Y'all can film from up here in the parking lot, but don't go any farther. We'll have a statement soon."

Otherwise, Winston had no comment at this time. He wouldn't speak a word to the press about the investigation until he'd sat down with Ed Bellamy and Rodney's widow. From where the news crew was setting up, they could see the airplane resting sideways on the runway, its back wheel broken off, and they could also see that the sheriff's office had something covered up out there on the grass. Any fool could surmise what had happened, but the questions were *how* and *why*, and Winston didn't have answers for those just yet.

He stepped inside Sweetney's empty office and picked up the telephone and called home. Marie answered on the first ring.

"Are you okay?" she asked.

"Yes," Winston said. "You? Did you get some sleep?"

"I did," Marie said. "But you weren't back when I woke up. It scared me."

"Well, you should've known that Glenn would come to the rescue, help an old man do his job."

"You're mad at me for worrying about you?"

"No, I'm mad at you for trying to do my job for me, Marie. I'm the sheriff, not Glenn. I don't need some kid checking up on me in the middle of the—"

"He's older than Colleen," Marie said, "and if he's some *kid* you shouldn't have made him captain."

"That ain't the point," Winston said, his voice louder than he'd meant for it to be. He looked up and checked the door to make sure no one had stepped into the office without him knowing. He turned back to the desk. "That ain't the point," he said again. "I'm up for reelection, Marie. My officers need to believe that I'm the best man for this job. They don't need to spend a second thinking I can't handle it."

"Well, I'm not one of your officers," Marie said. "I'm your wife."

"So, you're saying I can't handle it? You want me just to give up and drop out?"

"I'm not saying that, Winston. You just need to understand that when you go out alone in the middle of the night—"

"When I go out alone in the middle of the night I go out as the damn sheriff of this county," Winston said. "I plan to keep on being sheriff, and I'm asking you and Glenn and whoever else to let me keep this job as long as I'm elected to do it."

"Okay," Marie said. "I want you to keep the job."

"Thank you," Winston said.

The line grew quiet, and he regretted raising his voice and showing Marie how angry he'd been. Displays of anger had always embarrassed him, especially his own, but that didn't mean he was ready to apologize.

"I heard there's a body," Marie finally said.

"Who'd you hear that from?"

"A little birdy."

Winston wanted to be surprised that word had carried so quickly, but he wasn't. The island was small; the telephone made it smaller still. Word about the identity of the body would spread soon.

"It's Rodney Bellamy," Winston said.

He heard Marie gasp into the phone's receiver, and he knew she was now attempting to collect herself, probably staring out the kitchen window into the backyard, taking in the news and thinking .of how to respond. "That's Ed Bellamy's son," she said.

"I know," Winston said.

"He went to school with Colleen."

"I know," Winston said again. "And he just had a baby. His wife said he went out for diapers last night. I found him shot dead at the end of the runway. And there's an abandoned plane out here." He sighed. "It might've been full of drugs too. Could've been tons, hell, I don't know."

"Have you talked to Ed?"

"No," Winston said. "I'm about to call the high school, ask him to meet me over at Rodney's house so I can tell his wife."

"I'm so sorry you have to do this, honey."

Marie's voice had come out in a whisper, and he felt her softening toward him after their argument. He wanted to soften toward her too, but he felt a protective shell hardening around him in advance of sharing the news with Rodney's widow.

"Well, I hate that it has to be done," he said, "but I'll head home after that. You want me to pick up anything?"

"No, just come on home as soon as you can. I love you."

"All right," Winston said. "I love you too."

He hung up the phone, and then he looked around Sweetney's office, searching for a telephone book. He found one in a desk drawer, and he flipped through it until he found the number for the high school.

Winston called the school's office, and while he waited for Ed's voice to come onto the line, he pictured Bellamy inside the classroom that he had visited several times while Colleen was a student and a handful of times since. He figured Ed Bellamy was sitting at his desk, grading papers or flipping through a textbook, his thick glasses turned down toward the page, his black crew cut beginning to gray around his temples. A student assistant sent by the office steps into the classroom, whispers to Bellamy that he has a telephone call. Bellamy looks up from his desk, tells the students to continue working quietly, and then he steps into the hall.

While he'd been swept up in Korea, Winston had been too old for the Vietnam draft, and he knew he'd been lucky, but Ed Bellamy was younger than him, and he hadn't been so lucky. Ed still carried himself like a soldier: rigid, unsmiling, watchful, direct. That's how he appeared in Winston's mind as he marched down the hallway at the high school, his feet clapping on the dull linoleum floors, his straight shoulders passing the banks of olive-green lockers that lined the walls on either side.

"Hello," a man's voice suddenly said on the other end of the telephone line. "This is Ed Bellamy."

He'd made it to the phone faster than Winston had expected, and the sound of his voice caught him by surprise.

"Ed," Winston said, "this is Winston Barnes."

Silence.

"Ed, I'm really sorry, but I've got some terrible news."

Another moment, and then Winston heard Bellamy's voice again.

"Oh, Lord," Bellamy said. "Oh, Lord, oh, Lord."

"Ed, I'm sorry to tell you this, but Rodney's been—" But Winston stopped, corrected himself. "Rodney's passed away."

"Oh, Lord," Bellamy whispered again. "Oh, sweet Jesus."

Something in Bellamy's voice told Winston that his eyes were closed, his face downturned, his free hand raised to his forehead. Winston paused for a moment, considered what to say next. He heard Bellamy stifle a sob on the other end of the line.

"Ed," Winston said, "can you tell me his wife's name?"

The line remained silent. Winston waited.

"Janelle," Bellamy finally said.

"I hate to do it, but I have to talk to her, tell her what happened. I think it would be good if you could be there when I do it."

"She called me this morning," Bellamy said. "She said she hadn't seen him since last night." He fought another sob. Winston heard him swallow, clear his voice. "How did he— Where did you find him?"

"He's been shot, Ed. I'm out here at the airport."

"Shot?" Bellamy said, his voice louder than it had been before. "Shot? At the airport?"

"Yeah, Ed, and that's about all I can tell you because it's all I know right now."

"I want to see him."

"I know, Ed, and you will. I'm happy to come out to the high school and pick you up. We can ride out to Janelle's together."

"No," Bellamy said, his voice tightening. Winston knew Bellamy's brain was clicking away from his own grief toward the grief Rodney's widow would soon feel. "I'll meet you there, but give me a few minutes. Wait for me before you knock on the door."

"Okay, Ed," Winston said. "I'll see you there."

He set the phone back on its cradle. He looked around Sweetney's office. An entire bookcase was dedicated to meticulously constructed and painted model airplanes. Beside it sat two metal file cabinets. Sweetney's desk was neat and orderly, the chair pushed back as if he had just stood up to step outside. A chair for guests sat on the other side of the desk, and Winston considered taking a seat and calling home to talk to Marie again, but he decided not to. He knew his mind was searching for reasons to stall, for him not to climb into Marie's car and drive out to the area of Southport known as the Grove to deliver the worst news that Rodney Bellamy's wife would ever hear. Winston decided not to wait any longer, and he opened the door and stepped into the sunlight.

Outside, a crew from Channel 3 had set up a camera in the parking lot on the edge of the field that led toward the runway. The newly arrived reporter looked up at Winston where he stood outside Hugh's office. She didn't look a day older than twenty, her big, blond hair barely registering the breeze. "Sheriff?" the reporter called, but Winston waved her off. She'd talk to Channel 9's reporter. He knew they'd compare notes, coming to the conclusion that they had no option but to wait for his statement.

Winston looked out toward the runway. Kepler still loomed like a scarecrow over Bellamy's body, the tarp that covered it stirring almost imperceptibly in the breeze. Winston saw that Dorsey and Sweetney had begun walking back toward the office, and just as Winston and Dorsey locked eyes, Dorsey raised his hand and pointed at the television crews gathering in the parking lot. Winston raised his eyebrows and shook his head in warning. There was no way in hell he wanted Dorsey out in front of the investigation. Dorsey nodded as if he understood, and Winston followed the sidewalk toward Marie's Regal where it still sat parked beside Bellamy's Datsun. Before climbing behind the wheel, Winston heard Dorsey call out to him, but he let the breeze carry Dorsey's voice far away from his ear.

DEATH HAD BROUGHT Winston to someone's door on only a few occasions during his time as a police officer in Gastonia and as a member of the sheriff's department in Brunswick County, but it had rarely been murder that sent him. He was usually consoling mothers, fathers, and spouses, and then glossing over the details of car crashes, drownings, and other accidents. It wasn't often that he had to explain to someone that another person had taken the life of their parent or child or, in this case, husband.

After leaving the airport, he tried to calculate how long it would have taken Bellamy to leave the principal's office and go back to his classroom for his car keys, how much time would be required to find a substitute to take over his class for the day, and how many minutes a grieving father would need to drive the eighteen miles from the high school to Rodney's house in the Grove. Fifteen? Twenty? Certainly no less.

Winston drove as slow as he could down Howe Street into downtown Southport, the water rising up before him at the end of the street. Here the Atlantic Ocean merged with the Cape Fear River as it led northwest to Wilmington and the Intracoastal Waterway to the southwest, which separated Oak Island from the mainland, and here, centuries earlier, pirates had reigned. Now the sleepy town depended more on the treasure of tourists than it did on the bounty of pirates. At the end of Howe, Winston turned right and drove along the water where boats of all kinds and sizes were tied up in slips and restaurants that had been closed for the season sat empty and dark. He made another right and circled back toward North Lord Street, where he drove into the Grove and found a little white house with a well-manicured yard and a tan sedan parked haphazardly behind a pickup truck in the driveway. A little of the tension that had been building inside Winston released itself because he knew that Bellamy had beaten him there.

Winston parked Marie's car on the street in front of the house. Just up the road, a Black boy played with a little dog at the edge of a yard. The boy, who might've been three or four, must have held something in his hand that the dog wanted because the dog was leaping for it, and the boy was laughing, holding his clenched fist above his head. For a moment, Winston found himself back in Gastonia, sitting behind the steering wheel as a much younger man, the errand that brought him to park alongside the street just as tragic as the one that brought him to the Grove now. The little boy opened his palm and the dog took something from it. He wiped his hand on his shirt, and then he looked up the road at Winston. The sight of the little boy was almost too much for him to bear. The little boy ran back toward his house, the dog following, and Winston climbed out of the car.

He figured the truck parked in the driveway must have belonged to Rodney and that he had been driving his wife's Datsun last night. The irony of that discovery settled on his chest with a weight that surprised him. He closed his car door and made his way across the yard. He could hear Janelle's cries before he even stepped onto the porch.

On most occasions, the sound of a doorbell is loud and cheerful, loaded with mystery and curiosity and expectation. Doorbells have an element of surprise that feels manipulative—almost evil—

when announcing the news of death. Winston had spent a lot of time thinking about this over the years, and he thought about it again at that moment as he delivered three almost silent knocks on Janelle Bellamy's door. Inside, the woman's cries seemed to go silent, and Winston feared that, in her sudden grief, Janelle might believe that he was Rodney returning home, that there had been some great mistake and that her husband was still alive. He feared that she would open the door and find him instead.

But when the door opened, there stood Ed Bellamy, his eyes damp and his face already collapsed with the kind of exhaustion that only grief can bring. He nodded at Winston. "Sheriff," he said.

They shook hands, and for a moment Winston wanted to pull Bellamy into an embrace, but instead he just stepped into the living room, and Bellamy closed the door behind him. The interior of the small house reminded Winston of his and Marie's home back in Gastonia: the living room full of secondhand furniture; the short hallway on the left that led to a kitchen and probably a small laundry room; the hallway on the other side of the living room, the open bathroom door on the right, the three closed bedroom doors on either side of the hallway just beyond it. Something about the house— the arrangement of the furniture or the smell of new carpet—told Winston that Rodney and Janelle Bellamy had not been living here for very long, and now, if she stayed in their home, she would be living here without him.

Bellamy walked to the sofa and sat down. He closed his eyes and put his head in his hands. Winston had not been invited to sit, so he continued to stand by the door.

"Ed," Winston said, "I just want you to know how sorry I am. I can't imagine—" But he stopped speaking when Janelle opened one of the bedroom doors in the hall and walked into the living room. Winston saw that the woman he'd heard crying just moments before was now gone. This woman's face was shining, her bright eyes showing no trace of tears aside from the redness they'd left behind. Her face portrayed no sign of sadness, but also no shock that the Brunswick County sheriff was standing in her living room. She held a fussing baby that didn't look to be more than a few months old. She bounced the baby as she walked. She raised her eyebrows at Winston and nearly smiled, the gesture being the only false thing about her.

"He didn't sleep much last night," she said. Her voice was pitched and sharp, and Winston could feel her restraint and also the panic that fueled it. She patted the baby's back, rubbed her open hand up and down across it. "None of us slept." And that was the moment when her face changed, when she turned back into the woman Winston had heard. "He just went out for diapers," she said, her face collapsing, her mouth nearly swallowing her lips as she choked back a great, heaving sob. The baby in her arms began to cry louder. Bellamy stood from the sofa and stepped around the coffee table toward her, reached out his arms to take the child. Janelle turned away from him, began whispering over and over. "Shhh, it's okay, honey. Daddy's just gone for diapers. Daddy's just gone for diapers."

It was all too much for Winston, but the only thing he could do now was look away.

LATER, WINSTON'S NAME came over the walkie-talkie as he turned onto Howe Street. He pulled to the side of the road, wiped his eyes, took a breath, and picked up the walkie-talkie from where it sat on the passenger's seat. On the other end was Randy Taylor, a retired officer who often ran dispatch during the morning hours once Rudy had gone home. Everyone in the office called dispatch "The Randy and Rudy Show," and even though no one had ever said that to Randy or Rudy, Winston figured they probably knew just the same and probably even got a kick out of it.

"Sheriff?" Randy's voice repeated.

"I'm here," Winston said. He took another breath, rubbed his eyes and then his face with his free hand.

"Leonard Dorsey wants to talk to you," Randy said.

"You know what it's about?" Winston asked.

"He didn't say, but I reckon it's something about that airplane."

"Is he still out at the airport?"

"He is," Randy said.

"Well, do me a favor and call Hugh's office. Tell them I'm on the way."

"Ten-four," Randy said.

Winston tossed the walkie-talkie back onto the passenger's seat, where it landed on the campaign posters Marie'd had printed. He sat there on the roadside and watched as cars entered and left Southport. He rolled the window down, felt the warmth of the morning. He took another deep breath.

Although he tried to shake the image and the sound, Winston could still see and hear Janelle crying, the baby boy wailing in her arms. He had wanted to do something, but there was nothing he could do but watch Ed Bellamy wrap his arms around the young woman while turning his face away from Winston. Winston knew that he had muttered condolences and promises to do all he could, but he knew that Janelle and Bellamy either hadn't been listening or perhaps hadn't been able to hear him over the sound of the baby's cries and their own deafening sadness. Winston didn't blame them. He wouldn't have listened to himself either.

At one point, a bedroom door had opened in the hallway just past the bathroom, and the face of a teenaged boy peered out and made eye contact with Winston. His hair was cropped close, and his skin was darker than Janelle's, but their faces were similar. Winston wondered if they were siblings, although the boy seemed much younger. The boy had stared for a moment, his eyes moving from Winston to the spot where Bellamy stood, attempting to console both his daughter-in-law and his grandson. The boy in the doorway hadn't spoken. Once he'd finished looking, he'd simply withdrawn into the bedroom and closed the door behind him.

When Winston left, Ed Bellamy had followed him outside to Marie's car.

"What can you tell me, Winston?" Bellamy had asked.

"Not much," Winston had said. "Not because I can't or don't want to, but just because there's not anything to tell right now, Ed."

"Where'd you find him?"

"Out at the airport."

"*Where* out at the airport?"

"By the runway," Winston had said. "A plane landed out there in the middle of the night. Whoever brought it in abandoned it and disappeared."

"And that's who—" Bellamy had said, but he'd stopped, unable to force out the words he hadn't yet prepared himself to say.

"Maybe," Winston had said. "We just don't know, Ed. But I promise you I'll do my best to find out."

"People are going to think it's drugs," Bellamy said.

"It might've been, Ed," Winston said. "We don't have any idea."

"Rodney wasn't involved with drugs," Bellamy said.

"I'm not saying he was, Ed."

"I'm saying he wasn't, Winston. I don't even want to hear that or see that mentioned anywhere."

"Right now, all I know is that your son was murdered, and I want to find out who did it," Winston said. He'd looked back toward the house, saw that the blinds were parted in the room where the teenaged boy had appeared at the doorway. The boy must have understood that Winston had spotted him, because the blinds closed. "Who's that boy inside?"

Bellamy had looked back toward the house, the spell of his anger and grief broken for a brief moment.

"His name's Jay," he'd said. "He's Janelle's little brother. She brought him up from Atlanta."

"How old is he?" Winston had asked.

"Fourteen. He got into some trouble down there. Her folks didn't know what to do with him." He exhaled and put his hands in his pockets. "She and Rodney brought him up here this summer."

"What kind of trouble did he get into?"

"I don't know, Sheriff," Bellamy had said. His gaze turned back to Winston in what could only be perceived as a hard stare. "The kind of trouble boys get into everywhere. I tried telling Rodney not to take him in. I tried telling him how hard it is to—" He had stopped speaking for a moment, had crossed his arms and then raised a hand to cover his mouth. Winston waited. Bellamy crossed his arms again. He looked up at Winston. "I tried telling him how hard it is in this country to raise a Black boy into a man."

ON HIS WAY back to the airport, Winston went through the Hardee's drive-through for coffee. He knew he needed to eat something, but he couldn't imagine choking down a biscuit, even though he knew that black coffee wasn't going to be easy on his empty stomach.

When he turned left onto Long Beach Road, he saw the Food Lion sitting up ahead on his left, and he decided to pull into the parking lot. As far as Winston knew, this was the only business that was open twenty-four hours that also sold diapers. If Rodney Bellamy was heading anywhere in the middle of the night, this would've been it. Winston drove through the parking lot, his neck craning one way and another, his eyes scanning the horizon toward the southwest for any glimpse of the sky above the airport. He parked Marie's car at the top of the lot close to the road, and then he climbed out and stood there for a moment, taking sips of the hot, bitter coffee.

From where he stood, he could see the airport's beacon. It would have been even more visible in the middle of the night with its bright light and the absence of car headlights on the road. If Rodney Bellamy had been standing where Winston was standing now, he would have had an unobstructed view of the aircraft coming in. Winston walked to the middle of the lot and found that he could still see the beacon light, although he could no longer see the entire expanse of airspace over the runway. But the airplane had been loud enough to awaken him and Marie, loud enough to shake their house—or at least to have made them think their house had been shaken—so if Rodney had heard it, perhaps he had run out to the road in time to see it disappear beneath the distant tree line.

And what had taken him out there? The belief that he'd witnessed a plane crash? Winston couldn't explain it, but he knew Rodney hadn't been involved in drugs. That didn't make any sense. He and Janelle had only recently moved back to Southport. Rodney hadn't had the kind of time it would take to embed himself with an operation like this. But had it been dumb luck that found him standing in this parking lot at the exact moment that the aircraft had come in? Had it been simple curiosity that led him to climb back into his car and go check out what he'd seen and heard? Perhaps, like Winston, he'd expected to find a crash landing, a fiery wreckage, victims strewn along the runway. Instead, someone had shot him in the chest and left him to die, and what had Rodney thought in the seconds before that happened? Winston hated to consider it, but more than that he hated that Ed Bellamy and Rodney's widow would spend the rest of their lives considering it long after Winston's role in the investigation was over.

He swallowed the last bit of his coffee and walked back to his car. Since he was heading back to the airport, he figured he'd better have something to say to the news crews, who wouldn't leave unless he did. He found a pad inside the pocket of his jacket and jotted down a few notes about what he knew, what was safe to say without speculating.

When he got to the airport, he saw Bellamy's car where it still sat parked, the police tape that now cordoned it off blowing in the breeze. He pulled into an empty space in front of Sweetney's office. Dorsey's white Cadillac and Sweetney's truck sat unmoved from where they'd been parked that morning. There was Kepler's cruiser and a few other cars in the lot that Winston didn't recognize. Another news van had joined the other two, and it sat parked on the grass on the edge of the lot. It was a television station from Myrtle Beach.

Dorsey must have been waiting for Winston to arrive, because as soon as Winston got out of the car, notepad in hand, Dorsey opened the door to Sweetney's office and called out to him. He waved for him to come inside. "Come on in here, Columbo," Dorsey said. He stepped back inside the office and let the door close behind him.

Winston spoke to a couple of the reporters and promised to be with them in a few minutes. Inside the office, he found Sweetney sitting behind his desk and Dorsey standing by the bookshelf full of model airplanes, studying them as if they could reveal something about the abandoned aircraft just outside. Dorsey looked up and nodded at the chair in front of Sweetney's desk. "Have a seat, Sheriff," he said.

"No, I need to get back to work out there and talk to those reporters," Winston said. He felt something in the room change. "Dorsey, I hope you haven't brought me in here to tell me you've already been yapping at them."

"Hell, no, Winston," Dorsey said. "I know better than that." He slipped his hands into his pockets and stared at his feet. Winston could hear his fingers tinkering with keys or loose change. Otherwise the room was quiet. "FBI agents are here," he finally said.

"I figured they'd be here sooner than later," Winston said.

"Well, I called them," Dorsey said. He slipped his hands from his pockets and crossed his arms. "Just wanted you to hear it from me in case they mentioned it."

"*You* called them?" Winston said.

Dorsey slid his hands back into his pockets. He rocked back on his heels. "Look, Winston, I know you're coming up on a reelection, but this thing's too big for us, for you."

Winston closed the notepad he'd been holding, slipped it into his back pocket, and walked toward the office door. He pushed it open and stepped outside. Behind him, he heard Dorsey catch the door before it closed. Dorsey caught up with Winston, walked alongside him.

"Now listen, Winston, this is the federal government," he said. "They can take care of this thing. There ain't no use in ruffling feathers—" But Winston kept walking, didn't even turn to look at him.

The first person Winston encountered on the runway was Deputy Kepler. "Sheriff," Kepler said. He took his hat off and held it in his hands like he was entering a church for a funeral. "I tried to keep them out of the plane until you got back, but they said the investigation is being taken over, and I said—" But Winston didn't let him finish.

"Stay here," Winston said. "I'll be back."

Winston found the two agents inside the plane, one of them standing in the fuselage, and the other standing in the cockpit, looking down at the black, dusty remnants of Winston's search for fingerprints. Winston knew them both. He stood in the open cargo doors. He cleared his throat. "Gentlemen," he said.

Both men looked at him, but only the one standing in the fuselage smiled. Agent Avery Rollins was a few years younger than Winston, but the gray hair and gray beard made him appear older. Winston and Rollins had worked together many times over the years—mostly on cases when drugs had been brought in on boats, smugglers using the waterways and wharfs the same way marauders had used them in earlier times—and their relationship was quiet and easy, both of them understanding that the other had a job to do and knew how to do it. Rollins wore a white golf shirt and the clichéd navy blue wind-breaker with the FBI badge over the breast and "FBI Special Agent" printed across the back in yellow. He had the agent's standard SIG Sauer strapped to the leg of his tan cargo pants. The other agent, the one still standing in the cockpit, was outfitted in the exact same garb. He was Josh Rountree, a short, square man with brown hair and a closely trimmed mustache who always held himself out as being distant and aloof. Winston had never seen him smile or say a word that wasn't tied directly to an investigation at hand. It was too hot for the agents' jackets, especially inside the plane, but Winston saw it for what it was: a power play to broadcast to anyone who saw them that the federal government was now in charge.

"Winston," Rollins said. The two men shook hands. "You know Agent Rountree."

"I do," Winston said.

Rountree turned his head, and Winston nodded *hello*. "Your office do this?" Rountree asked. He pointed to the fingerprinting dust that covered the cockpit.

"Yeah," Winston said. "I did. I was the first on the scene." Then, feeling as if he were hedging against what might come next, he said something that both surprised and shamed him. "It was dark. Didn't quite know what we were working with."

"You find any good prints?" Rountree asked.

"Not a one," Winston said.

Rountree sighed and shook his head as if what he saw before him was the most disappointing thing he'd seen in days. Winston looked at Rollins, and Rollins winked and gave him a slight smile as if to encourage Winston to let go of any judgment or disappointment he may be feeling in that moment. Winston appreciated the gesture, and he did his best to smile at Rollins as if only the two of them were in on a joke about Rountree being too serious, but he knew that Rountree's reaction would stick with him for a while.

Over the years during which he'd worked with the FBI's local office in Wilmington, Winston had found almost all the agents to be the same, especially agents from the offices in Charlotte and Raleigh. They were outsiders hoping to move on to something bigger and better in the bureau; outsiders who looked down their noses at local law enforcement even more than they looked down their noses at locals. He'd always taken Rountree to be that kind of agent, but Rollins was different. He'd married a woman from Wilmington and had settled down years ago and raised a family.

"I heard you had a night last night," Rollins said.

"You could say that," Winston said. "I've had quite a morning too."

"I bet," Rollins said. He put his hands on his hips and looked around the empty airplane. "I bet."

In the cockpit, Rountree had opened a small notebook, and he stood there, his back to Winston and Rollins, writing something. Rollins looked at Winston and nodded toward the open cargo doors, and Winston turned and stepped out. Rollins followed. The two men walked a few yards away from the airplane. They stopped on the edge of the runway by the spot where Rodney Bellamy's body still rested beneath the tarp. The morgue was slow in coming, and Winston was frustrated that Bellamy's body was still on the scene, especially now that the FBI was there to witness it.

"Look, Winston," Rollins said, "you know we're going to—"

"I know," Winston said. "I know."

"I imagine you could use a big case before the election, and I think we can work together to—"

"I know," Winston said again. "I was just hoping that—" But he was embarrassed to say it, to say that he wanted to prove himself in front of his community before they made their decision about his fate. But he couldn't say it because it was a stupid thing to think, much less to say out loud. "Never mind."

"Well," Rollins said. He slipped a pair of aviator sunglasses from his breast pocket and put them on, and then he shrugged off his windbreaker and folded it and dropped it at his feet. He turned his head to the right and stared down the runway for a moment, and then he looked at the tarp. "Let's have a look," he said. He bent at his knees and lifted a corner of the tarp and peered beneath it. Winston looked away. He'd seen all he'd needed to see of Rodney the night before. "What can you tell me?" Rollins asked.

"He's a local man named Rodney Bellamy," Winston said. "Black, mid-twenties. His wife said he went out for diapers last night. They got a new baby boy."

"That's a shame," Rollins said.

"Yeah, it is."

From the corner of his eye, Winston saw Rollins let go of the tarp and pick up his windbreaker. He stood. "How'd he end up out here in the middle of the night? You think he was up to something?" Rollins nodded toward the airplane. "Maybe he was helping unload this aircraft, and then something went sideways?"

"I don't think so," Winston said. His gaze had turned back to the tarp, and he recalled seeing Rodney's face last night in the flashlight's beam, and then he recalled the faces of Rodney's father, his widow, and his baby boy that he'd seen just that morning. Winston wanted to tell Rollins that Rodney Bellamy wasn't just one more Black man taken out with a bullet, but what did that even mean? And why did he feel the need to say it, to even think of saying something like that? "I think he went out for diapers, and I think he saw a plane come in low in the middle of the night. He must've come out here to check it out."

"Any arrests or convictions?"

"No," Winston said. "He's clean. Always has been as far as I know. My daughter went to school with him, and I know his daddy. He teaches over at the high school. He's a good man."

"A lot of good daddies have bad kids, Winston."

"Not this one."

Winston felt the presence of someone behind him, and he turned and found Rountree standing just a few feet away. Rountree still held his open pad, but he clicked his pen closed and slipped it into his breast pocket.

Rountree looked at Rollins. "We'll send this out on the teletype back at the office," he said. "This aircraft needs to be processed in a covered hangar, and there's not one big enough here. Best bet's Wilmington."

"You going to fly it?" Winston asked. He'd meant for it to be a joke, but the words came out tinged with the anger he still felt after Rountree's dig at him over the fingerprints.

"No," Rountree said. His face portrayed neither humor nor amusement. "But we'll find somebody who can." He nodded toward Rodney's body. "And we'll find out what happened to him."

Winston followed Rountree's eyes down to the tarp at Rollins's feet. And that was when he saw it, when they all saw it. Perhaps the angle of the sunlight was perfect, or perhaps no one's eyes had come to rest on that exact spot just yet. Whatever the reason, all three men spotted the shell casing at the same moment. It rested in the grass only a few feet off the runway, but Rountree was the first to move toward it. He pulled the pen from his pocket and bent toward the ground and slipped the tip of the pen into the empty casing. He stood and held it up as if he were pinching a tick between a pair of tweezers. No one said a word until Rountree's gaze moved from the casing on the tip of his pen to Winston's face.

"I thought your office processed this scene, Sheriff," Rountree said.

"I thought we did too," Winston said.

Rollins stepped forward, lifted his sunglasses from his eyes. "Looks like a nine-millimeter," he said.

"It is," Rountree said. He took a baggie from his pocket, snapped it open, and dropped the casing down inside. "Maybe I can actually get us a fingerprint after all."

Winston and Rollins were quiet as they watched Rountree seal the bag and slip his pen back into his breast pocket. Winston looked at the two agents, and he understood that if he was going to have a role in this investigation then he was going to have to take it.

"I'd like to run point with the media on this," Winston said. "And I'd like to keep a deputy out here twenty-four hours a day until the plane's gone." Winston's office was already stretched thin, and keeping somebody out here on the runway around the clock to guard an airplane that wasn't going anywhere anytime soon was only going to stretch them thinner. But he'd already suggested it, and it was too late to take it back.

"I'm fine with that," Rollins said. "It's better you than me when it comes to reporters. And I appreciate the offer to keep eyes on the aircraft."

"It'd better not be the same officers who were supposed to be looking for shell casings," Rountree said.

Rollins sighed as if he wished that Rountree hadn't said what he'd just said. He looked at Winston. "That's fine with me," Rollins said. "It would help us out until we can get this thing moved. I'll give you a shout as soon as we know something about how that's going to happen."

Winston nodded at Rollins. "Let me speak to these reporters so they'll leave," he said.

He left the agents on the runway and headed back toward the parking lot. Winston stopped where Kepler stood and asked him to follow.

"Just stand beside me and look smart when I start talking," Winston said.

Kepler shrugged. "I'll do my best."

As the two men walked, an ambulance from Dosher Memorial drove through the parking lot. The gathered members of the press parted for a moment, and the ambulance passed through the open gate and rolled onto the runway. It slowed when the driver spotted Winston and Kepler in their uniforms, but Winston gestured for it to continue on and pointed toward the spot where the agents still stood by Bellamy's body at the end of the runway. He watched the ambulance for a moment, neither he nor Kepler saying a word, and then he turned back toward the parking lot, where the reporters—microphones, tape recorders, and cameras at the ready—were waiting for him.

He felt something familiar, something he had felt more often over the past couple of years; it was the knowledge that he could walk away from this job right now and go on about his life. After the shock of the decision, no one would begrudge him leaving the job, retiring, especially with Marie trying to recover and everything that had happened to Colleen. Winston knew it would be easy—perhaps practical—to give in to that urge. He felt like he was holding his breath instead of breathing, and he wondered why he was doing something he didn't want to do. But what would happen if he walked away? If he literally walked away from the reporters and the investigation and Kepler and simply climbed into Marie's car and drove home? They wouldn't have insurance, for one. They wouldn't have a steady paycheck. It would quickly become clear that Winston's big decision to walk away from the stress of his job would introduce untold stress into the remaining parts of his life. Best to keep things how they were, at least until the election was over and any choice Winston could make in this moment would have been made for him.

The television reporters and cameramen saw Winston as he approached, and they could tell something was afoot. They scrambled into a cluster at the edge of the asphalt. He recognized the crime reporter from the *Wilmington Star News* and the field reporter from the *State Port Pilot* just down the road in Southport. Nearly all of them held either a microphone, a tape recorder, or a camera.

Winston pulled the notepad from his back pocket and flipped through it until he found the page on which he'd jotted his talking points in the grocery store parking lot. He took a deep breath. "Good morning," he said. "I'm Sheriff Winston Barnes. Last night, a little after four a.m., the sheriff's office arrived on the scene here at the airport, where we discovered an airplane abandoned on the runway, along with the body of an individual."

"What was in the airplane?" asked the blond-haired reporter from Channel 3. "Can you tell us who was flying it?"

Winston lifted his hand to show that he wasn't done speaking, and then he continued. "At this time, the victim has been identified as Rodney Bellamy of Southport, and Mr. Bellamy's family has been notified. We have no information that links Bellamy or his death to this aircraft, but I want to stress that this is an active investigation, and that the airport will remain closed until it is completed. If anyone has any information on the events of last night, you are encouraged to contact—" Winston watched a Chevy crew cab dually pull into the lot. frye and son construction was labeled on the side. The truck parked at the end of the row of cars on Winston's right. "If anyone has any information, please contact the sheriff's office. I will not be taking any questions at this time. Thank you."

But of course that didn't keep the gaggle of reporters from calling out Winston's name and shouting questions at him as he and Kepler walked past them. Winston gave them all a pinched smile and a couple of patient nods, but he didn't stop to speak to them, and they didn't follow.

He and Kepler walked along the edge of the parking lot toward Marie's car, and as Winston removed his keys from his pocket, Bradley Frye climbed out of his truck. Winston watched as Frye straightened his pants and made sure his shirt was tucked in. He noted the pistol Frye had holstered at his side. *What in the hell is he doing with that?* Winston thought.

"Sheriff, Deputy," Frye said, nodding at Winston and Kepler. His smooth, tan skin, blue eyes, and parted blond hair made him look ten years younger than his forty-one. His white polo shirt and khakis were clean and pressed crisp and straight. A first glance would take Bradley Frye for old money, but anyone who hung around him longer than a few minutes would discover that his family's money was new, and it was spent on things like big trucks, expensive boats, and parcels of land where spec houses were thrown up overnight. Winston was more accustomed to arresting men like Bradley Frye for drunk driving or picking up prostitutes than he was accustomed to standing against them in an election.

"Brad," Winston said. He reached out and shook Frye's hand. Kepler did the same. Winston noted a sense of embarrassment on Kepler's behalf, and it endeared him to Winston, this small recognition of the awkwardness he found himself in as the two rivals stood toe-to-toe at a crime scene within earshot of the local media.

"I thought I'd come by and see if I could help out," Frye said. "I heard y'all might have your hands full this morning." He looked out toward the runway, and then he looked over at the gathered group of reporters. A few of them were recording the scene on the runway where the ambulance had parked. Two paramedics lifted a stretcher holding Rodney's covered body into the back of the ambulance. Rollins and Rountree stood by and watched.

"We're doing okay," Winston said. "Things are moving along. Ain't that right, Deputy Kepler?"

"That's right, Sheriff," Kepler said, his voice quiet. "Moving along."

Winston looked at Frye. "But we appreciate you coming by."

"Heard y'all had a dead colored boy out there on the runway," Frye said.

For the moment, Winston ignored him and looked at Kepler. "You mind heading back out there? I'll get somebody here soon to relieve you." Kepler nodded, and then he turned and walked back toward the runway.

Winston turned to face Frye. "Man," he said.

"What?"

"He was a man," Winston said. "You said 'boy,' but he was a man."

"Yeah, well," Frye said, "y'all thinking drugs?"

"We're not thinking anything right now, Brad," Winston said. "We've got an investigation to complete. There's plenty of time for thinking later."

"Well, I guess we'll see what the voters have to say about that next week, huh, Sheriff." He smiled.

"I guess we will," Winston said.

Frye squinted his eyes and looked out at the airplane on the runway. He smiled. "See some FBI fellows out there," he said. "I bet that means it was drugs." He crossed his arms. "Drugs from Mexico. And you got the coloreds out here waiting to unload them and move them through this county."

"That's a great theory," Winston said. "If you'll excuse me, I need to get back to work."

Frye put his hand on Winston's shoulder to stop him as he tried to step past him toward Marie's driver's-side door. Winston looked over at the reporters. Most of them were now busy winding cords and loading equipment back into their vans.

"You shoot him?" Frye asked.

"Don't touch me, Brad," Winston said.

"I know you took out a colored boy back in Gastonia. Good for you if you got this one too." The ambulance drove past on its way out of the parking lot. "You just let me know what I can do, Sheriff," Frye said. "I got a bunch of boys on my crew who'd be happy to lend a hand. I don't plan to wait until I'm sworn in as sheriff to protect this county."

Winston shrugged off Frye's hand. He looked down at the gun on Frye's belt, an expensive Browning Hi Power with a mother-of-pearl handle that Winston couldn't imagine Frye even figuring out how to hold, much less shoot.

"You can start by leaving that sidearm at home," he said. "It's illegal to open carry, and I'd hate to have to jail my opponent so close to the election."

"Would you now?" Frye said.

"I would," Winston said, "but I will. Get back in your daddy's truck, Brad. Go to work."

MARIE WAS STANDING behind the screen door when Winston pulled into the driveway. She waved, and he forced a smile instead of waving back. The truth was, his hands were shaking, just as they had been shaking since his stare-down with Bradley Frye. How had Frye known about what had happened in Gastonia? How would anyone know about that? To have it resurrected now was a shock that Winston was struggling to handle, compounding his worry over Marie, his grief for Colleen, and the appearance of this airplane that seemed to have fallen from the sky to land beside Rodney Bellamy's dead body. And now the investigation was being taken from him and turned over to the FBI, and everyone was watching him just as Marie stood at the door and watched him now.

He climbed out of Marie's car, and she opened the door as he stepped onto the porch.

"Are you okay?" she asked.

"Yeah," Winston said. He squeezed her hand and walked into the hallway and opened the closet door and put his holster and pistol away. When he hung up his jacket, he realized that he was still wearing his white T-shirt from the night before. He walked into the kitchen where Marie had set out a plate with a ham sandwich and some potato chips on it. She followed behind him. He went to the sink and washed his hands.

"How was Rodney's wife?" Marie asked.

"Bad," Winston said. "Bad, like you'd expect."

"Did you see the baby?"

"Yeah," Winston said. He snapped a paper towel from the roll where it hung beneath the cabinet.

"Did you talk to Ed?"

"I did, Marie." Winston turned and looked at her. He kept drying his hands. "I did. It was awful. All of it. All of it was awful." He bent and opened the cabinet beneath the sink and tossed the paper towel into the trash can that was hidden there.

"I'm sorry," she said. "Of course. Of course it was awful." She looked at the table, where the plate of food waited for him. "I made you a sandwich," she said. "I thought you could use something to eat."

"I'm really not that hungry," Winston said.

"Well, I think you need to try to—"

"Why'd you call Glenn, Marie? Really? Why'd you call him?"

He watched her step away from him as if his question had been a physical thing that had struck her. She put her hand to her chest as if to finger a necklace, but there was nothing there. She smoothed back her hair instead and set her face as if she were readying herself to take on whatever he was going to say.

"We already talked about this, Winston," she said. "I apologized."

"That's not what I asked you, Marie," he said. He leaned his waist against the counter, his hands reaching back to brace himself. "I asked why you called him. Do you not think I can do my job?"

"Of course you can do your job, Winston."

"Well, no one else seems to think I can. The Wilmington FBI is in on this now, Marie. They're taking over the investigation, making it look like I can't do this job anymore. And if I don't keep this job, then I don't keep our insurance, and then what's going to happen, Marie? To us, to you? I'm not going to work for Bradley Frye."

"And I won't ask you to," Marie said. "We'll find a way to make it." She raised her hands, dropped them to her sides. "I'll go back to work. I can go back next school year. There's bound to be—"

"Work?" Winston said. "Marie, you can't even get out of bed some days. We don't know what's going to happen next."

Her face changed. What had been hard suddenly softened, but not toward him.

"Well, I'm sorry, Winston. I'm sorry to be letting you down."

"Jesus," he said. He walked toward the kitchen table and took a seat where she'd left the plate of food waiting. He picked up half the sandwich, and then he dropped it onto his plate. "It's not about that," he said. "It's about me needing to keep this job. It's about people believing I can still do it. Leonard Dorsey called the damn FBI, and Bradley Frye's showing up at the scene as if he's already been sworn in." He picked up the sandwich again, took a bite. He chewed, the taste of it not even registering. "It feels like it's being pulled away from me, Marie." He swallowed, looked up at her where she still stood in the kitchen. "And I never thought you'd be one of the people pulling it."

"What do you mean, I'm pulling something away from you?" Marie asked. She walked to the table, sat down across from him. "I'm not trying to take something from you. I never have. Me calling Glenn has nothing to do with your job. It has to do with me loving you and not wanting you out there alone if you don't have to be. I mean, Jesus, Winston, somebody shot Rodney Bellamy last night. And you were out there. In the dark. That could've been you."

Marie put her hands on the table, intertwined her fingers. Winston stared at her hands, her wrists, registered how thin they were before they disappeared into the buttoned cuffs of her long-sleeved blouse. He knew she worried about him, and he knew he was taking out on her what he could not take out on Leonard Dorsey or Bradley Frye or the FBI or, hell, Rodney Bellamy for being there on that runway last night.

"I'm sorry," he said. "I'm sorry. It's just that—"

"Don't explain," Marie said. "Don't explain." She raised her eyes to his, her mouth curving up in a slight smile. "I was right, by the way."

"About what?"

"About it being an airplane."

Winston smiled too. "I don't remember there being a debate about that," he said.

"Well, I was the first to say it at least," she said.

"I can't eat all this," he said. He picked up the other half of the sandwich and reached across the table. Marie took it from him and allowed herself a small bite.

"I bet it was drugs," she said. She reached to the middle of the table and lifted a napkin from the holder. She wiped her mouth, crumpled the napkin in her hand. "Drugs from South America. That's probably what the FBI thinks too. That's why they're getting involved." She stared at Winston for a long moment as if doing so could get him to reveal everything he'd seen and heard and felt in the hours he'd been away from her. "You're not going to tell me, are you?" she finally said.

Winston looked down at his plate of potato chips. He knew that by now word had spread around the island. Marie's friends had probably been calling the house all morning, asking questions once they heard that a plane had crash-landed and been abandoned at the airport. By now everyone probably knew that a body had been found.

"Debbie said this happens where her sister lives down in Florida all the time. She said they're always catching Colombians trying to unload cocaine from airplanes."

Winston raised his eyebrows in mock curiosity. "Is that what Debbie said?"

"Yep," Marie said.

"Well, I sure hope these aren't the same Colombians," Winston said. "I'll talk to Debbie before I write my report."

"Don't be cute," Marie said. She smiled at him, and her smile felt good to Winston.

"Did Debbie ever see any photos of those boys from Colombia? I'll deputize her and give her a gun if she did. Let her take up the night watch out there on the runway."

"I'll put her on night watch in our driveway," Marie said. "Keep you in this house at night so I can get some sleep."

"I'm just glad to see you eating something," Winston said.

The phone rang in the kitchen.

"I bet that's Debbie with some hot leads," he said.

Marie stood from the table and tossed her wadded-up napkin at him. "You sit," she said. "I'll get it. You've done enough investigating today."

Marie picked up the phone from its cradle on the wall beside the sliding glass door. Her back was to Winston.

"Hello?" she said, and then she turned around and looked at him. "Hey, honey," she said, her words and the tone of her voice and the look in her eyes telling Winston that Colleen was on the other end. He stood from the table, but she raised her finger to send him a signal that let him know that she wanted to hear her daughter's voice for as long as she could. It would be his turn after that. She crossed her arms and leaned her back against the wall, the sunlight coming in the sliding glass door playing on her skin, hollowing out her cheeks, and glinting on her hair. "How are things down in Dallas?"

Winston sat back down and took another bite of his sandwich, suddenly hungry and willing to eat because he didn't know what else to do while he waited. He watched Marie as she knitted her eyebrows together. She looked at him.

"Oh," she said, "in Wilmington?" She put her hand over the receiver and said, "She's at the airport in Wilmington."

Winston stood up from the table and walked toward Marie, his mind alive with scenarios and possibilities. Had Colleen and Scott planned a surprise trip home? Had they separated? Did she need him to pick her up?

"What happened?" he whispered, but Marie raised her finger to silence him again.

"Don't worry, honey," Marie said, her voice softer than Winston had heard it in a long time. "It's okay, honey. We'll come get you." She looked at Winston, widening her eyes as if sending him a cue to speak a line that only he could speak or to take some action that only he could take. "Your father's already on his way."

CHAPTER 4

"Those white folks are probably going to eat you," Kelvin had said. "That's what they do to Black people up there in the country."

Jay wasn't supposed to have been hanging around Kelvin after what had happened, and he'd known he'd be in even more trouble if his parents caught them together. After all, it had been Kelvin's fault that Jay had been sent up to the country in the first place. Jay shouldn't have trusted him, but Kelvin was fifteen, a year older than Jay, with an older brother named Terry who'd already finished high school and had a job at the shoe store in the mall in Decatur. Terry had called them both babies whenever he'd seen them hanging out at Kelvin's house after school.

"Y'all babies found your peckers yet?"

"Y'all babies still watch cartoons?"

"Y'all babies getting sent to juvie?"

And, for a while, Jay thought for certain they would be sent to juvie.

The plan had been that they would walk into Wright's corner store just like they'd walked into it every day since they'd been old enough to walk home from school. Kelvin would distract Mr. Wright by talking to him, and Jay would make his way to the back of the store, where he would slip two bottles of MD 20/20 from the cooler and slide them into the waist of his jeans before cinching his belt tight. If anything went sideways, Kelvin would use their code word—Thriller—and the mission would be aborted. Jay had wondered why they couldn't switch places, why he couldn't distract Mr. Wright while Kelvin pinched the liquor. Kelvin had brushed that suggestion aside. "Because you can't talk like I can," he'd said. But it was his brother Terry's talking that had gotten the whole thing started.

Terry had told them both that girls liked MD 20/20, which he called Mad Dog, especially Banana Red and Electric Melon. Terry had told them both that if a girl drank Mad Dog, she'd let you kiss her and touch her wherever you wanted to touch her. Jay had never kissed a girl before, and he didn't know what to think about that advice, but Kelvin said he'd kissed a bunch of girls, and he knew that what Terry was saying was true. Kelvin said he'd hooked up with Robin Francis, a tall, skinny girl with buck teeth and braces who lived down the street from him. He'd told Jay they'd take the Mad Dog to Robin's house next time she had a friend over. He'd said Jay would see.

"I'll take Robin," Kelvin had said, "depending on what friend she's got with her."

"I ain't kissing Robin," Jay had said, mostly to sound defi nt, but also because he couldn't imagine kissing anyone, much less someone taller than him with braces on their teeth. "I don't want those big old buck-toothed braces in my mouth, clacking against my teeth."

Kelvin had laughed. "Come on, man," he'd said. "Pecking on those teeth is just like pecking on a typewriter." He raised his hands as if placing his fingers on the keyboard, and he began typing. "Click, click, click, ding!" he'd said. At that sound he thrust his hips forward before beginning to type again. Jay had laughed. "Come on, man," Kelvin had said again. "You're going to love it."

Alone in his bed at night, Jay had stared up at the ceiling, listening to the sound of the Braves game on the television in the living room, the squeak of his father's leather recliner as he leaned toward the side table and poured salted peanuts into his hand from the jar of Planters he always kept there. Later, he would hear the clap of his mother closing her book and getting up from the sofa to go into their bedroom, his father following behind her not long after. Once the house had gone quiet, Jay had lain there and imagined kissing Robin Francis, her breath warm and sweet with what Terry had promised would be the fruitiness of the Mad Dog, her braces shiny and sharp. Click, click, click, *ding*! he'd thought.

But once he was inside Mr. Wright's store, all the doubts he'd had about Kelvin's plan, his story of kissing Robin Francis, and the promise of the sugary sweetness of the MD 20/20 and all the things Terry had said it would get the girls to do, suddenly rose up in his chest like a sickness he feared would spill from his mouth.

After Jay had made his way to the back of the store and was standing in front of the drink cooler as if unable to decide what kind of soda to choose, he'd looked up at the convex circular mirror that hung above him in the corner of the store. In the mirror, he could see Kelvin standing by the magazine rack as if having the same trouble selecting what to read that Jay was having selecting what to drink. He could also see Mr. Wright in the mirror's reflection, at least he could see his hands where they rested on the counter by the cash register. From this angle—the angle at which the mirror hung and the angle at which Jay was standing—Mr. Wright's face was obscured by the bank of cigarettes that hung from the ceiling within easy reach of Mr. Wright's fingers. Jay had seen him find a pack of cigarettes for a customer without even raising his eyes from where his other hand accepted the bills before pecking away at the cash register and making change once the drawer opened.

Jay didn't need to see Mr. Wright's face to be reminded of what it looked like. He was Jay's father's age, good friends with Jay's father, actually. He had medium brown skin and a thin mustache and a head full of hair. Jay had grown up seeing Mr. Wright and his father and other men from the neighborhood sitting in his parents' driveway beneath the carport on Saturday afternoons, smoking cigarettes, telling stories, drinking beer, and talking about whatever it was they were always doing together: bowling or playing cards or fishing; the kinds of things men did when they got off work and got away from wives and kids. Those driveway sessions were just about the only times Jay saw his father smile. He'd even laugh. In fact, sometimes he'd laugh until he cried, tears glistening on his smooth, dark skin, his cap coming off and revealing his bald head whenever he removed it to slap his knee with it or use it to pop one of his friends in the chest as they laughed together, hunched over in their chairs, stomping their feet.

Jay had stared at the mirror and waited to hear Kelvin's voice speaking to Mr. Wright to distract him from what they were—from what Jay was—about to do. But Jay stared into the mirror and watched Kelvin just stand there by the magazine rack without saying a word. Mr. Wright's hands had disappeared from view, and without turning around Jay was unsure of what the man was doing.

He looked at his own face in the mirror and saw himself for what he was: a lanky, skinny kid with a smooth face, skin and eyes just as dark as his father's. His face looked scared no matter how much he tried to keep it from appearing that way. He didn't want to steal from Mr. Wright or drink Mad Dog or feel Robin Francis's buck teeth and braces in his mouth. But going through with the plan, even if the plan hadn't quite gone into effect just yet, was easier than saying the truth out loud, especially if he had to say it to Kelvin.

Jay's father's name was James, and Mr. Wright had always called Jay "Little J," and he'd always called Kelvin "Little K," although Jay had no idea what Kelvin's father's name was. He didn't know anything about Kelvin's father aside from the fact that he didn't live with Kelvin and Terry and their mother. Kelvin didn't really want to talk about his father, and Jay didn't push it. He understood. He didn't want to talk about his own father either.

It wasn't that Jay didn't love his father or that he thought his father didn't love him: quite the opposite. Jay knew he was loved, especially by his mother in her quiet, gentle way. She was a librarian, and throughout his life Jay would think of libraries when he thought of his mother: the fresh, clean smell of books in their bindings; the whispered voices; the confidence that whatever you needed or wanted could be found provided you had the time and the patience to wait for an adult to find it or to look for it on your own.

Jay's father's love was different, grumbling and marked by qualifiers like "because" and "but." *Boy, I'm doing this because I love you* and *Son, I love you, but*. Jay's sister, Janelle, had already been everything he knew his father now wanted him to be—smart in school, good at sports, self-possessed and certain—and by the time Jay was born, when Janelle was almost thirteen years old, Jay figured his father had spent one whole childhood confident that he had done the best he could and had, in fact, done well. And then Jay came along, and his father just didn't know if he could do it again. It's not that his father was an old man; he was only forty-eight, not that that really meant anything to Jay. But he did *seem* old. While other parents listened to Michael Jackson and Lionel Ritchie, Jay's father listened to the Temptations, the Platters, and the Supremes and kept the radio on all day in the carport, especially when his buddies were over, telling their stories on Saturday afternoons.

Jay lifted his right hand and put it on the handle of the glass door that covered the refrigerated drinks. He kept it there for a moment, his fingers closed tight around the handle, waiting to hear Mr. Wright call out from the front of the store: "Little J, what you doing back there?" But he heard Kelvin's voice instead.

"Mr. Wright," Kelvin said, "how much is this magazine?"

"Which one?" Mr. Wright asked. Jay had wanted to look up into the mirror again, but doing so would've required him to step away from the cooler, and he was already standing in front of it, had his hand on it, in fact, and he knew he couldn't turn back now without drawing attention to himself.

"Which one?" Mr. Wright asked again.

"This one here," Kelvin's voice said.

"What's that, a *MAD* magazine?"

"Yes, sir," Kelvin said.

Jay opened the cooler door, felt its cold air pour out and wrap itself around his fingers. He stepped forward and let the opened door rest against his right hip. He reached for a bottle of Mad Dog with each hand. He grabbed one of Banana Red and another bottle—he was never able to discover what kind—and then he lifted the front of his shirt and stuffed the bottles into the waistband of his jeans. His hands were shaking, and he was trying to unfasten his belt and cinch it tighter when Kelvin shouted, "Thriller! Thriller!" before Jay heard the crash of the door being slammed open and the bell atop it being rung and the sound of Kelvin's feet pounding across the sidewalk and into the parking lot at a sprint.

Jay had turned away from the cooler, his hands jostling the bottles stuck in his waistband, and made a break for the door. He ran up the aisle by the front windows, his peripheral vision noting the shape of Mr. Wright as he came out from behind the counter. Jay had his shoulder against the door when he felt Mr. Wright's powerful grip clench itself around his left forearm. He pulled Jay back toward him, and Jay let go of the bottles, which had worked themselves up from his waist to his stomach, where he'd clutched them to his body. One of the bottles came loose and shattered on the linoleum, splashing neon pink liquid across the floor and all over Jay's and Mr. Wright's pants.

"Jesus," Mr. Wright said, momentarily relinquishing his grip on Jay's arm.

Jay felt the slackening of Mr. Wright's fingers, and he tore his arm free and stepped toward the door, but his shoe slipped on the wet floor, and he found himself on his back, flailing in the nauseatingly scented liquor and bits of broken glass. Mr. Wright bent down and helped him to his feet, his strong fingers once again closed around Jay's arm.

"Come on, Little J," he'd said. "Come on. Let's stand you up."

The first call Mr. Wright had made had been to Jay's mother.

"I should call the police," he'd said to Jay, the phone pressed to his ear while he waited for someone at the library's circulation desk to answer. Jay, the back of his shirt and blue jeans soaked through with Mad Dog, sat on the wooden stool Mr. Wright kept behind the counter. Mr. Wright stood, his back leaning against the window that looked out on the gas pumps and the otherwise empty parking lot. "You better be glad I know your daddy," he'd said. "And you'd better be glad I ain't calling him right now."

But Mr. Wright had ended up calling Jay's father anyway because his mother had been in a meeting and wasn't able to leave work to come pick him up, and Mr. Wright refused to let him leave the store without talking to one of his parents. But he'd looked just as worried about calling Jay's father as Jay was. His father worked as a mechanic for DeKalb County, and Jay pictured his father being called out from under one of the county's cars that he had up on a lift, tools in hand. Jay knew his father would raise his head at the sound of his name, set down his tools, and wipe his hands on the towel he always kept hanging out of his back pocket regardless of whether he was at work or at home. He would walk across the garage, pick up the phone, clear his throat, and then have one of his best buddies tell him about the awful thing his only son had just done.

"J," Mr. Wright said, "it's Connie down at the store. I got Jay here with me. I'm going to let him talk to you."

Jay had refused to turn rat on Kelvin, even though he knew that Mr. Wright knew that the boys had been in it together, even though he knew that Mr. Wright would tell his father exactly what had happened.

And that was why Kelvin's comment—the one about white folks eating him—really pissed Jay off.

"Man, it's your damn fault I got in trouble with my pops."

"Shoot," Kelvin had said. "Nobody held no gun to your head. Nobody told you to drop that bottle and make it look like you pissed yourself with Mad Dog." They'd been having this same argument for weeks since the event, but the part about Jay pissing was new.

"You shouldn't have run out on me," Jay said. "A friend wouldn't have done that."

"He was coming."

"He was coming because you acted a fool and hollered crazy shit and ran out."

"Shoot," Kelvin said.

"If you'd have stayed cool, we'd have been sipping on that Mad Dog with Robin and one of her girls, and then 'you-know-what.' But you acted a fool instead."

"Shoot," Kelvin said again.

But Jay couldn't imagine it, neither the "you-know-what" nor the sipping on the syrupy, caustic-smelling liquor. The smell of it had baked itself into his nose, and no matter how many times he had washed his clothes he'd still been able to smell it, and that seemed fitting, because the smell of the Mad Dog made his stomach feel the exact way the memory of that day still made him feel: sick, nauseated, alone.

The ride home in his father's truck had been quiet and uncomfortable.

"Can't believe you'd steal from Connie like a damn thug" was all his father had said. Instead of saying more, he'd lit a Winston Light and cracked the driver's-side window. The only other thing he'd said was when Jay had turned the radio on, the tinny jangle of the oldies station crackling through the truck's old speakers. "Turn that off," his father had said. So Jay had turned it off.

The decision had been made swiftly and quietly and without Jay's input. His mother and father had been planning a trip to North Carolina in June to see their new grandbaby for the first time, and while Jay had never been left home alone and figured he was expected to go along, he knew for certain they would not leave him home alone now after what had happened. And then, one morning a few days before school let out for the summer, Jay and his father were sitting at the breakfast table when his father closed the newspaper and looked across the table at Jay, where he sat pushing scrambled eggs around on his plate with a piece of toast that had nearly gone soft.

"Go ahead and pack you a good suitcase for when we go to Janelle's," his father had said.

"What's that mean?" Jay asked.

"You're going to be staying awhile."

Jay looked to his mother where she stood at the counter with her back to them. She was pouring coffee into a thermos for his father's lunch.

"Mom," Jay said.

"Listen to your father," she said.

Jay turned back to his father. "How long?" he asked.

"Long enough to learn not to steal," his father had said. He sat back and crossed his legs, flicked the newspaper open again. "Or until I can find Kelvin and kill him."

"James, it took two to tango," Jay's mother said. She had turned around, and she was standing with her arms folded, looking at Jay's father. "Kelvin's not one bit more guilty than Jay is."

"I bet he ain't being sent out to the country," Jay had said.

"You probably right," his father had said. "And that's why you'd better thank God you ain't Kelvin."

"It ain't fair," Jay said. He tossed the toast on his plate and slammed his back against his chair.

His father closed the newspaper slowly, deliberately, as if he was putting off something he either didn't want to do or perhaps wanted to relish. "Boy, you break that chair I'm going to break your ass." He laid the newspaper across his knee, raised his closed fist so Jay could see it. "I've got three jobs when it comes to you, and ain't none of them to be fair to you." He unfurled his index finger. "Job number one: Keep you safe, which also means keeping you alive. Job number two." He extended his middle finger. "Keep you healthy: Feed you. Give you a roof. Keep clothes on your back." His ring finger slid free next. "Three: Keep you happy." He sat back in his chair and picked up the newspaper. "And I ain't really interested in keeping you happy anymore."

"It still ain't fair," Jay said.

His father set the newspaper by his hat where it rested on the table. He stood. Jay inhaled deeply as if his body were warning him that he may need extra oxygen for flight. His father had never hurt him, but Jay had never done anything this bad. He could remember his father whacking him on the back of his legs with a belt when he was a young boy, but it had never really hurt, and even then Jay knew those punishments were designed to instill fear instead of pain. But now, if his father hit him, with either an open hand or a closed fist or a belt, pain would be the only goal.

His father loomed above him.

"Your mother and I work too hard to worry about what you think is fair. Connie Wright works too hard to think about it too. You have stolen from all of us, Jay, and we are deeply, deeply ashamed of you." He stood there for a moment, and Jay feared he would say more. But instead of speaking he raised his hand and touched the breast pocket of his county work shirt as if making sure his packet of cigarettes was where it always was, alongside his various pens and a shiny, metal tire pressure gauge. He snatched his hat from the table and slapped it onto his head.

His father picked up his lunchbox from the counter and walked out of the kitchen, but Jay could hear the crinkling plastic of the pack of cigarettes as his father shook one loose, followed by the sound of a lighter being struck. His father opened the front door and stepped outside, leaving behind a nearly undetectable remnant of smoke. Jay heard him start his truck and back out of the driveway.

His mother was still standing with her back against the counter, arms still folded across her chest. When Jay looked into her eyes, he knew what his father had said about his being deeply ashamed was true for his mother as well.

What Jay also discovered to be true was that his parents did not care about whether or not he was happy, because the prospect of living out in the country in Southport, North Carolina, did not make him happy.

As to their visit, his parents only stayed at Rodney and Janelle's house for a long weekend before heading back to Atlanta without him, although Jay knew his mother had wanted to stay longer to make sure Janelle and the baby were settled, but his father had never been one for vacations, which really meant that he'd never been one to allow himself to take any time off work, and by Saturday he was openly questioning whether or not he and Jay's mother should just leave on Sunday afternoon instead of Monday morning.

"Less traffic on Sunday," he'd said.

"No, James" was all his mother had said, not even raising her eyes from the baby's face where he slept, cradled in her arms.

Janelle's husband, Rodney, had sensed his father-in-law's restlessness and the strain it was putting on Janelle and her mother, so on Sunday, Rodney borrowed a jon boat from a friend and took Jay's father fishing. Janelle had tried taking the family to the beach on Saturday, but that had been a challenge. The baby had cried in the sticky sand and hot sun, and Jay's father had sat on a lawn chair, reading a newspaper he had folded into a tiny square to keep it from being rattled loose from his grip and carried away by the wind coming off the ocean, his only concession to his daily wardrobe being the shorts he wore. He still wore his same black work shoes, black socks, and long-sleeved shirt buttoned at the wrists, and, of course, his cap.

They were the only Black family on the beach that day, and Jay could feel the eyes of the white tourists upon them, and he couldn't help but remember what Kelvin had joked about white people doing to Black folks out in the country.

Once he and Rodney had walked down to the ocean and crashed through the breakers and were floating far from the shore, Jay had asked him, "Where are all the Black people at?"

Rodney had turned back toward the beach, its gray sand littered with pasty white bodies except for the dark clump where Jay's mother and sister sat on beach towels and his father sat on his chair, fighting against the wind as he turned one of the pages of his newspaper. Rodney laughed and looked back at Jay.

"Working," he said. "Or hunting, maybe fishing." He looked back at the beach. "None of those people on the beach are from here. People from here don't come to the beach."

"What do they do?"

"I don't know," Rodney said. "Same thing you do in Atlanta, I guess," but Jay knew that couldn't be true. In Atlanta, he played video games at Kelvin's house, hung out at the mall, shot hoops on the court that was walking distance from his house. He looked at

Rodney, who was now floating on his back, his eyes closed and his arms thrown wide as if welcoming the sunlight. Jay couldn't imagine Rodney being a kid his age, couldn't imagine him growing up in a place like this.

And then Jay's parents were gone, leaving him behind in a small house with a much older sister, who'd become a mother and who now felt more like a stranger than she ever had before. He was also left with a nephew who made him feel much too young to be called "uncle" and a brother-in-law whose cool, calm distance made him feel younger still.

It was late June, and while Jay did not know how long he'd be staying with his sister and her family, the fact that Janelle took him to the mall in Wilmington to shop for a backpack and new school shoes gave him a good idea. And then, in early August when classroom assignments were released by the county schools, Rodney drove him over to South Brunswick High School, where his father, a gruff, surly old man who reminded Jay of his own father, had his father worn glasses and gone to college, gave him a long, nearly silent tour of the school.

There wasn't much to do during the bright, white-hot August days while Jay waited in dreadful terror for school to start. Rodney left for work at Brunswick Electric early in the morning, and by the time Jay left the guest room, Janelle would've already fed the baby and put him down for his first nap of the day. Jay would find bland, unexciting cereal in the pantry and milk in the refrigerator before sitting down at the small kitchen table and pouring himself a cold breakfast.

Sometimes, Janelle had sat with him while he ate, and she'd ask about life back in Atlanta. How were Mom and Dad? What did he and his friends do when they weren't robbing convenience stores? What did he like to study in school? Jay understood these questions as honest attempts to know him, but they merely pointed out the gulf in their ages and the fact that the two of them had been raised by two seemingly different sets of parents and that life had been and would be very different for them both as a result.

In the instances in which he had been at the house alone, Jay had taken the opportunity to explore its contents, which meant he scoured the drawers and shelves in Janelle and Rodney's bedroom. What he'd found there had embarrassed him: Rodney's underwear; Janelle's panties; a pack of condoms; and a bundle of love letters Rodney had written to Janelle that featured descriptions of sex that seemed more real and romantic, and therefore more embarrassing, than anything Terry had described to him and Kelvin back in Atlanta.

Most often, Jay spent time in Rodney and Janelle's narrow walk-in closet, where Rodney's clothes hung on the left and Janelle's on the right. Above the racks, shelves rose all the way to the ceiling, and it was there, on the top shelf above Rodney's clothes, that Jay found the rifl .

It was resting inside a hard, powder-blue case, but Jay knew what lay inside as soon as his fingers swept over the hard, plastic shell that was as finely dimpled as gooseflesh. He found the handle, and he lifted the case down and set it on the floor in the middle of the closet. When he opened it, he caught the scent of the rifle's oiled metal barrel and its polished stock. The weapon was hard and cold and beautiful, and he imagined Rodney carrying it in the woods around Brunswick County, sighting down a deer or squirrel or rabbit or bear, whatever it was that men like Rodney hunted with a gun like this. Jay had grown up hearing his father tell hunting stories about his life as a country boy down in Norcross, Georgia, and Jay remembered that when Janelle first began dating Rodney, their father felt that he finally had someone with whom to share his stories, someone who would appreciate them in the same way their father did. Jay had felt left out, had felt that Rodney was just one more person who had more in common with Jay's father than he did, but he'd also been certain that he could've never enjoyed hunting the way the two of them did. But now, gazing down at the rifle where it begged to be handled, Jay finally understood. He wanted to load it, aim it, and fire it, but it was weeks before he did any of that. In the meantime, he left the open case on the floor of the closet, never going farther away than Rodney and Janelle's bed, never pointing the rifle at anything other than the image of himself holding a weapon in the bedroom mirror that hung on the wall above the dresser.

When his sister had been home, there hadn't been much for Jay to do aside from riding Rodney's old bicycle up and down the hot, humid road past old, quiet houses or dribbling his basketball in the driveway, which, thankfully, was paved, unlike so many other drive-ways in the Grove, many of which were made of gravel and shells or white, powdery sand. He planned on trying out for the basket-ball team in the fall, aiming for varsity, but planning for JV. Rodney had told him that kids in the county took basketball seriously, but Jay figured none of them could possibly be as good as the kids he'd played against on the playground at school or at the boys' club in his neighborhood. Even the white kids he'd played against at the YMCA on Saturday afternoons when he could convince his mother or father to drop him off had been good, all of them wanting to be Larry Bird, throwing elbows and camping out on the three-point line and clap-ping their hands at whoever had the ball.

Jay had tried to model his game on the swift-footed guards in-stead of the lumbering post players: Isiah Thomas, Walt Frazier, and even Michael Jordan, the college kid at UNC who'd made a name for himself that spring after sinking the championship-winning shot against Georgetown.

One hot afternoon when he was out in the driveway dribbling his basketball and thinking about the toll the cement was taking on the soles of his new black Adidas, he paused in his routine and detected the rhythmic *thump, thump* of a ball being dribbled somewhere close by. Then he heard the unmistakable *clang* of a ball bouncing around the inside of a rim before falling through the net. He walked to the end of the driveway, his ball held against his hip, and stood there, craning his neck to turn his ears in both directions up and down the otherwise silent street, searching for the source of the sound.

Since moving into his sister's house, he had seen no other kids his age on her street, and he'd grown bored of his loneliness and equally fearful of the possibility of not laying eyes on another boy his age before school began at the end of August.

A few houses down to his right, their road connected to a perpendicular road that led farther into the community. On his left, the road in front of Janelle's house continued on past several houses before turning to dirt—sand, really—and disappearing into the woods. The sound of the ball bouncing and hitting against a rim seemed to be coming from that direction, so Jay set out in search of it, his own basketball still held to his hip as if he were holding a baby there.

The noise grew louder and Jay more certain of its cause when the road turned from asphalt to earth. He had never walked or been driven this far. Up ahead he could see outbuildings and work equipment and cleared land, and he wondered if he'd stumbled upon some kind of farm. He continued walking past pine trees fronted by dense bushes clumped with Virginia creeper and thick, woody vines until a clearing gave way to a small, paved patch of land, where a white boy about Jay's age stood, sinking bank shots against a wooden backboard on a goal that, just by looking at it, Jay knew was a few inches under regulation height.

Jay stood there, watching, until the boy must have felt Jay's eyes on him. He stopped shooting, picked up his old, dusty ball, and turned to face Jay. The boy's eyes were big and dark; his brown hair was short but grew in a long tuft down the back of his neck. He wore black shorts and a black mesh tank top so dirty with dust that it appeared gray.

The boy looked at the basketball that Jay held, and he nodded by way of hello. "Want to shoot?" he asked.

Jay didn't speak or move. He waited for the boy to turn his back and resume his jump shots, and then he left his spot by the dirt road and walked to the opposite side of the crude half-court from where the white boy stood, still shooting jump shots, the ball bouncing back to him as if its path were preordained.

Jay took his first shot, and the ball hit just inside the rim and bounced around before popping out.

"It's a tight rim," the boy said. "That's why I bank them, get them to fall right through."

"It's low too," Jay said, the first words he'd spoken. "By a couple inches."

"Easier to dunk on, though," the boy said. He hadn't looked at Jay since inviting him to shoot, and he didn't look at him now.

Jay rebounded his shot and dribbled back out. He stopped and looked at the boy. "Can you dunk that?"

"I might could," the boy said. He paused and looked over at Jay. "Can you?"

"I might could get the rim," Jay said. He set his ball down, and then he stood straight. He charged toward the goal and sprang off his left foot and closed the tips of his fingers around the rim, pulling on it just enough for it to vibrate against the backboard. When he landed, he turned and looked at the boy, expecting something, but he didn't know what.

"Want to play 21?" the boy asked.

"Yeah," Jay said. "Let's use my ball."

And they did. The boy was strong, stronger than Jay, and surprisingly so given his skinny arms and legs and what his mesh tank top revealed of his bony, bird chest. He was a good shot, but Jay was a little quicker and a better dribbler. But even with those advantages, the boys nearly played one another to a draw, with the competition going to a decisive third game, which the white boy won with free throws that took him to 21.

The boy's name was Cody, and he was fifteen and would be going into the tenth grade at South Brunswick, where his mother worked in the school cafeteria, doing what, Jay never asked and was never told. Cody's father was a handyman of sorts, at least that was what Jay had been able to discern given the tools and unfinished projects strewn about the outside of the trailer where Cody lived with his parents, an only child, much like Jay now felt himself to be.

They spent the last few weeks of summer in this manner, playing 21, with Cody pretending to be Larry Bird and Jay pretending to be Magic Johnson, which would have been more fun had he had a teammate to pass the ball to. Jay did his best to keep his new Adidas high-tops clean, the ones Janelle had bought for him at the mall using the money his parents had left her, but at least he was breaking them in before the season began, and he figured that, as the new kid on the court at school, it would be more important to be good than look good. Each afternoon, after walking home from Cody's, Jay would stand at the kitchen sink and clean his shoes, wiping down the black leather with a damp paper towel. That was where Rodney had found him one evening when he'd arrived home early from work.

Rodney had been holding the baby in his arms, jostling him gently and making funny faces at him. The baby's wet, black eyes stared up at his father, his tiny fists curling and uncurling. Rodney turned his body so that Jay could see the baby as he cradled him. "Want to hold your little nephew?"

"Nah," Jay had said. He tugged on the hem of his damp T-shirt. "I'm all sweaty."

"What are you doing?"

"Cleaning my shoes," Jay said. "Trying to anyway."

"You been shooting hoops with that Rivenbark boy at the end of the road?"

Jay did not know Cody's last name and had never asked it and had never heard him tell it, but as far as he knew, Cody was the only boy on their road aside from himself.

"Cody?" he asked.

"That white kid."

"That's Cody," Jay had said. "Yeah, we play ball sometimes."

Rodney had looked down at the baby, and then he'd looked up at Jay. Jay could feel his brother-in-law's eyes boring into the side of his face.

"Just be careful," Rodney said.

With what? Jay had wondered. Playing with a white kid? Playing with a poor kid? Getting injured before tryouts? He'd wanted to ask Rodney what he meant, but he hadn't said a word, had just continued wiping down his shoes, squeezing the paper towel so that the dirty water dripped into the sink.

"His folks," Rodney said. He'd shrugged. "You know, just be careful."

The next day, when Jay came home from shooting ball at Cody's, he'd found Rodney mixing cement in a wheelbarrow. He'd already used post-hole diggers to dig a hole to install the goal he'd purchased at the sporting goods store in Southport. The pole was lying on the grass, the shiny red rim already attached to the white fiberglass backboard where it leaned against Rodney's truck.

Rodney, the hose in his hand trickling water onto the powdery mixture in the wheelbarrow, had nodded at the collection of pieces spread out around him.

"Pretty sweet, huh?" he'd said. He knocked the basketball out of Jay's hands and shot it, one-handed, through the goal where it rested at almost ground level. "This old boy's about to ball you up."

But Rodney never shot baskets with him after that. He had always left for work before Jay got up for school, and he'd come home in the evening just before dinner. Jay always had homework, and Janelle was insistent that he do it all without getting up from the kitchen table after they'd put everything away after dinner.

Jay and Cody shot baskets and played one-on-one on the new goal, intuitively ending their play before Rodney came home from work, although Jay never mentioned why and Cody never brought it up. Janelle had never mentioned Cody either, and Cody never saw her, never stepped foot in the house, even leaving early one day to go home to use the bathroom, although Jay had invited him to use theirs. Jay went so far as to count the number of times Cody had watched him drinking water from the hose before he accepted Jay's offer to take a sip. It had taken six days for Cody to say yes.

Occasionally, Janelle had asked Jay if he'd made friends at school, and he had usually answered "Not really" or "Not yet," which was true for the most part. Given their separate grades, he and Cody hadn't really seen one another at school, but even when Jay had passed him in the hallway or stood near him on the blacktop after lunch, they had done little more than nod at one another before looking away.

After basketball tryouts had passed and neither of them had made varsity or JV, Cody because he decided not to try out and Jay because the country boys who did were bigger, faster, and better than he had anticipated, they stopped playing basketball at either Cody's house or Jay's. Jay kept to himself, watching television as the days grew shorter and slightly cooler, occasionally riding Rodney's old ten-speed into Southport to buy a Coke and a bag of chips at the convenience store if he had money or if Janelle was willing to give him some. She'd been gentle with him, and he'd known it was because she'd felt badly that he hadn't made the basketball team and that he missed his friends and had not made new ones to replace the old. The kids in Brunswick County, whether they were Black or white, seemed suspicious of him and his closely shaved head and his long shorts and the quick way he spoke to them when and if they spoke to him. The kids he met at school walked and talked slowly, laughed quietly and rarely, and wore blue jeans and T-shirts no matter how hot it was outside.

Rodney had seemed to sense Jay's loneliness with more acuity than anyone, and it was clear to Jay that Rodney had tried to trace his disposition back to his not making the basketball team. "Look, man," Rodney had said. "I didn't make it my freshman year either. And then I played varsity for the next three."

Jay had shrunk down in the sofa cushions, shrugged his shoulders. "I ain't going to be here next year," he'd said. "So it don't matter anyway."

"Well, Michael Jordan got cut his freshman year too," Rodney had added. "And look at him now."

But Jay had known he was no Michael Jordan. He was a gangly teenager with no friends who'd already lost interest in basketball, who spent most of his time watching television and riding a dorky bike and the rest of his time handling his brother-in-law's rifle in secret, trying to gather the nerve to load it and take it into the woods behind the house.

By the time Jay and Cody had begun hanging out again, the air had grown cool, and Jay was finally wearing blue jeans like the rest of the kids, and so was Cody, although he regularly wore his black mesh tank top as if it were a required uniform, his skinny arms browned by the sun, his bone-white belly and chest seeming to glow through the screenlike fabric.

Although the high school, college, and NBA seasons had begun, basketball was over in Jay's mind, and it must've been over in Cody's too, because they never played and never talked about playing. Instead, they explored the woods surrounding the Grove and the piece of land where Cody's family's trailer sat. If they walked far enough, the trees—pines mostly, racked with vines and scrubby shrubs—gave way to an enormous swath of cleared acreage where expensive homes were being built. They could reach the water here where the ocean opened to the waterway that separated Southport from Oak Island. Cody talked about fishing, but he never brought a rod, and he talked about setting up tin cans for target practice, but he never brought a gun either.

They spent more of their time either throwing things into the water, looking for things the water may have washed ashore, or slinking around the construction sites, doing their best to steer clear of the carpenters and various contractors pouring concrete, installing windows, or hooking up HVAC systems on the cement pads that sat alongside the houses, many of which appeared close to being finished.

Cody always kept his eyes out for tools—hammers, screwdrivers, staple guns: the more expensive, the better. And he always came away with a bit of copper wire or a handful of unused nails or a strip of rolled carpet: things that had clearly been left behind but held value to him.

One late afternoon, on their way home from the water, Cody had spotted a heavy framing hammer that had been left behind on the front porch of a home that had been framed up but not yet walled in. Cody had picked up the hammer and bounced it in his hand as if testing its weight and ability to do the job.

"Man, you'd better leave that where you found it," Jay had said.

"If they'll miss it, they shouldn't have left it."

"That's no reason to steal it," Jay had said, realizing that he sounded more like his father than himself.

"They're tearing down my woods," Cody had said. "Used to be we could come down here and fish without nobody running us off."

"Nobody's running us off now."

"Not yet," Cody had said, "but I'm keeping this for when they do." He'd turned, the hammer still in his hand, and walked toward the woods that would lead them home.

Cody had no idea what Jay had done back in Atlanta that had caused him to be sent to live with his sister and brother-in-law. He wasn't necessarily embarrassed by what he and Kelvin had done, though his guilt over the fact that he'd done it directly to Mr. Wright and indirectly to his mother and father had done nothing but grow over the intervening months. The reason he hadn't told Cody wasn't the implied stamp of criminality that something like that would garner, but instead the expectations that an act like that brought with it. Jay didn't know Cody well enough to know whether or not he was a bad kid—a thief, a bully, a liar—and he hadn't seen him at school enough to discern anything from his actions there. But Jay did not want Cody to know that he, in fact, was capable of being a thief, because perhaps that would trigger something dark and malevolent in Cody that Jay had not yet seen surface, and then Jay would be expected to rise and meet it.

But nearly the opposite happened: the more Cody stole from the new development—the more tools and bits of wire and other materials he was able to secret away—the more Jay felt something angry and resentful and dangerous rearing itself inside him. His sister and Rodney had not sensed it, and he'd known they did not know him or understand him well enough to perceive anything real or true about him, and he knew for certain that the same could have been said of his teachers and the kids at school. Cody had become Jay's sole fulcrum of expression, the one person who'd kindled in him the desire to impress.

The first time Jay had taken Rodney's rifle out of his and Janelle's bedroom, he'd walked out the front door and stepped off the porch, the powder-blue plastic case bouncing against his thigh where he held it down by his side. Cody had been waiting for him in the driveway. The day had been warm, the sun having already settled below the trees. Fall had come, and the afternoon had taken on a soft, gauzy light.

"Woah," Cody had said, his eyes locked on the case. "Is that what I think it is?"

Jay had tried not to smile or flush with pride. He'd looked around, making sure no one had seen them. Janelle had gone to the grocery store and taken the baby with her, and Jay knew they had at least an hour before she would return. Rodney wouldn't be home until closer to dark.

Jay had walked around the corner of the house, past the gate that led to the backyard, and along the narrow strip of sandy soil tufted with grass that separated the neighbors' fence from theirs. He had not spoken and did not stop walking until he and Cody were in the woods.

By the time they'd stopped, Jay had led Cody deep into the trees behind his house, well out of earshot of anyone's backyard. Jay had knelt and set the case gently on the earth, making sure there was nothing beneath it to scratch the plastic shell. He unfastened the clasps and opened the case. Cody stepped behind him and looked over his shoulder.

"Well, looky there," he'd said. Jay stood and looked down at the rifle. Cody stooped to touch it, but Jay beat him to it, scooping it up with his left hand and letting the barrel drop into his right.

"That's a Springfield," Cody had said.

"Yeah," Jay said, although he had no idea what that meant or if it was true.

"Do you have any cartridges?"

Jay looked at him. The only time he'd ever used a cartridge was to play Atari with Kelvin in Terry's room when Terry wasn't home.

"Bullets," Cody said. "They hold the bullets."

"Yeah," Jay said. Cody smiled. "There's a couple boxes of them in the closet."

"In the closet?" Cody repeated. "Go get them. Let's fire this thing."

Jay looked at the gun in his hands, thought about the sound it would make, what kind of attention that might draw. If someone found out, he wouldn't be able to explain it to Rodney and Janelle, not the taking of the rifle or the showing it to Cody or the shooting it with someone Rodney clearly didn't want him hanging around. And worse, he knew they'd tell his father, and Jay couldn't bear the thought of that.

"I just wanted to show it to you," he said. "We can shoot it some other time."

"Let me see it," Cody said. He reached out his open hand. Jay hesitated for just a moment, but then he passed the rifle over.

Cody bounced the rifle in his hand the same way he'd bounced the hammer he'd stolen, and for a moment Jay feared that Cody might tear off toward home and that he would never see Rodney's rifle again. But instead, Cody lifted the rifle in a firing stance, closed one eye, and sighted down the length of the barrel.

"Man, I wish you had some cartridges," he said. He squeezed the trigger, something even Jay had not yet done, but nothing happened. "*Pow*," Cody whispered. He kept the rifle pointed into the distance, and he turned his head and looked over at Jay. "Your brother-in-law hunt deer?" he asked.

Jay opened his mouth to say something in response, but he wasn't able to say it before the two of them heard a voice they had not heard before.

"Drop that rifle, boy."

Jay spun around to face the woods leading to the development, and that was where he saw a white man standing, pointing a huge pistol at Cody. From the corner of his eye, Jay could see that Cody had lowered the rifle. He was staring at the man too. "You keep that rifle down, boy. You raise it and I'll blow your goddamned head off," the man said. Cody seemed to realize the implication of what holding the rifle meant, and he lowered it even more until it was pointing at the ground. The man crept forward, his pistol pointed at Cody's chest. With his free hand, the man gestured toward the rifle, his palm upturned, his fingers curling in the air as if trying to catch something floating there. "Give me that rifle, boy."

Cody turned the rifle sideways in his hands and held it out like an offering.

Panic pushed Jay forward. If the man took the rifle, Jay knew he would never get it back, and Rodney would discover that he had taken it, and everyone would consider it stolen. Without thought of either the danger or his own foolishness, Jay lunged for the rifle, but the man lunged too, and he snatched it from Cody's hands before Jay could reach it, and then he swept his pistol through the air until it was pointing at Jay's chest.

"What the hell are you doing, boy?" the man asked. "You trying to get your goddamned brains blown out?"

Jay's heart roared in his chest, and he could feel it beating in his ears, his body pulsing with terror. Although his vision felt sharper than ever, he could feel tears beginning to rim his eyes. He stared at the pistol's barrel where the man held it pointed at his chest, and he imagined the sound of the bullet leaving the chamber, coursing through the long cylinder, and striking his body. He looked up at the man's face; the man was smiling.

"You going to cry, boy?"

"Give that back."

"This?" the man said. He holstered his pistol, and then he studied the rifle. He opened the bolt to see if it was loaded, and then he closed it. "Where'd y'all steal this from?"

"We didn't steal it," Cody said.

"Oh, yeah?" the man said. "How about I call the police and ask them."

"It's Rodney's," Jay said, immediately regretting it.

"Rodney's?"

"Yeah," Jay said. His breathing had slowed and steadied, and his heart, while still racing, was not governing his body in quite the same way it had been just moments before. He could smell the man's body—either his cologne or aftershave—and he feared that even if he were able to get the rifle back, the man's smell would forever taint it, and Rodney would immediately know it had been taken out and handled, and he would suspect Jay.

"You Rodney Bellamy's little brother?" the man asked. He propped the rifle on his shoulder as if he were a soldier preparing to march, but Jay could tell that he was no soldier. He appeared too casual, one hand in his pocket, his hip cocked to the side. It seemed that relaxing in this way after pointing a gun at two boys was the most natural thing he could do.

Jay wasn't Rodney's brother, not really anyway, but he wasn't clearheaded enough to think of the term *brother-in-law*. He simply nodded his head.

"Well, damn, I know who your brother is," the man said. "Your daddy too." He laughed as if this fact should be funny to all of them. "Jesus," he said to himself.

"Give me that gun back," Jay said.

The man widened his eyes as if shocked by what Jay had just said to him. He bent slightly at the waist and lowered his voice as if speaking to a dog. "Come and take it, boy."

Jay felt Cody's hand on his elbow. "Don't," Cody said. "Don't."

The man smiled, looked from Jay to Cody. "Y'all are like salt and pepper," he said. "Jesus, it's cute." His face went flat and his eyes suddenly narrowed. "If I catch you back here in this neighborhood again, I'll kill you both, I promise you that." Neither boy said anything, but Jay's mind flashed back to the many things Cody had stolen, the times they had tracked mud into a house under construction, and the one time Jay had thrown a rock through a window that had not yet been installed.

"These ain't your woods," Cody said. Jay looked over at him. Cody's nostrils flared and his chest heaved as if he couldn't gather enough breath in his lungs.

"You're wrong about that," the man said. He raised his free hand and pointed behind him. "I own every stretch of this land from the waterline"—he swept his arm around and pointed toward the Grove behind the boys—"to the little shantytown right there, and I'll come to own it soon enough." He lowered his arm and looked at Jay, and then he tossed the rifle on the ground at Jay's feet. "Get home, boy." He looked at Cody. "I know your daddy," he said, "and I don't think he'd look kindly on you running around with colored boys. Don't let me catch y'all back here again." He stared at them for another moment, and then he turned and disappeared into the trees.

Jay and Cody stood there until they could no longer hear the man's feet moving through the woods, and then Jay bent to gather the rifle in one hand and the case in the other. They ran in separate directions: Jay headed back between the fences that separated Rodney and Janelle's property from the neighbors', while Cody tore along the edge of the woods toward his family's land. Neither of the boys had said a word.

Jay squatted next to the house before rounding the corner to the driveway, and he quickly checked the rifle for scratches or smudges or fingerprints. Seeing none, he laid it carefully back in its case and closed it. He picked it up by the handle and carried it around to the front of the house and through the front door. Once he was inside, he'd inspected the case with the same quick meticulousness with which he'd inspected the weapon, and seeing nothing that caught his eye, he set the case back on the top shelf on Rodney's side of the closet.

The man's cologne seemed to linger in the small closet, but Jay thought it possible that the scent had either become trapped in his nasal cavity or perhaps had burrowed into his brain. He spent the rest of the day in this jittery, adrenaline-driven state of apprehension and fear, waiting for a knock on the door or a telephone call that would relay to Janelle or Rodney exactly what had transpired in the woods right behind their house. But neither the knock nor the call came that afternoon or evening, and by the time he was brushing his teeth and getting ready for bed, Jay felt certain that the only person he would ever talk to about what had happened in the woods was Cody himself, and he doubted that Cody would say a word to anyone, mostly because, like Jay, he didn't seem to have anyone to say it to.

It was hours later, well after Jay had drifted off to sleep, that he was awakened by the baby's crying and kept awake by the whispers of his sister and brother-in-law. He looked at the clock on his bedside table. It was a few minutes before 3:00 a.m. Jay had never been awake in Janelle's house that late at night, and he wondered if the whispering between Janelle and Rodney was something that happened every night, or if the baby always woke and cried each night at this time.

And then he feared that something else had kept Janelle and Rodney from sleeping. Perhaps the man from the woods had called Rodney at work and told him what had happened. Jay replayed every conversation he'd had with his sister and Rodney that evening during dinner and later when they'd carved two pumpkins on the front steps, searching each discussion they'd had for any hint that either of them knew something. Or perhaps Rodney had sensed something in the closet, perhaps he had caught a whiff of the man's cologne and asked Janelle about it. Perhaps they had sought out the source of the smell and opened the rifle's case and discovered something different about it, although Jay couldn't imagine what that would be. He'd put it back exactly as he'd always put it back each time he'd taken it down from the shelf. But then fear gripped him by the neck when he realized he could not remember which way the case had been facing when he'd taken the rifle down, and he could not remember which way he'd left it facing when he'd put it back.

He lay in bed listening to their quiet voices, and then he heard Rodney's heavy footsteps in the hallway, and then the sound of the front door opening and closing quietly. In the driveway, Janelle's car started, and the yellow glow of the Datsun's headlights illuminated the blinds that covered the window above Jay's bed.

He wondered where Rodney was going this late at night, and he wondered if Janelle was still awake, still staring at the rifle inside the open case that Rodney had left on their bed, her mind doing its best to decide whether or not Jay was to blame. Jay decided that he would wait to see what they asked him in the morning, and he hoped that he could catch the school bus without seeing either one of them so that he could find Cody and they could get their stories straight.

And school was where he'd been the next morning when Mr. Bellamy, Rodney's father, opened the door to his math class and gestured to the teacher to join him in the hall. It wasn't uncommon for a teacher or the principal or another administrator to interrupt a class to speak with a teacher, but even though he knew this, Jay could not stop the thrumming of his heart nor deny the sudden clamminess of his skin. Why did it have to be Rodney's father at the door?

Jay's teacher stepped halfway through the doorway and looked at him, and then she said his name and waved him out into the hall. "Get your things," she said.

Jay stood, his body and legs feeling rubbery and cold, and slid his book and papers into his backpack. He could feel the other students' eyes on him, and although none of them were speaking, he knew they were all wondering what the quiet Black kid from Atlanta had done.

His teacher was waiting for him at the door, and she put her hand on his shoulder as he passed through the doorway and into the hall, where Mr. Bellamy stood, his hands in his pockets. Jay had never spoken to Mr. Bellamy at school and had spent very little time with him outside of it, so he did not know how to read the man's face.

"Jay," Mr. Bellamy said. "Something terrible has happened."

CHAPTER 5

The airport in Wilmington, North Carolina, especially in 1984, was small, and Colleen couldn't help but think of it as a miniature model of a real airport. After getting off the phone with her mother, she found a bench near the curb outside baggage claim and took a seat, her suitcase on the ground at her feet and her purse resting on her lap. She wore a jean jacket over the T-shirt she had slept in the night before and a pair of white jeans with black Keds. She slid her headphones over her ears and pressed *play* on her Walkman; Pat Benatar's "Shadows of the Night" came on in mid-song. She remembered a pair of black sunglasses in her purse. When she looked for them, she found the dog-eared copy of T. Berry Brazelton's *Infants and Mothers* that she'd been carrying around in her purse for nearly a year like some kind of talisman that could change her fate. She thought about pulling out the book and flipping through its pages, but instead she found her sunglasses and slid them on, and then she sat there and cried.

A handful of taxis was lined up by the curb. A middle-aged Black man stood with his elbows propped above the driver's-side door of the taxi closest to Colleen. He looked at her across the roof of the car and nodded *hello*. He wore black sunglasses too, and he also wore one of those yellow-tinted visors that you picture card dealers wearing in dark, smoky rooms where men hide out from their wives and the police.

The man mouthed something, and Colleen could tell that he was speaking to her. She took off her headphones and waited for him to repeat himself. She was still able to hear the tinny whine of Pat Benatar's voice.

"You need to go somewhere?" the man asked.

She looked down and pushed *stop* on the Walkman, then she wiped her eyes behind her sunglasses. She looked back up at the man. "No," she said. "My father's coming to get me."

"That's good," the man said. "That's good." He turned his head forward, and she knew that from where he stood he could see the spot on the runway where the airplanes were turning around after landing before taxiing to the airport's one terminal. "Fathers should come get their daughters when they're crying."

She wanted to tell him that she wasn't crying, but she was, and what did it matter if this man she had never seen before and would never see again watched her cry? She also wanted to tell him it was none of his business, but his business was picking people up from the airport, and she very much looked like someone who needed that business. As to her father coming to get her, that seemed to imply a rescue, and she would have to admit her father did have a history of rescuing her.

When she was twelve years old and in the seventh grade, she had saved up her babysitting money to buy a new outfit from Belk's Department Store for the school photo. She could still picture the outfit now: a pale yellow blouse, a bright yellow skirt with a matching yellow cardigan. A white flower had been stitched over the left breast. The stitching of the flower's blue stem ran down the front, under the left arm, and across the back of the sweater.

She was incredibly proud of the outfit, and it was easy for Colleen to recall her devastation, along with her humiliation, when she felt the warm dampness of her first period seep into her cotton underwear and wet her thighs where she sat at her desk in Mrs. Roberts's English class. Colleen and her mother had already talked about her getting her period, and she knew exactly what was happening, but she couldn't stop a mixture of shame and shock from overtaking her. She resisted raising her hand and calling Mrs. Roberts over for fear of having to tell her what had happened and having anyone else hear. Instead, she slipped off her cardigan and did her best to bunch it around her to hide the stain that she knew was spreading across the front and back of her skirt. Everyone else in the class was bent over their desks, working quietly. She stood and pushed back her chair. Her underwear felt heavy, as if its weight could cause it to slide down her legs to the floor.

"Mrs. Roberts," she said. The teacher looked up at her. "I don't feel good. I need to go to the office and call my mom." She backed away, opened the door, and stepped into the hall. Neither Mrs. Roberts nor anyone else in class had said a word. She fled as soon as she'd pulled the door closed.

Colleen had hidden out in the bathroom while the school secretary called home to tell her mother what had happened and to ask her to bring a new outfit to the school. The nurse had given Colleen a sanitary pad, and she sat down on the toilet, her stained underwear on the floor beside her, and held the pad between her legs. Her sweater and skirt had been folded inside a paper bag that sat on the floor beside her underwear. The outfit was ruined. Colleen cried at the realization that she would not wear it in her school picture, and she wondered when her mother would arrive and what outfit she would bring to replace it. She didn't know how long she sat there, but she remembered the bell ringing and knowing that she would have to return to Mrs. Roberts's classroom to gather her things and that she would have to answer questions from her teacher and her friends.

When Colleen heard the door open, she snatched her damp underwear from the floor and held it before her with the tips of her fingers as if it were a dead animal. She expected to hear her mother's voice, but instead she heard the sound of handcuffs clinking and the squeak of her father's rigid belt, the heavy footstep of his hard-soled shoes. Her heart sank.

"Honey," he said. "Are you in there?"

"Yes," Colleen said, choking back a sob. She had never been embarrassed to cry in front of her father, but sitting there in a closed bathroom stall, naked except for a rumpled blouse and a pad held between her legs, she was humiliated. "You're not supposed to be in the girls' room."

"Well," he said, "I've been given a special dispensation by the principal." The stall creaked, and she imagined her father leaning his body against it. "They told me what happened, and I brought you something to wear." He sighed. "I hope I got it right."

She pictured her father in her room at home, opening the closet and her dresser drawers, pulling out skirts and sweaters and blouses and placing them on the bed as if trying to fit them into some kind of puzzle that made sense to him. She could not imagine what he had chosen, and she was terrified at the thought of hurting his feelings, but she was even more terrified of leaving the bathroom and sitting for photos in whatever he had brought.

Colleen looked up to see him lowering down an outfit on a hanger. It was the same yellow sweater set she had purchased from Belk's, the tags still attached. She stood up, still holding the pad between her legs, and took it from his hand. She remembered crying with relief. Her father had never been shopping with her—she didn't know that he had ever been shopping by himself—and she could not imagine him at the department store alone, wandering through Belk's until he found the outfit she had ruined.

"How did you know to get this?" she asked.

"You think I don't pay attention?" he said. "Your mother thinks the same thing. I pay more attention than y'all think I do." He bent down and slipped an unopened pack of underwear beneath the stall door.

"I'm sorry," she said.

"Honey, why are you sorry?"

"Because they called you at work," she said. "Because you went all the way to the Belk's in Shallotte."

"Don't be sorry," he said. "Don't ever be sorry. You needed me, and I came. I'll always come when you need me."

And here he was, on his way once again.

The man who stood by the taxi was chewing gum, and he blew a pink bubble before pulling it back into his mouth. Colleen had had two more beers in the Charlotte airport during her layover and another one on the flight to Wilmington, and she didn't want her father arriving and smelling alcohol on her breath. He wasn't the kind of person to scold or judge someone for having a drink or two, but Colleen didn't want him to learn that the law school graduate who didn't practice law and who'd just lost a child and who might be losing her marriage had also become a day drinker.

"You got any extra gum?" she asked.

The man stopped chewing for a moment. He looked away from the runway and back at Colleen.

"I do," he said.

"I'd love a piece if you don't mind."

"I don't."

He stepped around the front of his taxi and onto the curb. He pulled a package of gum from his pocket and passed a wrapped, pink square of Bubblicious to her.

"Thank you," she said. She unwrapped it and popped it into her mouth.

"You're welcome," he said. "I hope your day gets better."

"Me too," she said.

"It will."

He stepped off the curb and walked back around the front of his car to the driver's side. He opened the door and climbed in. Colleen heard the radio come on inside the cab. He leaned back in his seat.

She put her headphones back on and pushed *play* and closed her eyes too. The taste of the gum was almost overwhelming in its sugary sweetness. She thought of the Bubblicious commercials and how the kids on television blew bubbles that lifted them up off the ground and allowed them to float through the air and even carried them into outer space. She kept her eyes closed and listened to Pat Benatar's voice and turned her face up toward the sky and blew a bubble, pictured her body leaving the bench and her feet leaving the ground. She would look down and search for her father's car on the roads around the airport, and she would somehow lower her body back to the earth just seconds before he arrived. She stayed like that, eyes closed but lifted toward the sky. A tear rolled down each cheek and met at the bottom of her neck.

On the flight from Charlotte, Colleen had finished her beer and then closed her eyes and laid her head back on the seat. She had imagined the spirit of her dead son flying alongside her outside the plane's window, going extra fast to stay abreast of the airplane so he could keep his eyes on her. She knew this would sound crazy—insane, in fact—if she were to say it out loud, but a few months ago she'd been a woman waiting on a baby, and she was just a woman who'd lost one, and somehow it felt like now she was less than what she'd started out being. As the airplane had prepared to land, she opened her eyes and looked out the window to see its shadow on the clouds beneath them. When the clouds broke, the plane's shadow fell to the earth below, skimming over the faces of waterways and the waving heads of sawgrass and the tops of scrub oaks. The spirit of her son merged with the shadow of the airplane, and she knew he had returned to the place where she and Scott had spent so many hours skirting his parents' boat through these waters, the place where they had planned to make their home so very far from Dallas, Texas.

But this area hadn't always been home, at least not to Colleen anyway; it was Scott's home. He had even looked like the North Carolina coast the first day she'd laid eyes on him four years earlier in the registration line at Carolina. They'd been grouped together because their last names both started with B, and she'd spotted Scott with a folded class schedule sticking out of the back pocket of his shorts. Unlike the other guys in line to register for classes—most of them with shaggy hair and in blue jeans and boots—Scott looked as if he'd just stepped onto the dock after a day on the water: canvas boat shoes that were tied so loosely they appeared to have been slipped on; the tan shorts and the baby blue polo shirt tucked into them; the braided leather belt; the Ray-Ban aviators that sat atop the white cotton sun visor. It was easy to see him for what he was: a rich kid from the eastern side of the state whose parents didn't quite have the financial pull necessary to get the prodigal son into an Ivy League law school or even somewhere like Wake Forest or Duke, but a family nonetheless with just enough political clout with the board of governors to encourage Chapel Hill to look the other way while opening its doors for their boy.

Colleen certainly didn't have the grades, connections, or financial backing to attend Wake Forest or Duke, but she'd done well on the LSAT and maintained a solid GPA, so Chapel Hill had thrown a little scholarship money her way. North Carolina Central had offered her a full ride, and although she had to admit to herself that something vaguely liberal and progressive spoke to her about the prospect of attending a historically Black university, she always knew she would end up choosing Chapel Hill. It was the late 1970s, and the thought of being a minority among minorities validated whatever it was inside her that made her feel that, so far, her life had been far too comfortable.

Life had been comfortable for Scott too, but the more she watched him that first semester and the more she learned about him the clearer it became that he found law school especially challenging. It was evident that he wasn't going to be the smartest student in their classes, and, after a few weeks of listening to him stumble around his answers when called on in Property, Colleen understood that Scott had never been the smartest student in any of his classes, even if he had more than likely been the richest and the best looking. But there was something in his willingness to try to talk through tough questions that attracted her, and by the time their first semester was halfway over she and Scott and a handful of other 1Ls were regularly meeting for beer and pizza on Wednesday nights at a basement dive called the Rathskellar, just off Franklin Street.

The group—there were six of them: three guys and three girls—would drink Coors Light and eat pizza and occasionally go to the jukebox and play Duran Duran or Springsteen to drown out the voice of Ronald Reagan, who so often appeared on the television above the bar. The place was a dive, and the bar didn't yet have cable, but the bartender would continually clamber up and down the beer kegs to switch the stations and adjust and readjust the rabbit ears to get the reception just right.

Only one person in their group liked Reagan: Brantley Suttles, a staunch Baptist from Shelby who'd gone to Campbell as an undergrad. The rest of them believed themselves to be Democrats, although it was clear to Colleen that none of them but Scott knew exactly why. Unlike their parents—hers included—who were still mourning the assassinations of John and Bobby Kennedy and still pissed at Nixon for too many reasons to count, Scott's mother and father were blueblood conservatives, products of the old money that seeped from the once-decaying and now-gone plantations in the eastern part of North

Carolina. But that power was fleeting and recentering itself politically and geographically in Raleigh, Charlotte, Greensboro, and Chapel Hill. Scott seemed to understand this, and he was more than willing to discuss the waning powers of his parents' worldview. Unlike Colleen's political ideologies, which were based on protests, headlines, song lyrics, and domestic bombings by fringe groups, Scott's political ideology was much simpler. What he didn't possess in inherent brilliance or revolutionary zeal he made up for in his simple understanding of people: their motivations, fears, and frustrations.

Theirs was a strange generation. They grew up with headlines about marches, protests, and sit-ins; they watched the Vietnam War and Woodstock live on color television; they all wanted to be H. Rap Brown and Jane Fonda and Patty Hearst; and when they turned eighteen and felt the full conviction of their revolutionary duty, they all voted for a soft-spoken peanut farmer who was systematically humiliated from his earliest days in office until what seemed his very last. *And what did we do then?* Colleen asked herself. They turned their gazes inward, a turning that had begun much earlier than they realized.

Colleen had never wanted to be Bernardine Dohrn; she wanted to dress like Bernardine Dohrn, to talk like Bernardine Dohrn, and to be desired like Bernardine Dohrn. Scott seemed to understand this posturing before Colleen did, but he never called her on it, never tested her liberal ideologies beyond those Wednesday night conversations in the months before and after Reagan's election.

Their courtship began with Scott and Colleen leaving the library together on Wednesday nights, walking out to their separate cars, and driving back home to their separate apartments before meeting their friends on Franklin Street for pizza and beer. But soon enough Scott was asking Colleen if she'd like to ride with him, and they'd leave her car on campus, then stop by her place so she could drop off her books and change clothes before heading to the bar. Afterward, he'd return her to her car late that night and sit behind the wheel of his own while she cranked the engine and gave him a wave. But by Thanksgiving she was being dropped off at her car in the early mornings before class, always in the clothes she'd worn out the night before, Scott now leaning against her driver's-side door and giving her a long kiss for the hour or two they'd go without seeing one another. Soon she found herself staying at Scott's apartment nearly every night, driving over after leaving the library when it closed its doors at midnight, finding Scott sitting at the table in his tiny kitchen, a cassette of Bruce Springsteen's *Nebraska* playing relentlessly on the small stereo he kept on the counter. They'd ride to campus together the next morning, enter the building together, unafraid of anyone noticing, knowing, or imagining what went on between them when they weren't in class.

And so they carried on that way throughout their first year of law school at Carolina, and that summer Colleen returned to her parents' house in Oak Island and began a paid internship at a real estate law office that a friend of her father's had lined up for her. Scott was just up the road in Wilmington, where he lived with his older brother Don and his wife and found an unpaid internship at Legal Aid, a job that took him into some of the most depressed neighborhoods in the city to meet some of the poorest people in the state. The stories he told Colleen over the phone during the week made her worry about him: his safety, his sense of justice that could easily be taken advantage of, his heart that let in too much at once. But she also worried that what he was doing actually mattered, and not just in the grand scheme of the careers they often talked about but couldn't really imagine awaiting them at the end of their third year of school.

But Colleen hadn't thought or worried about these things on the weekends when she drove her crappy hatchback Cavalier north on Highway 17, and she, Scott, Don, and his wife, Karen, would launch Don's boat from the waterway at Wrightsville Beach and head out to Masonboro Island, where they'd hitch to one of the other dozen or so boats that were captained by similarly tanned, well-dressed, attractive twenty- and thirty-somethings. On the way out Don would follow the coastline and point out the gorgeous homes that had once hosted guests like the Vanderbilts and the Astors on Masonboro Sound, and Colleen couldn't help but feel that in pointing out the absence of these families, perhaps Don was pointing out the fact that his and Scott's family was still there, present and accounted for, not quite as glamorous or as famous, but every bit as capable of impressing Colleen with their wealth, standing, and dedication to leisure.

Once they reached Masonboro Island, they'd stay around the boat drinking and swimming and sunning themselves to a ruby red until dusk. Then they'd go ashore and make a fire and sit around with many of the same people they'd spent the day with, grilling hot dogs and hamburgers, drinking beer, and listening to music, eventually sneaking off in couples to go farther up the beach to spend the night atop a sleeping bag with nothing but a thin cotton sheet to protect their sunburned skin from the warm breeze that came off the water. They'd fall asleep to the sounds of conversations around the fire that would not die down until just before dawn.

Colleen thought that would be her life. Back then she wasn't thinking about marrying Scott or having a child with him; she was simply living a life that she thought would last forever. And now here she was back in the place where she had thought that life would continue, sitting on a bench alone and waiting for her father.

COLLEEN KNEW THAT her father was not the kind of man who'd sit behind the wheel of a running car at the curb and wait to be found. He was the kind of man who parks and comes to find you, and that's what he did. Colleen looked up, and suddenly he was there. The last time she'd seen him, he and her mother had arrived in Dallas for their grandson's birth, and now something about her father seemed or looked different, but Colleen knew that it was she who was different. Everything about her had changed.

"Hey, bean," her father said.

She stood, and he opened his arms to her. She left her sunglasses on and hugged him, smelled the familiar scent of him—his old man aftershave, wood smoke from the fireplace, something of the salty air. She closed her eyes. "Hey, Daddy," she said. "Thanks for coming to get me."

"Of course," he said.

"I know it's a surprise."

He pulled away from her but kept hold of her arms. He looked directly into her eyes.

"It's a good surprise," he said. "It's always good when you come home."

Colleen did her best to smile, and then she bent down to pick up her suitcase. Her father took it from her hand when she stood.

"How's Scott?" he asked.

She sighed. "Let's talk in the car," she said.

He'd parked the Regal in the short-term lot, and, while she waited for him to unlock the passenger's-side door, she spied the posters and flyers bearing her father's face in the backseat.

"How's the campaign?" she asked.

He laughed, shook his head. "Let's talk in the car," he said.

ONCE THEY LEFT the airport, Colleen and her father made small talk as he drove through Wilmington:

"How's the weather in Dallas?"

"Hot. How's it been here?"

"Cooler than you'd think."

"How's Mom?"

"About the same."

It wasn't until they were crossing the bridge over the Cape Fear River and into Brunswick County that he put his rough palm over the back of her hand and gave it a squeeze. Colleen looked at the river below them where it snaked inland from the ocean. She'd missed bridges and open water, although she'd grown up terrified of both. She felt her father's hand on top of hers, and suddenly she recalled what he would say to her each time they crossed a bridge when she was a girl, no matter where they were. She looked over at him.

"Are you going to say it?" she asked.

"Say what?"

"Don't look down," she said.

"Don't look back." He smiled, kept his eyes on the road, gave her hand another squeeze.

"Why don't you say it anymore?" she asked.

"I don't know," he said. "Maybe it's because you're not scared anymore."

But was this true? Was she not scared anymore? Or was it possible that the intervening years had found them rarely in the car together, certainly not crossing bridges together? That possibility filled her with sadness, and she chose to believe that she was no longer afraid instead of believing the truer thing: that she was no longer a girl who spent time in the car with her dad.

Her father cleared his throat, took his hand off hers, and moved it back to the steering wheel.

"Colleen, I'm not going to ask you what made you decide to come home. That's not my business." He coughed as if he were buying time to consider what he would say next. The sun was directly overhead, and Colleen knew the river probably looked beautiful in the brilliant light, but she didn't turn to see it. "But your mother's probably going to ask a lot of questions. That's just how she is, and she doesn't mean a thing by it. I'm just telling you so you can think of whether or not you want to give answers."

"I might wait and see what her questions are first," Colleen said. "Then I'll decide if I want to answer them."

"That's fair," her father said. He looked over at her and smiled. "That's fair."

"Are you playing 'good cop' before we go into the interrogation room?"

"No," he said. "No. I just don't want you walking in the door and being caught off guard or upset by anything your mother says. She's been worried about you, and I know you've been worried about her, and I just—I don't know."

"It's okay, Dad," she said. "I know."

He nodded toward her Walkman.

"I see you got one of those radios."

Colleen had forgotten that she'd clipped the Walkman to her belt loop and left the headphones around her neck.

"What's it sound like?" he asked.

"You want to hear it?"

"Sure."

She slipped the headphones from around her neck and placed them on his ears, and then she pushed *play*. She heard the music come on, and she sat back and watched him bop his head up and down. He passed his hand through the air in front of him as if he were groping for something in the dark, and Colleen understood that this was his idea of dancing.

"Groovy," he said.

She laughed and pushed *stop*.

"That's enough, Dad," she said. "I don't want you getting too hip. I don't want Mom having questions for you too."

COLLEEN'S FATHER DIDN'T tell her about the airplane he'd found the night before or the body of Rodney Bellamy until they were driving past the tiny airport where the abandoned airplane waited like a subject that could not be avoided. Although the day was bright, Colleen could see the distant glimmer of the beacon light in its rotation as they drove past.

"You knew Rodney, right?" he asked.

"Yes, I knew him," she said, "but not well. He was nice. Everyone liked him. His dad is—"

"Ed Bellamy," he said. "I know, but your mother reminded me in case I didn't."

"How do you think he ended up out there?" she asked. "I can't imagine him being somebody who'd deal drugs or meet airplanes in the middle of the night."

"I don't think he was that kind of guy," her father said. "His wife said he'd gone out for diapers."

"Gone out for diapers?" Collen repeated. She turned away from her window and looked at her father. "He had a baby?"

With that question, Colleen felt the weather change inside the car; it became cold and quiet, and she could feel that her father understood that whatever wound he feared her mother would uncover had been uncovered before they'd even arrived home.

"Yes," he said. "He had a baby."

"How old?"

"Five months, I think his wife said."

"Boy or girl?"

Her father inhaled, held it. Although her gaze had moved to the windshield, from the corner of her eye Colleen saw her father look out the driver's-side window as if he could not risk seeing her face.

"Boy," he said.

Colleen closed her eyes. She felt her father's rough palm on the back of her hand again, felt his fingers closing over hers.

HER MOTHER WAS in the kitchen when they arrived home, but by the time she and her father made it inside and were standing at the bottom of the stairs, her mother had left the kitchen and was walking toward Colleen with her arms open wide.

"Colleen," she said, "I was so surprised when you called!"

Her mother wrapped her arms around her, and Colleen hugged her back. They rocked from side to side as if it had not been just a few months since they'd seen one another, but much longer. Her mother's body felt slender and frail, and Colleen was afraid of hurting her, even more afraid of acknowledging the changes in her mother's body in such a short time.

They released one another, and Colleen stepped back and hitched her bag farther up her shoulder. "Well, I hope you like surprises," she said.

"I do," her mother said. "I do, especially good ones, good ones like this."

Colleen's mother looked her up and down, reached out and touched the bob of Colleen's hair where it fell along her jaw, fingered the Walkman's headphones as if they had come from the moon. She sighed.

"Scott called," her mother said. "He wants you to call him as soon as you can."

"Okay," Colleen said. She slipped the headphones from around her neck, set the Walkman on the table inside the door, and shrugged off her jean jacket and hung it on the post at the bottom of the stairs.

"He was surprised that you were here," her mother said, "but surely you told him you were coming?" Her statement ended in the lilt of a question, but it felt more like an accusation.

Colleen realized that her father had fled upstairs with her suitcase. He had predicted this trap, and he'd had the sense to retreat before it was sprung. Her mother held out a small slip of paper, and Colleen reached for it. It was a phone number with a 469 area code: Scott's office telephone number, a number Colleen had not yet called enough times to memorize.

"Are you going to call him?" her mother asked.

"Yes, Mom. He's my husband. I'm going to call him."

"Well, good, because I think you should, because he seemed really surprised when I told him you were here."

"I've got it, Mom. Thanks."

As Colleen walked up the stairs, she passed the framed eight-by-ten photograph of her and Scott on their wedding day. She hitched her bag over her shoulder again and reached out and took the frame off the wall and held it before her. In the photo, Scott is wearing a black tuxedo with ruffles over the buttons on his shirt, and she is in a white dress dotted with silver sequins and topped by sleeves that are bunched up into what appear to be shoulder pads. They are both smiling smiles that are more nervous than happy, the slight bump of her pregnant belly imperceptibly rising against the dress's sequined middle.

Seeing the photo did not remind her of her wedding day; it reminded her of standing at the sink in their shared bathroom in Chapel Hill with a pregnancy test sitting on the counter while she spent an hour staring at the clear plastic box, wondering at its chemistry, willing it not to reveal a brown circle the instructions described as a doughnut, but of course that doughnut had appeared.

During their final year in law school, she had moved into Scott's too-small two-bedroom, one-bathroom apartment in Carrboro. The bathroom was a repository of their personalities and emblematic of their lives: the tiny shrapnel of beard left in the sink after Scott shaved each morning; the toothpaste they shared simply because he never bought his own; the bevy of shampoos and conditioners she would buy, try, and leave in the shower for Scott to pillage; the deodorants, shaving creams, and toothbrushes that crowded the laminate countertop around the small sink. Right in front of that sink was where she had been standing when she learned that it would no longer be just the two of them; and when she looked from the pregnancy test to her own eyes in the mirror, she did her best to see past the shock of her personal devastation and to imagine how Scott would react. Would he want to have a baby with her? Would he want to marry her? Did she want either of those things, now or ever?

Like all soon-to-be mothers, both those who plan it and those who don't, Colleen had immediately done the math in her head: it was November, and, depending on how long she'd been pregnant, that meant the baby would arrive sometime in the early summer, right when she and Scott were supposed to begin studying for the bar exam, something she had thought of as certain and impending, something that seemed much more daunting and real than the baby the test had revealed to be growing inside her—the proof of it floating in a plastic test tube right there on the bathroom counter.

Colleen tucked the framed photograph under her arm and walked up the stairs into her old bedroom. It had remained virtually untouched since she'd left for college. A four-poster bed with a white lace canopy rested on the same brown shag carpet that covered the floors in the rest of the upstairs. The bedspread was an orange quilt she had used since junior high. Posters covered the walls: a moppy-headed David Cassidy leaning against a tree as if posing for a senior photo; a Fleetwood Mac poster in now-dull neon colors; Joan Jett leaping into the air against a yellow background, a white guitar in hand, her lips puckered in enviable confidence. Her old, olive-green rotary phone rested as if waiting for her on the white wicker table beside the bed.

Colleen slid her bag from her shoulder and tossed it onto the bed beside her suitcase. She looked again at the wedding photograph of her and Scott, and then she opened the top drawer of her dresser, moved lonely, mismatched socks and old underwear out of the way, and slid the photograph inside—facedown—before closing the drawer.

She picked up the telephone and carried it over to the tan bean-bag chair that sat beneath the window, the paper with Scott's office number curled in her hand like a scroll. She lowered herself onto the beanbag chair and felt the tiny Styrofoam balls give way to her weight. The sticky leather rose up and closed around her body. She placed the phone in her lap and stared at it.

They had decided to get married and have the baby. Somehow, they had also decided that she wouldn't sit for the bar since she wouldn't be taking a job after the baby was born. All that—the bar exam, the job, the career—would come later, at least for her anyway. Scott had the federal job waiting for him in Dallas. He'd begun interviewing and had been offered the position—and others—not long after becoming president of the Student Bar Association at Chapel Hill. He had wanted to be editor of the *North Carolina Law Review,* but he didn't have the grades, so he settled for running for president instead. It suited him better anyway. People liked him. He could build consensus, and, no matter what he said or did, he never made waves, even when he talked about using the association's limited budget to lure Jesse Jackson to speak on campus. In the meantime, Colleen had been a dutiful first lady, although no one called her that or thought of her that way, especially when it became clear that she was a pregnant 3L without a job offer who would not be sitting for the bar that summer.

She didn't tell anyone—she still hadn't—but she'd had better grades than Scott. She'd pulled straight A's except for the B in Con Law I and the C+ in Secured Transactions. But Scott was president. He had a job waiting for him. He would soon be a father, but of course you wouldn't have known it by looking at him unless Colleen had been standing by his side. It was supposed to be her turn after the baby was born. She was supposed to spend the fall and winter studying for the Texas bar. Scott was going to help with the baby so she could prepare. They would find a good day care once she began working. It would be everything she had never considered wanting but felt she was getting nonetheless.

And now, sitting in her old bedroom with more than half the country separating her from Scott, she knew that the only thing she wanted was her son, and no matter what happened after this was over—whatever that meant—he was the only thing she could never have.

She lifted the phone from the cradle and held it to her ear. She listened to the dial tone and took a deep breath and began to dial. While she dialed, she pictured Scott in his office in the federal courthouse in downtown Dallas, the silvery sheen of glass windows reflecting the setting sun, the dull noise of traffic echoing below. She could not help but compare their current views: the stale, musty bedroom of an adolescent girl against the dignified office of a man who'd grown up to do exactly as he'd wished. Scott had made it all seem so easy because things were easy for him. Colleen could think of nothing that he had reached for that he had not grasped.

The phone rang a few times, and then Scott answered. "Where are you?" he asked.

"I'm at my parents'," she said. "My mom said you called."

"Well, I called our house all morning," he said. "And then I drove home at lunch, and you weren't there."

"Can you call me back?" she asked.

"Call you back?"

"This is long-distance," she said. "From my parents' house. Can you call me back?"

"Yeah," he said. She heard him sigh.

"You don't have to," she said. "You're the one who called here. I'm just calling you back."

"No, I will," he said.

"Okay," she said. She hung up.

She realized her heart was racing, her blood pounding in her ears. She looked down at her hands. They were shaking slightly. She closed her fingers over the phone, waiting for it to ring. And then it did.

"Hey," she said.

"Hey," Scott said.

"Hello?" her mother's voice said. Colleen could hear her from the kitchen phone as her voice snaked its way up the stairs. "Scott?"

"Hey, Marie," Scott said. "I was just calling Colleen back."

"Mom, I've got it," Colleen said. The heat in her body broke toward a cold, sweaty frustration.

"Okay," her mother said. "Okay," she said again. "I hope everything's okay."

"It is," Scott said. "Thanks."

"Okay," her mother said again. "Bye."

"Bye," Scott said, but Colleen's mother hung on, waiting a beat for someone else to speak before relinquishing her role in their lives.

"Okay," she said.

"Mom," Colleen said, "I've got it. Please." She heard the phone hang up. "Jesus," she whispered.

"How's it being back home?" Scott asked.

"About how it sounds," Colleen said. "I literally just walked in the door."

"When did you decide to do this?" he asked. "I called home and couldn't get you, and then I drove all the way there at lunch, and you weren't there. It scared me," he said again.

"Sorry to put you out."

"You're not—" But he stopped. "Colleen, listen." He pulled the receiver away from his mouth and spoke to someone else in the room. *Okay,* he said, his voice muffled by a hand he must have placed over the receiver. *Okay. Thanks.* Colleen pictured a flustered secretary or a young clerk standing at Scott's door, a handful of papers for him to sign. Or maybe it was a seasoned attorney who Scott was anxious to impress, who was perhaps already frustrated that Scott had taken the time to drive home to check on his still-mourning wife.

"Am I keeping you from doing something?" Colleen asked.

"No," Scott said, getting back on the line. "It's just—it's nothing. It's just busy here. That's all."

"I planned on calling you once I got here," Colleen said. "I didn't know you'd leave work and drive home to find me."

"No," he said. "It's fine."

"I just don't want to be there right now because it makes me think of him, which is so crazy because he was never even there, there at home, I mean. He was definitely here. It's just that—"

"No," Scott said. "I understand. I know it's hard, and I know I've been working a lot and you've been alone. Colleen, if you need to—"

"But do you?" Colleen asked.

"Do I what?"

"Do you know it's hard?" she said. "Do you?"

"I do," he said. "I know it's hard on you, and it's hard on me, but I can't imagine what it's like for you."

"You have no idea what it's like for me."

"I know I don't. That's why I—"

"Because you haven't asked me."

"Colleen, am I— Am I just supposed to—"

"You're not supposed to do anything," she said.

"Well, was there some magic thing I was supposed to say?"

"Jesus, Scott, really? Really? You don't have to say anything, but sometimes things need to be said—" But what she meant was *heard*. She needed to hear something from him. She did not know what it was, but she knew he would not say it.

The phone was silent. She could hear Scott breathing on the other end.

"I can still feel him," she finally said.

"I know. I can too," he said.

"But I mean *inside me*, Scott. I can still feel where he was inside me. And now he's not there, and he's not here, and I don't know where he is."

They were silent for another moment. Colleen waited. She heard something squeak on the other end of the line, perhaps his office chair.

She could not control what happened next. Her body heaved, and she began to shed enormous, unstoppable tears.

"Honey," Scott said. He waited. "Honey," he said again.

"Did you hold him?" she asked.

"Hold him?"

"Yes," she said. "In the hospital. After he was born. Did you hold him?"

"Of course I held him, Colleen. Of course I did."

"I don't remember it," she said. "I don't remember you holding him. I wish I remembered it." She choked back a sob and coughed. She wiped her nose with her T-shirt. "What did he smell like?"

Scott lowered his voice as if doing so could get her to lower her own. "I don't—" He stopped speaking, and Colleen could sense that he was adjusting the phone in his hand or turning away from someone or something. "I don't know, Colleen. I can't describe it. I wish I could."

"Yeah," she said. She sniffed, gathered herself as if pulling all her parts together. "I've wished for a lot of things."

"We'll get through this, Colleen."

She laughed, and then she sniffed and used her shirt to wipe at her nose again. "Yes, Scott," she said, "*we* will get through this."

"I'm not your enemy, Colleen. I'm your husband. And I'm his father. Just because I'm dealing with this in a way that's different from yours doesn't mean that I'm not going through my own shit apart from yours."

"Sorry to drag you into my shit," she said.

"I'm not asking you to apologize for anything," Scott said. "I don't think either one of us needs to apologize for anything."

She looked at the bed where her bag was lying, the Brazelton book peering out as if spying on her, as if asking her why she had not yet opened it that day.

"He'd be four months old now," she said. "The book says that at four months he would be cooing and chewing on toys. The book says he would be able to recognize our faces. He'd be able to read our emotions."

"Colleen, honey, I don't know if you should still be carrying that book around."

"Why not, Scott? Why shouldn't I? What do you want me to carry instead? I can't carry our baby."

"No," he said. "Of course not. Let me explain. I understand what the book means to you."

"It doesn't mean a damn thing to me, Scott. It's a book. I'm learning about—" She stopped for a second, and then she whispered, "I'm learning about *babies*. Who doesn't want to learn about babies?"

"I know it comforts you, but I'm wondering if it's helping."

"I fell asleep on the plane today, and when I opened my eyes, I thought I saw him outside the window. He was watching me."

"Who? Who was watching you?"

She sank lower into the beanbag chair and rested her head against the wall. She closed her eyes. "Him, Scott," she said. "Our son. I pictured him flying beside me, right outside the window. I wanted to open the window and touch him, but I couldn't open it. Of course you can't open the windows on airplanes."

"Colleen," he said. He lowered his voice to a whisper. "Colleen, have you been drinking?"

"Jesus, Scott. Really?" She sat forward, struggled to stand up from the beanbag chair. "I'm talking about our son recognizing my face and that's what you want to ask me? Jesus, Scott."

"I'm sorry," he said. "I'm sorry. Of course not. Of course that's not what I want to ask you." He paused, and Colleen stood beside her bed. She knew that Scott's eyes were scanning his office, his mind churning through ideas in the hope of finding something to say to her. "You just mentioned seeing him outside the plane. It just seemed like, I don't know. How's your mom?"

"She's sick, Scott. She's got cancer. She's skinnier than hell and she's already annoying the shit out of me. It's been a great visit so far."

"What did she say about you showing up at home?"

"She said, 'Holy shit, Colleen, you showed up at home. Now, go call your husband.' I don't know, Scott. Hang up and call back and ask for her."

"No, I want to talk to you," he said.

"Then let's talk," she said.

"I love you," he said. "I wish I was there, or I wish you were still at home so I could see you."

"It's better this way," she said.

"What's that supposed to mean?" he asked. "It sounds like—" He lowered his voice, and Colleen imagined him hunched over in his chair. "Are you leaving me?"

"I'm not doing anything, Scott. I'm visiting my parents. You're working. I'm here. You're there. It's better that way."

"For how long?"

"I don't know for how long."

"Did you buy a return ticket?"

"No," she said.

"But you will?"

"Of course I will," she said.

"Okay," he said. "I love you. Even if I don't know what to say, I can tell you that."

"Okay," she said.

"I love you."

"I love you too," she said.

They hung up and she put the phone back on its cradle, and then she lifted her suitcase from the bed and set it on the floor. She climbed onto the bed, lay down, interlocked her fingers and placed her hands on her flat stomach, and closed her eyes.

IT WAS FULL dark in Colleen's bedroom when she opened her eyes again. She was lying on her side, curled into the fetal position, her hands still cupped to her stomach. It took her a few moments to recognize where she was, but as soon as she realized she was in her bedroom back at her parents' house, she was able to hear the sound of their voices drifting upstairs from the kitchen below. She rolled onto her back and stared up at the dark ceiling. She had lain right here in this bed and listened to those voices for more than half her life, but this was the first time they had felt strange and foreign. She did not feel like she belonged anywhere or to anyone, and in that moment a glimmer of freedom slashed through her like a knife.

When she sat up, she realized that her head was pounding, and she left her room and walked into the bathroom and sipped water from the sink. She splashed water on her face and opened her eyes as wide as she could and looked at herself in the mirror. She smiled a grotesque smile. She frowned. She whispered, "Oh, I just felt like coming home. I thought y'all would enjoy the surprise."

Dinner was being made downstairs, and she knew by the smell of it that her mother was making country-style steak, mashed potatoes, and some kind of green vegetable. She knew they would all sit down at the table, where a green plastic pitcher of sweating sweet tea would be waiting. She knew her mother would ask her everything she could think of except *How are you and Scott?* and Colleen would do her best to answer without rolling her eyes or crying or staring into her lap until her mother got the hint, and the whole time she would be thinking about borrowing her mother's car and driving to the store for a six-pack of Budweiser and parking by the beach and climbing into the dunes and drinking every single one of them before burying the bottles in the sand and driving home.

But first Colleen would go downstairs. She would eat dinner and drink sweet tea. And she would answer the questions that she was able to answer. And she would say over and over, "We're fine, Mom. I'm home now. Everything's fine."

She turned the water on in the sink again and splashed it over her face. When she turned it off, she heard the sound of someone coming up the stairs. She dried her face and hands with the towel hanging by the sink, and then Colleen peeked into the hallway and saw her mother carrying a tray toward her bedroom.

"Mom," she said. She turned off the bathroom light, and the hallway fell into near darkness. She could see her mother's hands where they gripped the tray; the boniness of her arms made her hands appear monstrous. "Mom," she said again, "are you bringing dinner to my room?"

"Why not?" her mother said. "You've been traveling all day. You don't need to sit downstairs with two old people and listen to them gossip." She turned and pushed Colleen's bedroom door open with her foot. Light cut into the dark hallway. She looked back over her shoulder and gave Colleen a nod. "Come on," she said, "before it gets cold. I'm not carrying this down the stairs to reheat it."

She set the tray on Colleen's bed. It was just as Colleen had expected: country-style steak, mashed potatoes, green beans, and a glass of sweet iced tea. Her mother had wrapped a knife and fork in a paper napkin and left it resting beside the plate.

"You didn't have to do this, Mom," Colleen said. She sat down on the bed and picked up the glass of tea and took a sip.

"No, I didn't have to do this tonight, but I did," she said. She sat down beside Colleen. "You didn't have to fly all the way home from Texas today, but you did."

"That's true," Colleen said.

"And I'm glad you did," she said.

"I feel bad. I should eat with you and Dad."

"Why?" her mother asked. "So you can hear him grumble about driving back to the Wilmington airport tomorrow morning? Listen to me annoy him with my theories on that crashed airplane?"

"Why's he going back to the Wilmington airport tomorrow?" She unwrapped the silverware and scooped up a forkful of mashed potatoes. They were salty and warm.

"There's an FBI guy from Florida who's coming up to fly that airplane out of here," she said. "Your father's picking him up tomorrow morning." She sighed. "And he's staying with us for a few days."

"Here? Where?"

"In the office, I guess," she said. "I'll tidy it up in the morning. We'll worry about it then."

Colleen cut a piece of steak and swirled it through the potatoes.

"I'm glad to see you eating," her mother said. "It doesn't matter how old you get, you're always happy to see your child eat the food you've made for them."

"It's good," Colleen said. "It's been a long time since I've had food like this."

She could actually feel her mother wanting to ask what she and Scott ate for meals in Texas. Colleen had never been a very good cook, and Scott wasn't either. She would've been ashamed to tell her mother that they heated up foil-covered TV dinners in the oven or went out for dinner on nights when Scott didn't work too late. At that moment, Colleen couldn't picture a single meal they'd made together in the kitchen since they'd moved to Dallas. Colleen imagined Scott coming home to the empty house and opening the freezer and turning on the oven. She wondered if he was feeling the same heavy loneliness she felt, or if he felt anything at all. It was too much to take with her mother sitting on her bed watching her eat, so she shook the image of Scott from her mind.

"You said Dad doesn't want to hear your theories on the plane," she said. "What are they?"

"Drugs," her mother said. She sat up straighter. "I think it's a drug plane."

"You think Rodney Bellamy was flying a drug plane?"

"No, I don't think that," she said. "I don't know how he was involved. That just doesn't make any sense to me."

"Me either," Colleen said. She wanted to bring up what her father had told her about Rodney and his wife having a little boy, but she didn't. She didn't want her mother to read her face and turn the conversation toward her and Scott and what had happened to them.

"Do you remember the story I used to tell you when you were really little about the Magic House?" her mother asked.

Colleen laughed, more out of surprise than humor. The story of the Magic House had lingered in the corners of her memory since childhood, and she knew she might never have thought about it again had her mother not just mentioned it. "Yes," Colleen said. "I remember it."

In the story, Colleen's mother would be lost in the woods, and she would discover a house that was an exact replica of their own. She would be surprised when her key fit the lock, and she would go inside to look around. In each room—the kitchen, the living room, Colleen's room, her and Colleen's father's bedroom—she would find a different version of Colleen, some older, some much younger. Colleen's mother called it the Magic House because it was a place she could always go to find all the Colleens that Colleen had ever been.

"I was thinking of that story just now," her mother said. "I was thinking of it when I walked up the stairs and saw that your bedroom door was open. I thought you were in here, and I thought of the Magic House and I wondered which version of you I would find." She stopped talking and looked around the bedroom. She unfolded the napkin and laid it across Colleen's lap. "I always told you that whatever version of you was in front of me was my favorite version. That's still true," she said. "Right now, you are my favorite version of you."

Colleen smiled.

"So we're in the Magic House?"

"Yes," her mother said. "We're in the Magic House."

WEDNESDAY,
OCTOBER 31, 1984

CHAPTER 6

It was Jay's feeling that something was happening outside the house that woke him in the middle of the night, but it was the bright light that found its way through his window and past his blinds and onto the wall on the other side of his room that made him sit up in bed and listen. He could hear car engines and voices. He heard someone laugh. He thought of what he'd heard the night before when he'd woken to Janelle's and Rodney's whispered voices, and he wondered if he had stumbled into another nighttime event that would have eluded him had he slept through it. And then he heard what sounded like a gunshot. Seconds later, someone's fist was beating on the front door.

The light came on in the hallway, and he heard Janelle call his name. She'd spent the day in tears, setting the baby down only when Mr. Bellamy or a neighbor or friend of the family could convince her to rest, to sit on the couch, to lie down on her bed, to hold the phone to talk to their mother. He did not know whether or not Janelle had slept, but her voice sounded clearer and stronger than it had since they'd learned the terrible news that morning.

Another bang on the door.

"Jay!" Janelle called from the hallway.

"I'm in here," he said. She opened his door and clicked on his light. Her hair was messier than he'd ever seen it, and her eyes, though puffy with sleeplessness and grief, were wide with uncertainty at the sound they had both heard.

"What's going on outside?" she asked.

"I don't know," Jay said. "I just woke up. There's somebody at the—" But he wasn't able to finish before the window behind him exploded and pieces of glass blew through the blinds and something heavy landed on the floor by his bed. Janelle screamed, and Jay rolled off his bed and onto the floor, his feet touching whatever it was that had just been thrown into his room through the window. It looked like a tree trunk or a piece of firewood, and for just a moment Jay allowed himself to understand that he would have been killed had it hit him on his head.

"Come on out!" a voice called from outside.

"Oh, my God," Janelle said. "Oh, my God."

The sound of the log crashing through the window must have awakened the baby where he slept in the nursery, because he began to cry. Janelle seemed suddenly reminded that there was another soul in the house aside from hers and Jay's, and she left Jay's doorway and ran to the baby's room on the other side of the hall. Jay crawled across his bedroom floor, reached up, and turned out his light.

"Janelle," Jay called out. "Leave the lights off." He could hear her in the nursery, trying to calm the baby, trying to calm herself.

"Come out here, boy!" the voice outside said. "We ain't here to hurt nobody."

Jay stayed low, and he half-walked/half-crawled into Janelle's bedroom, where he went straight to her closet and reached for the top shelf on Rodney's side. He took the case down and opened it, and then he stood again and took one of the boxes of cartridges that he had not yet touched until that moment. He opened the rifle just as he'd seen the man in the woods do it, and with a shaking hand, he popped a cartridge inside and slid the bolt closed. He picked up the rifle in one hand and the box of cartridges in the other, and he bent at the waist and moved from the bedroom to the hall on his way to the front door.

Janelle must have seen him as he passed the nursery, because she stepped into the hallway behind him and cried out for him, but Jay didn't turn around. He knew he was going to open the door and confront whoever was out there.

Jay stopped at the door and set the box of ammunition on the table against the wall, and then, in what seemed like one motion, he turned the lock, opened the door, shouldered the rifle, and pointed it outside into a blinding light. He could not tell the source of the light, but he imagined that spotlights were being trained on him because the light came from many directions, and it was brighter than head-lights. He could not see beyond it, but something alerted him to the presence of other people, perhaps a dozen, perhaps more. He could hear their voices over the sounds of truck engines, and he could hear other engines revving and other voices calling out in other parts of the community.

Although Jay could not see the face belonging to the voice that he heard next, he knew exactly to whom it belonged.

"Boy, I thought I told you I didn't want to see you carrying that rifle again." It was the man who'd pointed the pistol at him and Cody in the woods.

Jay moved the rifle to point it in the direction of the man's voice, but he could not see anything beyond the porch landing where he stood. He was shirtless in a pair of old basketball shorts, and he was suddenly aware of the vulnerability of his body, and he was also aware that he had never fired a weapon and did not know what would happen if he fired this one. He heard someone laughing out in the yard on the other side of the light.

Jay moved the barrel of the rifle again, doing his best to track the source of the laugh, but there was only more laughter.

"He looks like a goddamned deer," someone said.

"Take that little buck down," another voice called. More laughter.

"Listen here, boy," the man from the woods said. "We don't need y'all bringing drugs into this county. We think it's time y'all pack up, get on back down to Georgia, take that peach of a sister back where she belongs."

Jay felt something wet on his arm, and he realized it was a tear and that he'd been crying. He did not know how long he stood there, but it seemed that hours passed. He kept his finger on the rifle's trigger, kept it raised and pointing blindly into the light.

"You think about what I just told you," the man's voice finally said. "You think about it."

There was the sound of car doors opening and closing, and suddenly the bright light waned as vehicles backed out of Janelle's yard and swung around in the street in front of the house. Jay kept the rifle raised, but when he looked to the road, he saw men in the back of the trucks, some of them sitting on the sides of the trucks' beds and holding Confederate flags on long poles, others standing behind spotlights fastened to the trucks' roofs. A few trucks spun their tires and kicked smoke into the air, and then they tore off down the road toward Southport. The last truck to leave their yard was a big dually with lettering on the side. It flew a Confederate flag from the back of its cab. There was the sound of a gun being fired into the air, and Jay flinched and ducked from the doorway back into the darkened house. He heard laughter, more squealing tires, and then the night went silent and dark.

He closed the door and locked it, even though he knew it offered them absolutely no protection from whoever the people were who had been waiting for him outside. They were gone, for now, but Jay knew they would return, and he would be ready.

CHAPTER 7

Marie was still sleeping soundly when Winston slipped out of bed the next morning. After getting dressed, he fought the urge to open Colleen's door to peer in at her while she slept. He told himself that he'd decided not to open her door because he was afraid of waking her, but he secretly knew that he was afraid of seeing a woman who would leave home again instead of a little girl who might just stay forever.

The night before, he'd gone to sleep with worry strapped to him like a dynamite vest, each of the worries packaged like a tiny bomb that he either had to snuff out or face the possibility of it blowing a hole through his heart while his mind wrestled itself toward sleep. He thought about his time in Korea, thought about how—although he'd seen no live combat—he was always aware and afraid of the possibility of something being tossed his way. How would he have responded? Would he have run? Thrown himself on top of it? Picked it up and tossed it back? Later, he would hear of guys in Vietnam launching their bodies on top of hand grenades that had been thrown by villagers—women and children who hated the soldiers as much as their fathers and husbands did. He imagined those men's hollowed-out bodies, their forever unseeing and unblinking eyes, and he thought of Ed Bellamy during his time in that country. He knew that Bellamy had been a marine, but he did not know in what capacity he had served.

Winston had closed his eyes, pictured Ed Bellamy as a young man, alone in a rice paddy as a helicopter hovers overhead, the winds from its rotors bending the limbs of trees and fluttering Bellamy's flak jacket. In this vision, Ed Bellamy is even younger than the son who'd be found dead on a runway all these years later. Winston thought of Rodney Bellamy as just a child, and he knew that he saw the man as such because he'd been in school with Colleen, whom he would always see as a child no matter how old she grew to be.

And in thinking of Colleen, Winston was forced to finger another tightly packed package of explosive. When he'd first laid eyes on her at the airport, the weight of her sadness had overwhelmed him, but unlike Marie's sadness, which caused him to withdraw, Colleen's grief pulled him closer, and the closer he got the more he realized he could not defuse Colleen's bombs because he could not even defuse his own.

Downstairs in the kitchen, Winston brewed a pot of coffee as the world lightened outside, and then he stood and stared out the windows toward the waterway while he drank his first cup of the day. Little more than twenty-four hours had passed since he had stood there wondering what he would find at the airport, and he could not believe all that had happened. The airplane. Bellamy's body on the runway. Glenn's stumbling upon him and nearly getting shot. The sudden phone call from Colleen that had surprised him more than anything he could have discovered at the airport in the middle of the night. And now here he was, setting off on another errand that would inevitably surprise him just as much as the others: an FBI agent from Florida who could supposedly fix and fly the airplane, a man Rollins had said was named Tom Groom, was expecting Winston to pick him up at the Wilmington airport. And Groom would be staying with him and Marie in what suddenly felt to Winston like a full house.

He'd tried his best to hide his frustration with Rollins over the phone last night. It was true that the hotels had closed up shop for the winter, but he knew other arrangements could've been made, and there were better options than having a stranger stay with him and Marie. This option was just the cheapest and the least disruptive to the day-to-day operations of the FBI's Wilmington field office. Winston was certain that Marie was excited by the idea of having someone stay with them, but he was afraid that it—along with Colleen's visit—would take a toll on her, although she'd never show it, especially not in front of a guest.

After leaving the island, Winston drove past the airport, and he could see a cruiser parked on the runway, the airplane still sitting sideways not far away from it. He knew Glenn had been out there for most of the night, but he couldn't remember which deputy had relieved him, meaning he couldn't picture the face of the deputy who was now probably fighting sleep, his head lolling against the driver's-side window as the sun climbed in the sky.

As he drove north on Highway 133, Winston's mind was quiet for the first time since the airplane had come in and woken him from sleep, and that meant it was open to things he did not want to think about or recall. He'd been fighting it, but Rodney Bellamy's murder had been on the edge of every thought Winston had had since he'd found Rodney's body. While the fact of Rodney's murder was enough to send explosive jolts of panic through him, it was the imagined moment of Rodney's murder—the moment at which Rodney knew he would be killed—that was haunting Winston. Had Rodney known he would die the moment he saw a gun pointed at him? Had he thought of his wife's face or spoken the name of his baby boy?

In all his years of police work, Winston had never had the experience of believing that his own death was imminent, and the one time he had taken a life he had not considered the possibilities of what that man was thinking. It had all happened so fast—at least he wanted to believe that was the case; he wanted to believe that the man had not had time to think of his wife or his children or the set of circumstances that had landed him behind the counter in the pharmacy on Franklin Boulevard back in Gastonia, his pistol held on the pharmacist and the young girl who worked the register, Winston's pistol pointed at the man's chest from where Winston stood on the other side of the counter.

But there had been time enough after it was over for Winston to think of everything panic had not allowed him to consider. The man's name; it was James Dixon. He'd been thirty-one years old, married, with two young children. No record of arrests or convictions. He'd been laid off, but for years he'd worked as a mechanic at the Firestone Mill and lived in the Black section of the mill village, and a few days after his funeral, that was where Winston had driven, parking his car up the road from Dixon's house and wondering what he'd expected to gain from being in such proximity to the dead man's home.

The first time Winston had sat in his car near Dixon's house, he'd sat behind the wheel clutching an envelope stuffed with nearly five hundred dollars, which was as much money as he could afford to offer without making things tough for him and Marie and Colleen. He'd also sat there with both an explanation and an apology prepared to deliver to Dixon's wife. He couldn't understand her grief, and he was awfully, inexplicably sorry for it. He just saw the gun in her husband's hand. How could he have known it was unloaded? It had all happened so fast, and there was not time to notice that the magazine was missing, that the pistol was so rusted as to have been incapable of firing. Winston could not possibly have asked about Dixon's job or his family or his desperation or what that thirty-seven dollars in the till would mean to them.

That day, while Winston sat in the car, a little boy no older than six or seven had stepped out the front door of the mill shack with a child's slingshot in his hand. He'd walked to the edge of the yard and stopped to pick up bits of gravel that he loaded into his toy. He aimed for a tree in the middle of the yard, and from inside his car, Winston could hear the slap of the rocks each time one smacked against the tree's trunk. Soon, a woman came outside, a young baby on her hip, and she said something to the boy. The boy turned to go in, and the woman looked up the street and saw Winston. Had she known who he was, what he had done? Her eyes settled on his for a moment, and then she turned and followed her son inside the house.

Winston's hand went to the handle on the car door, his other hand holding the envelope of cash, but something kept him in the car, gave him permission to wait, to come back tomorrow, to put off the apology and the errand that had sent him there. The next day, there was a truck parked in the driveway, and Winston watched an older Black man walk in and out of the house a couple of times. He didn't know who the man was, and he thought it best to come back when Dixon's wife was alone. The next day, the family was gone, but Winston had never forgotten Dixon's family, and he knew that even though they had never met him, they had never been able to forget him either.

WHEN WINSTON PULLED up to the near-empty arrivals area at the Wilmington airport, he didn't even have a chance to put the cruiser in park before a man stepped off the curb, opened the passenger door, and leaned inside.

"Hey," the man said, extending his hand across the seat toward Winston. "Agent Tom Groom. Your pilot."

Winston reached out and shook the man's hand. The man wore a navy blue polo shirt tucked into khaki pants. He wore the standard-issue SIG holstered at his side, and he had the same standard-issue bearing of the other agents Winston had met over time, the same rigidity, the same distance and withdrawn air about him.

"Nice to meet you, Agent Groom. I'm Sheriff Winston Barnes," he said. "I hope you didn't wait too long."

"Not at all," Groom said. He lifted up an army-green duffel bag so that Winston could see it. "Mind if I toss this in the back?"

"Go ahead," Winston said.

Groom opened the back door and set the bag on the floorboard, and then he slid onto the passenger's seat and closed the door. He was medium height with a slender build and a full head of thick auburn hair. Something about him seemed vaguely familiar to Winston, and he considered that Groom could easily pass for one of the Kennedy brothers if not for his accent, which Winston was already trying to place.

"I just deplaned," Groom said. He raked his fingers through his hair in an attempt to get it off his forehead, just like Winston remembered Jack Kennedy doing in the old newsreels. "Perfect timing."

"Good," Winston said. He pulled away from the curb. "We've got about an hour drive down to Oak Island."

Tom Groom told Winston he was forty-three years old, was born outside Ames, Iowa, and joined the air force at eighteen just in time to be sent to Vietnam. During the war, he would eventually fly the military version of the same aircraft that now sat sideways on the runway at the airport in Brunswick County. "It was a C-47," Groom said, "outfitted with mini guns. Flew ground support, dug them out when the Viet Cong came in." Groom said that after the war, he went to college back in Iowa, and when that was over, the FBI came calling.

Winston felt Groom turn and look at him as if he were sizing him up, taking the measure of him in some way.

"Did you serve?" Groom finally asked.

"Yeah," Winston said. "Navy in Korea."

"I figured. You can always spot a veteran."

"That was a long time ago."

"I bet it doesn't seem like it," Groom said. "Vietnam won't ever seem like a long time ago to me."

"It sticks with you," Winston said, but Winston didn't want to talk about the past, his or Groom's. He didn't want to talk about war any more than anyone else who'd ever been through it.

"Are you the FBI's aircraft specialist?" Winston asked, only half-joking.

"It seems like it sometimes," Groom said. "Once you find your niche, it's hard to get out of it."

They were crossing the bridge over the Cape Fear River and heading into Brunswick County when Winston asked Groom how he knew Agents Rollins and Rountree.

"I don't," Groom said. "Not really, anyway, not beyond a quick talk on the phone. The teletype came into the Miami office, and we deal with downed aircraft all the time down there."

"You ever deal with them sitting sideways on a short runway?"

"No," Groom said. He laughed a little, the first real emotion Winston had seen him express since he'd gotten into the car. Winston felt himself relaxing. "I can't say I've seen that. But if that rear landing gear can be fixed—and I think it can, based on what your airport manager told me—I believe I can get this aircraft out of your hair. If I've done it during monsoon season out in the jungle, I can for sure do it on a nice October morning."

They rode in silence for a moment. Winston tapped his fingers against the steering wheel as if listening to a song in his head, but the only thing he heard was the rumble of the engine as the cruiser whipped down the winding curve of Highway 133, the swamps on either side glowing in hues of yellow in the morning light. On the left-hand side, far past the trees that obscured the view, the Cape Fear River divided Brunswick County from the city of Wilmington.

Historical markers dotted the roadside, announcing the fact that settlers, slaves, and Indians had once inhabited this land over the span of centuries.

Groom broke the silence. "Mind if I smoke?" he asked.

"No, not one bit," Winston said.

Groom reached into his breast pocket for a pack of cigarettes. Winston looked over and saw that the pack was blue and gold and featured some kind of Asian lettering on it. Groom shook one loose and lit it with a lighter that he slid back into his pocket. He took a drag, and then he rolled down the window and blew smoke from the side of his mouth.

"What brand is that?" Winston asked.

Groom kept the cigarette between his fingers, but he held it in front of him and studied it for a moment. "Hero," he said. He took another drag and exhaled. "They're harder than hell to get in the States, but it's the only bad habit I brought home from the war, so it's worth the trouble."

"There are worse," Winston said.

"That there are." Groom flicked an ash out the cracked window. "You from around here?"

"No," Winston said. "Up the road a piece, just west of Charlotte."

"What brought you down here?"

"Oh, I don't know," Winston said. "Just wanted to live at the beach, I guess."

"You fish?" Groom asked.

"No," Winston said. "I don't fish, and I have to tell you, I haven't been on a boat in years, and I can't remember the last time I set foot on the beach when it didn't involve work."

Groom smiled a little. He took a drag off his cigarette. "Well, I understand that," he said. "I've lived in Miami almost twenty years, and I can't recall the last time I did any of that stuff either."

"Work keep you busy?"

"Oh, yeah," Groom said. "Plenty of work."

"I know you get a lot of drug planes down in South Florida," Winston said. "I'm wondering if you've ever heard about one this far north."

"It happens," Groom said. "But up here I think they're more likely to use boats."

"You're right about that," Winston said. "You're right about that."

"You think this is drugs?" Groom asked.

"I don't know what I think just yet," Winston said. "I really don't."

"If it was drugs, they would've had a local, somebody waiting on them," Groom said. "Agent Rollins told me you had a body out there."

"That's right," Winston said. "But something tells me he didn't have anything to do with it."

"It would be hard for an innocent man to explain being out on a runway in the middle of the night to greet a drug plane. He might be your local."

Winston looked over at Groom. "You got a lead you're keeping from me?" he asked. He smiled and looked back at the road.

Groom took another drag from his cigarette. "Not yet," he said. He picked a fleck of tobacco from his tongue, flicked it out the window. "But I just got here."

ROLLINS AND ROUNTREE must have assumed that Winston would bring Groom to the airport, because he spotted them on the runway as soon as he parked the cruiser outside the office. He wondered why they couldn't have just picked up Groom themselves, why they had to send him on an errand as if he were their gofer, but he'd already done the errand, so maybe he was.

The door to Sweetney's office opened and Leonard Dorsey stepped out as if he'd spent all morning waiting for Agent Tom Groom to arrive. Dorsey clapped his hands together and smiled. "Is this our pilot?" he called out.

"Jesus Christ," Winston said.

"Who's that?" Groom asked.

"County commissioner. He sells insurance for a living."

"He looks like he sells insurance," Groom said. He opened the back door and lifted his duffel bag from the floorboard.

Dorsey walked down the sidewalk from the office toward the parking lot. "I hope you know more about planes than your fellow FBI buddies do," he said.

"We'll see," Groom said. "I know a good bit."

The office door slammed and Winston looked up to see Hugh walking toward them.

"Hugh," Dorsey said. "This here's our pilot."

"That's what I figured," Hugh said. He shook Groom's hand. "Hugh Sweetney."

"Agent Tom Groom."

"You want to get a look at this aircraft?" Hugh asked. "Check out that back wheel?"

"You bet," Groom said.

"Like I told you on the phone, you're more than welcome to use anything we've got in the shop here."

"I appreciate that," Groom said.

Hugh smiled, and then he turned and started out toward the runway. Groom adjusted his duffel on his shoulder and turned toward Winston. "Thanks for the ride out here," he said.

"You bet," Winston said. "I'm going to head over to the office, get some stuff done. Just call over there when you need me to carry you home." He felt like he was dropping off a teenager at a sleepover. "Rollins knows how to get ahold of me."

Groom nodded, gave a little wave, and set out toward the runway to follow Hugh.

"You think he'll do it?" Dorsey said. He was still standing beside Winston, his hands in his pockets and his tie loose around his neck.

"I think he'll try," Winston said. "But it's hard to predict just what will happen."

THE SHERIFF'S OFFICE was part of the Brunswick County courthouse complex, a collection of squat, redbrick buildings sequestered off in clumps of tall pine trees alongside Route 88 in the town of Boiling Springs. Winston had always thought the buildings looked like what they were: a place where civic responsibility was decided upon, written down, enforced, and when infringed upon, punished. Perhaps that was why the sheriff's office had always felt institutional to Winston, and entering it always gave him the same feeling he had when entering a school or a church or another building where a set of expectations had been clearly defined before he ever arrived.

He opened one of the glass double doors and stepped into the reception area, the faded orange-and-white checkered linoleum running the length of the hallway, the soles of his shoes squeaking against the polish that lifted the sharp, antiseptic scent of cleaning solution from the floor. Three chairs rested against the wall on his left, and this was where people sat when they were waiting for the business of the office to work for them or against them—mothers and fathers picking up teenage vandals; attorneys waiting to question clients arrested on DWI; victims of violence or duplicity or chance, nervous or uncertain or thrilled by the prospect of filing a complaint. A sliding glass window was built into the wall on his right, and on the other side of it the office secretary, Vicki, sat behind a desk littered with paperwork, schedules, and calendars. She slid the reception window open when she saw Winston. "I heard our pilot made it up from Miami," she said.

"You heard right," Winston said. He stepped through the doorway next to the glass window and stood beside Vicki's desk where his mailbox, the one on top, was affixed to the wall right inside the door. He looked through its contents, removing the papers and sealed envelopes that looked important, tossing the rest into the wastebasket at his feet.

"And I heard he's an FBI man."

"You heard right again," he said. He looked down at Vicki. He had no idea how old she was, but he knew she was past middle age, her chin-length brown hair too dark not to be dyed, the skin around her eyes and lips papery and spiderwebbed with wrinkles from decades of smoking. He'd known her for more than twenty years, knew her husband, Clint, her high school sweetheart. He'd worked over at the munitions depot at Sunny Point before going on disability after a back injury and eventually retiring. Winston knew Vicki's kids too, one of whom lived in Charlotte and another, a son with kids of his own, who lived here in Brunswick County. Winston's relationship with her was built on gentle teasing and the unspoken understanding that he needed her to play the role of den mother for him and his deputies and staff, and he, in return, would make her job as easy as possible by always trusting her to run her administrative ship efficiently. She was the keeper of schedules and reports, messages and requests, and all she asked for in return was to be left to her solitary work while being allowed the freedom to rib her boss at any opportunity she could find.

"This is a mess, Sheriff," she said. She lowered her voice and leaned forward. "We're lucky the FBI's taking over." She smiled again, sat up, went back to shuffling the papers on her desk. "Marie called. She's looking for you. The way she talked, she might be looking for your pilot too."

"He's out at the airport if she needs to get ahold of him," Winston said. "He's all hers."

"How's she doing?" Vicki asked.

"She's doing good," Winston said. "She's good."

"Well, let me know if y'all need anything. You know I can bake."

"I do know that," Winston said. He smiled. "Any other messages?"

"No, sir," Vicki said.

Winston tapped on the door frame by way of goodbye, his wedding ring pinging against the metal with a tinny report.

He turned right and walked toward his office, which sat at the end of the hallway past the restrooms, the water fountain, the deputies' shared offices, and the break room. He unlocked his door and tossed the papers onto his desk, and then he slid his holstered weapon from his belt and hung it from the coatrack. Winston closed his door and sat down at his desk. He looked around his office for a moment, his mind trying to decide exactly where to begin.

On the wall to his left hung a dozen or so framed photographs that Marie had carefully placed not long after he'd moved into the office almost thirteen years ago. There was a photo of him in Korea and another photo of him in his dress blues—his first uniform—just a few years later when he was back in Gastonia and a young, fresh-faced police officer. In the photograph he is standing outside his mother and father's house, Crowder's Mountain looming in the background, the canopy of trees above him broken just enough for the slash of sunlight coming through the leaves to cause him to narrow his eyes against the brightness at the exact moment the photograph was taken. In another photograph he is a few years older, wearing a white jacket and black bow tie, standing at a car wash and spraying the shaving cream off the back windshield of his Mercury. Marie, still in her wedding dress, her hair pinned up in an immaculate platinum beehive apparent even in the grainy black-and-white photograph, is sitting in the front seat. Beyond those pictures, there were framed photographs that traced Colleen's childhood from newborn to high school, her face and eyes appearing the same to Winston in each photograph.

He turned his eyes from the wall of framed pictures to the pile of papers and envelopes on his desk, and he spent an hour or so listening to the muffled sounds of Vicki answering the phone at her desk while he leafed through the reports Glenn and a couple of other deputies had put together, all of them containing detailed accounts of leased storage facilities and rented trucks, vans, and trailers. All the information began to blur together, and Winston knew his exhaustion was affecting his concentration.

Other reports waited on his desk as well: a domestic assault at a trailer home somewhere out in the woods near Winnabow; a stolen car found burned in the woods on Highway 133 by Orton Plantation; a fourteen-year-old boy missing from Shallotte whose parents thought he had run away to Wilmington or Fayetteville.

The phone rang on his desk, and Winston picked it up. The call was from Sheriff Oren Petty, just across the border down in Horry County, South Carolina.

"You sitting down?"

"I sit down when I can," Winston said.

"Well, I hope you're sitting down right now."

"I am."

"Good," Petty said, "because I think we found your cargo, some of it anyway."

Winston leaned forward and picked up a pen and flipped to a clean page in the notebook that sat on his desk. "Go ahead," he said.

"We just had us a big bust," Petty said. "It's a house way out in the county that we'd been watching for a while. We moved on it this morning and found the mother lode."

"What was it?"

"About twenty kilos of cocaine so far," Petty said. "They were packaging it up to move."

"Tell me you found some suspects."

"Oh, we found plenty of those, Sheriff. Made four arrests so far."

"And tell me you found some weapons."

"Plenty of those too," Petty said.

"Well, I'll be," Winston said. "You mind sharing those names, prints, and those weapons?"

"No, sir," Petty said. "As soon as we get them processed down here I'll make sure my office is in contact."

"If we can match the bullet that killed our guy up here to one of those guns down there then we'll be getting somewhere," Winston said.

"I got my fingers crossed," Petty said.

"Me too," Winston said.

CHAPTER 8

After finishing her dinner, Colleen had carried her tray down to the kitchen once her parents' lights had gone out for the night, and she had taken five bottles of her father's Old Milwaukee and brought them up to her room. She'd found her senior yearbook and sat on the bed, drinking the beers and leafing through the yearbook and finding every picture of Rodney Bellamy that she could. There he was in his senior photo wearing a tuxedo jacket and bow tie, a thin mustache above his lip. In another picture he was leaning against a car in the school parking lot, laughing at what someone was saying off-camera.

Before she turned off her light, she had taken the rotary phone from where she'd left it on the table by the beanbag chair and set it beside her pillow. Its ringing was what woke her, and with her eyes closed, her hand frantically searched for the handset. She found it and lifted it to her ear.

"Hello?" she said.

"Colleen?" It was her father's voice.

"Yeah?" she said; her throat was scratchy and dry, and her mouth tasted terrible. She kept her eyes closed tight, afraid of the light seeping around her curtains, afraid of what time the clock on the dresser would reveal.

"You sleep okay?"

"Just fine," she said.

"Good," he said. "I had to run out, pick up this fellow at the airport, but I'll be home later. Maybe we can all go out for supper or something. Just got a phone call from the sheriff down in Myrtle Beach. Might be some good news on Rodney's case."

Colleen's yearbook still sat on the bedside table, and when she stood from the bed, she placed her palm on it to steady herself. She forgot that she had hidden the empty beer bottles beneath her bed, and she kicked one over. It landed with a soft thud against the shag carpet.

"Colleen?" her father said.

"Yes," she said. "I'm here. Dinner sounds good. I'll talk to Mom."

"All right," he said. "Is she home?"

"I don't know," Colleen said. "I haven't seen her."

"She might've decided to walk a little. I almost wish she wouldn't do that."

Colleen's hand was still propped on the bedside table. Her head was bowed and her eyes were closed. She waited, but her father didn't say anything.

"Thanks for picking me up yesterday," she finally said.

"Of course," he said. "I'm glad you're home."

"Me too," she said, then, "I just hate that you had to drive back up to the airport today."

"That's okay," he said. "Tell your mother I'll be home as soon as I can. And mention going out to eat tonight."

"Okay," she said. "Bye."

"Bye," he said.

Without lifting her head, Colleen reached behind her and dropped the handset back on the cradle. She stood up straight, used her toes to push the empty bottles as far under the bed as she could without losing her balance.

Downstairs, she heard the sliding glass door that led from the kitchen to the back deck open and close. She didn't know what time it was, but she knew her mother was back from wherever she had been. Colleen kept her eyes closed, but she felt the room turn, and she realized that her head was splitting. She swallowed, passed her tongue over her lips. She took a breath, held it for a moment, and then she left her room and crossed the hall to the bathroom.

She pulled back the shower curtain and turned the water on, making sure it was almost hot enough to burn. She slipped out of her clothes and stepped into the shower, letting the scorching water run through her hair and over her face. Then she turned her back to the water, sat down in the tub, and let it pour over her.

After the shower, she got dressed and pulled her damp hair back into a short ponytail and came downstairs to find her mother sitting at the kitchen table with an empty coffee cup. She walked to the coffeepot and poured its remnants into an old cup with a fading picture of a lighthouse on it.

"Good morning, honey," her mother said. She was flipping through a magazine. Colleen noticed again how long and thin her mother's fingers looked, how frail her knobby wrists seemed where they disappeared into the loose sleeves of her soft pink sweatshirt. Colleen knew her mother was always cold now, so she wasn't surprised to see the collar of a light yellow blouse peeking out from the neck of her sweatshirt.

"Good morning," Colleen said.

"Did you sleep okay?"

"I did." She took a sip of the coffee, suddenly reminded of how weak her father always made it. "Dad called."

Her mother sighed. "I'm sure he was checking in on me, making sure I haven't lifted a finger in his absence."

"He's just worried, Mom," Colleen said. "I'm sure he's worried about me too."

"Well, imagine his surprise when he learns that women keep the world together." She looked up at Colleen and smiled. "His and Scott's both. We don't need their worry."

"Just their surrender."

"Or at least their silence," her mother said.

"I'd take that," Colleen said. She took a sip of her coffee. "I would take silence."

Her mother looked back down at her magazine, turned a page, then another.

"I bet you didn't expect to have a full house when you woke up yesterday morning," Colleen said.

"I've stopped having expectations," her mother said. She smiled as if realizing the darkness of her words. "But let's get out of here and go to the grocery store. I'm sure there's something special you'd like, and Lord knows we'll need something to feed the mystery man. And we need some candy for the kids."

Colleen had forgotten that today was Halloween, but then she found herself wondering why she should have remembered. "You never have trick-or-treaters, Mom," she said. "I don't think you need candy."

"Well, we never have pilots and FBI agents stay in the guest room either. So I guess anything can happen."

TO GET TO Food Lion they had to drive to the end of the island and take the bridge across the waterway. Colleen drove her mother's car, her mother sitting upright in the passenger's seat, talking non-stop about people Colleen either didn't know or didn't want to know about, telling stories of death and illness and unforeseen catastrophes as if the tragedies of other people held incredible and imminent bearing on their lives. Every story paralleled Colleen's mother's life in some way: a woman had cancer; an older couple had an adult child who lived far away; someone was struggling with the question of retirement and Social Security and Medicare.

"And I told Sylvia, I said, 'Sylvia, if your daughter's helping you it means that she wants to.' Her daughter lives all the way in Raleigh, but she and her husband get off work on Friday and drive down here and spend every weekend with Sylvia since Ralph died. Isn't that something?"

"That is something," Colleen said, only half-listening. They were driving past the airport now, and Colleen craned her neck, looking out at the crash-landed airplane and trying to imagine the spot on the grass where her father had found Rodney's body. Her mother kept talking as if she'd already forgotten about the plane, the mystery of it, and the tragedy her father had discovered.

"So that's why I told Sylvia, 'Let yourself be taken care of.' Lord knows she's done enough taking care of Ralph and the kids."

Colleen tried to focus on her mother's story, but her headache had not abated.

"Who's this?" she asked.

"Sylvia," her mother said. "Sylvia Webb."

"Where do you know her from?"

"The gym," her mother said. "The gym here on the island, at the rec center."

"You've been going to the gym?" Colleen asked. She looked over at her mother, tried to imagine her lifting weights or riding an exercise bike in the midst of her illness.

"Well, I *was*," her mother said. "Before, you know, all this. All this being sick."

"And what did Sylvia's daughter do?"

"She just comes to visit a lot," her mother said. "Since Sylvia's husband died, her daughter just comes down a lot to check on her."

"When did her husband die?"

"Gosh," her mother said. "I don't know. Maybe two years ago."

Colleen quickly picked up the pieces and threads of what her mother was telling her, ran dates through her mind, made associations from loose connections, and gauged the timing of what she was hearing. Her mother had had cancer for over a year, and Colleen knew she didn't have the strength to go to the gym. Her mother's friend's husband had been dead for two years, so the story of her daughter returning home on weekends was not a new one. So why would Colleen's mother be telling her that story now?

"What's Sylvia's daughter's name?" Colleen asked.

Her mother paused for a moment and looked out the passenger's-side window as the car whipped past stands of pine trees, the clustered businesses of the Food Lion shopping center appearing ahead on the right.

"I don't know," she finally said.

"It seems like you would know her name if she's so great." Colleen looked at her mother, but she was still looking out the window. "And what does she do? In Raleigh, what kind of work does she do?"

"I don't know," her mother said. She inhaled as if about to release a sigh, but she held it.

"Well, I'm sorry I don't live closer," Colleen said. "I wish I could come home more, but Dallas is a good bit farther away than Raleigh."

Colleen could tell that her mother had turned her head to look at her, could feel her eyes on her now. "That's not what I'm talking about," her mother said. "I'm just telling a story. It's not about you or what you should do. Everybody's different, Colleen."

"No," Colleen said. "Everybody's not different, Mom. Sylvia's daughter, whatever her name is and whatever she does for a living, wants to see her mom. I want to see you too. She can drive home on the weekends. I can't. We're not different. Our situations are different."

"That's what I meant," her mother said, her face now turned away from Colleen and back toward the window. "Anyway, it's just a story."

Colleen pulled her mother's car into the parking lot in front of Food Lion. Her mother refused to hang a handicapped tag from the rearview, but Colleen parked as close to the store as she could. They climbed out and walked across the parking lot without speaking.

Once inside, Colleen's mother found a cart and set her pocketbook down inside it. Colleen tossed her pocketbook in as well.

"Is there anything you want?" her mother asked.

"Nothing comes to mind," Colleen said, "but I'll look around." And with that they were off in separate directions, each one burning with anger and perhaps a little embarrassment from the turn their conversation in the car had taken.

Colleen found herself on the breakfast aisle, and her eyes scanned boxes of cereal, Pop-Tarts, instant grits, and oatmeal as she walked toward the back of the store. She'd had only dry toast for breakfast, and her stomach clenched at the sight of some of the sugary offerings. Her headache now squeezed at her temples and narrowed her vision, and she found her forehead sweating and felt her neck grow fl shed.

When she reached the end of the aisle and turned left to round another, she spotted a woman at the far end pushing a young baby in a stroller. Colleen recognized her immediately. It was Myra Page, a girl she'd been friends with in high school but had hardly seen since they both left home for college. Myra didn't see her, and Colleen stood for a moment, watching the baby in the stroller, who looked to be a little boy. He was chewing on something as if his teeth hurt, and Colleen thought of the Brazelton book and tried to gauge his age, but something in her stomach turned, and she suddenly feared that she was going to vomit right there on the floor.

She spun away from Myra toward the meat counter, where great slabs of steaks and ground hamburger sat on crushed ice behind thick glass. She tried to remember the layout of the store, to recall where the restrooms were. She scanned the back wall for a sign, and then she saw it on her left and made a beeline for it.

Colleen was barely able to close the stall door and lift the lid of the toilet seat before that morning's coffee and dry toast and whatever remained from last night's dinner left her stomach in a weak, brown stream that trickled into the toilet. She coughed, spit what was left in her mouth into the water. She flushed the toilet and grabbed a fistful of toilet paper and dabbed at her face and neck. She opened the stall door and walked to the sink. She ran the water and splashed it over her face, cupped some of it into her mouth, swished, and spit it out. Her pale face stared at her from the mirror. She winced at the dark circles under her eyes. Her blond hair still looked damp where she'd pulled it back in the stubby ponytail. Her pocketbook was in her mother's shopping cart, so she didn't have anything with her. No lip gloss. No brush. Nothing to improve what she was seeing before her. She pinched her cheeks to bring color back into them, gave them a few light slaps. She opened her mouth, smiled gruesomely at herself.

Outside the bathroom, Colleen saw that Myra Page had reached the end of the aisle and was now standing by the butcher's counter, a woman beside her. To her great horror, Colleen discovered that the woman with Myra was her own mother, and she was holding Myra's baby in her arms, her fingers clasping the teething toy and passing it in and out of the baby's mouth while its flailing arms reached for it. Myra and her mother were laughing. Both women looked up and saw Colleen at the same time. Her mother smiled a smile that looked like elation to Colleen. Myra simply waved as if she and Colleen were still girlfriends.

Myra, as if remembering or intuiting the great upheaval of Colleen's life, cocked her head to the side and looked at Colleen as if she were a child. "And how are *you*?" she asked once Colleen was close enough. "You're in"—she paused as if trying to remember something—"Texas now, right?"

"Yeah," Colleen said. "Dallas. My husband took a job there."

"Wow," Myra said. "I bet it's really beautiful out there."

"It's nice," Colleen said. She tried to smile, tried to keep her eyes off Myra's baby boy. "It's growing on me."

"Well, now she's home visiting her mama," Colleen's mother said, rocking her body and the baby from side to side at the word *mama*. She laughed a little and looked at Colleen. Her face changed. "Are you okay?" she asked. Colleen nodded her head and did her best to smile. "Honey, did you just throw up?"

COLLEEN WAS CRYING by the time they made it out to the car. Her mother sat in the passenger's seat while Colleen lifted the paper bags full of groceries into the trunk. When she was finished, she slammed it closed and left the cart sitting where it was. She pulled her shirt-sleeves over her hands and wiped her eyes, and then she opened the driver's door and climbed inside. She started the engine and backed out of the space without looking at her mother.

"I'm sorry," her mother said. "I don't know what I was thinking."

"It's okay," Colleen said. She sniffed, wiped at her eyes again.

"I wasn't thinking at all," her mother said. "I just saw Myra and didn't think a thing about holding her baby. I just forgot."

"Forgot what?" Colleen asked. They had come to a stop at a red light before leaving the parking lot and turning onto Beach Road. "Forgot that I was with you? Forgot that I lost my son? Forgot that you lost your grandson?"

"I don't know, Colleen," she said. "Maybe, for a minute, I forgot to be sad." Her face broke and she closed her eyes. Colleen knew she was fighting tears. She had rarely seen her mother cry, and seeing it now surprised her.

Colleen reached out and closed her hand over her mother's. "It's okay," she said. "I'm not mad. I'm definitely not mad at you. I'm just sad, and I know you are too. It just is what it is."

The light turned green, and Colleen eased onto the gas and turned out of the parking lot. They rode in silence for a moment.

"I shouldn't have held that stupid baby," her mother finally said.

Colleen smiled a little, looked over at her. "It did look stupid, didn't it?" she said.

Her mother smiled too. "Yes, it did. It looked pretty stupid."

Colleen laughed. She reached for the radio. "Stupid baby," she said.

THEY LEFT THE radio on once they crossed the bridge and returned to the island, and Prince's song "When Doves Cry" played while they drove up and down the gridded streets, leaving campaign leaflets in people's mailboxes, the cold and frozen groceries almost forgotten in the trunk. And they talked, really talked. About Scott's new job and how much he was gone. About her mother's uncertainty over whether or not she wanted Colleen's father to take on another term as sheriff. About the airplane and what it could mean for her father's reelection, for the investigation into Rodney's death that would now take so much of his time.

Colleen wanted to stay in the car with her mother, their windows rolled down, the radio on, their conversation moving freely and loosely among topics that were connected by memory and shared history and kinship. But they had the groceries to unload, and Marie had a round of medicine due with her lunch, and so Colleen was forced to point her mother's car toward home.

The phone was ringing when they walked into the house, and Colleen, carrying a bag of groceries in each arm, walked into the kitchen and set them down on the counter. She answered the phone, immediately recognizing the man's voice on the other end.

"Hey, girl," he said. It was Danny Price, her first best friend, and also the first boy she'd ever slept in a bed with. The first boy she'd ever danced with until she was certain she'd drop from exhaustion or exhilaration. The first boy she'd ever seen stare at himself in a rearview mirror while applying mascara outside the Pterodactyl Club in Charlotte, strobe lights flashing on the other side of the building's nearly blacked-out windows, the music pulsing through the walls and into their chests. They had just turned eighteen, and as Colleen had watched Danny swipe the makeup wand across his eyelashes, she realized that she had never felt freer or more certain about her freedom at any other time in her life.

Now, all these years later, Colleen smiled, turned, and leaned her waist against the counter.

"I was wondering when you'd call," she said. She twirled the cord around her finger.

"I'm calling to check on you. Myra Page says you threw up at the Food Lion."

Colleen laughed out loud now, the first real laugh that had escaped her body in what felt like years.

"Word travels fast," she said.

"It does on this island," Danny said. "You want to go out tonight, make some bad decisions? Give Myra and them something else to talk about?"

"I do," Colleen said. "I do."

CHAPTER 9

After getting off the phone with Sheriff Petty, Winston called Glenn and then Agent Rollins and told them what he'd learned. Both were happy with the news, but Winston could tell that neither one of them had high hopes that anything at the scene down in Horry County would prove to be connected to their own investigation. Sure, the cocaine from Petty's bust might have been flown in on the airplane that now sat on the runway here in Brunswick County, but without fingerprints or ballistic evidence connecting the two scenes there was just no way to know. So, they'd have to wait until all the samples were turned in and tested and then tested against one another.

"We'll know something sooner or later," Rollins had said, but Winston didn't have any use for later. He didn't want to acknowledge the ticking clock of next week's election, especially not to Rollins, but the ticking was there, even if he was the only who could hear it.

After hanging up with Rollins, Winston heard Vicki raise her voice out in the lobby, speaking loudly as if trying to get someone's attention. "Sir," she said. "Sir!"

Winston leaned forward as if being closer to Vicki's voice would give him a better idea of what was going on on the other side of his closed door.

"Sir!" Vicki said. "You can't go in there!"

Footsteps rounded the corner and pounded down the hallway toward Winston's office. As if commanded by instinct, Winston stood and braced his body for whatever was about to come through his door, understanding that his gun hung just out of reach. Without thinking, he moved from behind his desk and readied himself to face the person that Vicki had been unable to stop.

He winced when the door flew open, not so much because the force of the swing made him blink, but because of the person the door's opening had revealed: Ed Bellamy stood just a few feet away from him, breathing heavily, his face gleaming with sweat, from either anger or exertion, his glasses slipping down the bridge of his nose. Neither man said a word, each seemingly surprised to be in such close proximity to the other after the stir Bellamy's march into the station had caused. Winston could see Vicki standing in the middle of the hallway, her face a combination of fear and anger. Winston looked from her to Bellamy, and then he looked back at her. "It's okay, Vicki," he said. "It's okay. I've got it."

She nodded her head slightly and turned the corner to make her way back toward her offi e.

Winston watched her go, and then his eyes settled on Bellamy's. He'd left one hand on the doorknob, and with his other he pushed his glasses back toward his eyes, and then he raised a hand and pointed his finger at the dead center of Winston's chest. Bellamy didn't say a word. He just stood there, pointing.

It was clear to Winston that Bellamy was not someone looking for a fight; he was very clearly someone who'd had the fight taken out of him: a father who'd lost a child, a man whose life had been destroyed in the course of a single day. Behind his thick glasses his eyes were damp with tears garnered by grief and rage, and in that single moment of silence that passed between them, Winston understood just how close and inextricably tied together the two emotions are.

Winston did not whisper, but he did speak quietly. "Ed," he said, "you can close the door."

Bellamy stood there for a moment, and then he pushed the door closed behind him, his other hand still pointed at Winston in what seemed like an accusation.

"What's going on, Ed?" Winston asked. He stepped back, felt his desk brush his thighs. He leaned against it as if he were about to relax into a conversation with a colleague who'd stopped by to swap gossip.

"We're not going to do this again, Winston," Bellamy said. He waved his finger as if scolding a child, and then he folded his fingers into a fist. "We're not going to do this."

"Do what, Ed?" Winston said. "I don't know what you're talking about." He gestured to a chair in front of him, and then he bent slowly and picked up his hat where it sat on the seat. "You want to sit down? Talk this over?" He stood slowly and walked behind his desk to give Bellamy more room to do whatever he decided to do.

Bellamy did not sit, choosing instead to put his hands on the back of the chair and grip it as if preparing to throw it against the wall. He leaned toward the chair, his voice coming out even and clear.

"We're not going back, Winston," he said. "We're not going back to night rides and gunshots. We're not going to stand for it."

"Jesus, Ed," Winston said, "what in the world are you talking about? What gunshots?"

"Last night," Bellamy said. "Bradley Frye and all his good old boys. They showed up at Rodney's house and threw something through a window, demanded that boy Jay come out. They were driving through the Grove in the middle of the night in their trucks, revving their engines, shooting off guns. Had their rebel flags flying." He pushed his glasses up again, and Winston saw that his hand trembled. "They came by my house too, and I was waiting for them. Anybody firing a weapon in front of my house is going to take fire in return."

"Wait," Winston said. "Wait, are you telling me that Bradley Frye came to the Grove and shot at people?"

Bellamy's face changed suddenly, and Winston saw that, for the first time since he'd burst into his office, Bellamy was angry. He stepped out from behind the chair and pointed at Winston again. His voice was louder, more defi nt.

"I'm telling you that he came into the Grove like the goddamned golden days of the Klan." He stopped, his breathing coming rapidly, his forehead again damp with sweat. "And I'm telling you this too: we will not be run out of our homes. Not again. Not by him."

"Jesus, Ed," Winston said. "I had no idea."

"You should've," Bellamy said. "I called 911 last night. It took some fat-ass deputy of yours over an hour to get out there; they'd all left by then. Your deputy didn't even get out of his damn car, Winston; wouldn't even come up on my porch and talk to me. I was out there with a rifle. He made me set it down, threatened to arrest me if I didn't. He said the night looked quiet as far as he could see."

Bellamy turned and looked at Winston's closed office door. He lifted his finger as if pointing through it. "And I've called her about five times this morning trying to get you on the damned phone, and every time she tells me you're busy. And I get here and find you sitting on your ass while my son—" He stopped, choked back something, and then continued. "While my son is sitting up in the funeral home because his widow can't stop crying long enough to make a decision about when to lay him to rest. And now she's got a bunch of white boys shooting off guns in front of her house in the middle of the night, busting out windows. We're not going to stand for it, Winston. I'm telling you. You listen to me now."

"I'm sorry, Ed," Winston said. "This is the first I've heard of what you're telling me."

"Jesus Christ Almighty," Bellamy said. He pulled a handkerchief from his back pocket and took his glasses off and cleaned the lenses.

"You know as well as I do that Bradley Frye is an asshole," Winston said. "He's always been an asshole."

"Yeah," Bellamy said. "He was a little asshole back in high school when he was loading up white boys to drive up to Wilmington to jump Black kids in the parking lot at the junior high school. He was an asshole when he was throwing eggs at our houses and cars and burning bags of shit on the front porch." He finished cleaning his glasses and passed the handkerchief over his forehead and then stuffed it back into his pocket. "But he's a man now, and he might still be an asshole, but he's an asshole with a gun and a truck and a rebel flag and a whole bunch of other assholes who'll do anything he tells them to do."

Winston attempted to say something, but Bellamy held out his hand to stop him, and he continued.

"And here's what he's telling his people, Winston, the people he's convincing to vote for him: he's telling them that my son was flying drugs into the airport, that Black people in this county are responsible for every bit of crime or violence or drugs that goes on here. And he's terrorizing the people in the Grove to try to get us to do something stupid, and, Winston, I'm ready to do it.

"You know he's developing that land on the water that backs up to the Grove. That's what this is going to end up being about. If he can terrorize us, turn people in this county against us, force us to sell our land and move, he'll be sitting on a whole lot of land, and when he uses this to get you voted out, he'll be sitting on a whole lot of power."

Winston's vision narrowed to the fine point that Bellamy was making, and he knew without reflection that everything Bellamy was saying was true. As a kid, Bradley Frye had reveled in the racial violence that trickled south like a poisoned stream from Wilmington, where there were fires and shootings and attacks on Black students and Black communities. It had been a war, and many of the battles had been waged by Bradley Frye and his buddies right here in Brunswick County. For people like Frye, angry boys who'd grown into wealthy men, the war was still raging, but now it was being fought with checkbooks and votes instead of fists and baseball bats.

"A deputy came out to your house last night?" Winston asked. Bellamy nodded his head *yes*. "You remember his name?"

"No," Bellamy said, "and I don't think he told me, even though I asked for it after the bullshit he pulled."

"And you called here today?" Bellamy again nodded his head. "And you spoke with Vicki out there, and you told her about what happened last night." Another nod. "Excuse me," Winston said.

He stepped around Bellamy and opened the door, and then he closed it softly behind him. He knew Vicki was back at her desk; he could hear her moving papers around as if she had suddenly become as busy as she had ever been. Winston walked down the hallway, turned the corner, and stopped at the open glass window in front of her desk.

"Vicki," he said. She paused in her work and raised her head slowly. They made eye contact for a moment, and Winston could not recall ever looking at her as clearly or as seriously as he looked at her now. She sighed and sat back in her seat as if knowing a long conversation was about to unfold. Winston finally spoke. "Ed Bellamy in there says he's been calling all morning, Vicki. Is that true?"

Vicki moved her hands into her lap, and Winston saw her interlock her fingers. She crossed her legs. She leaned her left elbow on the arm of her chair.

"You've had some calls, Sheriff," she said. "I was planning to give you all the messages. All of them too, not just the ones from him."

"Who else called? You told me Marie called when I came in. Who else called?"

Vicki dusted something off her lap. She repositioned herself and looked back up at Winston. "No one," she said.

"Let me see the messages."

"What?"

"The messages from Ed Bellamy," he said. "The ones you were going to give me."

"I didn't write them down yet," she said.

Winston sighed and stepped away from the window. He put both hands in his pockets, his fingers moving through his keys and loose change. He kept his eyes on the floor, the linoleum catching the glow of the fluorescent lights above him.

"Vicki," Winston said, his voice coming out quiet and even. He didn't know if he was speaking this way so that Bellamy would not hear him or so that Vicki would understand his seriousness. "This isn't just some other case." He looked up and stepped closer to the desk.

"That man just lost his son. He's devastated. And now he has Bradley Frye out there trying to terrorize his family and his community." He took his hands out of his pockets and put them on the counter. "When someone calls about something like that, Vicki, especially when they call three, four, five times, I need to know about it, okay?"

It seemed that Vicki did not even think about what she said next, and Winston knew that the words that came from her mouth were the purest expression of who she was.

"No law against driving around, Sheriff." She held Winston's stare, breaking it only to unfold her hands and scoot her chair closer to her desk. When she looked at Winston again there was something cold and final in her eyes that he had never seen before, but he understood that what he was seeing had always been there, had always been a part of Vicki and her life and her view of people like Ed Bellamy and her opinion of men like Winston who believed they deserved justice and equity. It was clear to Winston that his certainty was and had always been an affront to Vicki and people like her, and even more than surprise, Winston felt foolish for believing differently.

A door had closed between them, and Winston could feel that a coldness had seeped in. He now foresaw a relationship with Vicki that would be cast in the full light of their prejudices. There would be a sudden stop to small acts of kindness and shared joys, which could never transpire again without an unease that would color their every interaction.

Winston removed his hands from the counter and stood up straight. He kept his eyes on Vicki's. "Vicki," he said, "you are not an officer of the law in Brunswick County, and it is not your job or responsibility to decide what is and what is not illegal. It is your job to share all messages with me, regardless of who they are from and regardless of what they are. Is that clear?"

Another moment passed between them, their eyes still on each other, and in that moment Winston understood that, at least on this issue and probably many others that would be revealed and come to bear on their lives in significant and insignificant ways, Vicki had sided with Bradley Frye and people like him, and he knew that she would vote for Bradley Frye next week. Nothing had changed, but something had been revealed, and Winston had not seen it coming, although he had lived with it and worked alongside it every day of his life for almost two decades. This new knowledge diminished him, and he felt smaller standing in front of Vicki now than he had when he arrived at her desk buoyed by the righteous anger of justice and accountability. Winston found himself suddenly and acutely aware that he had run out of allies and that he was alone, both the arbiter of justice and the witness to justice gone awry.

"Vicki, listen to me," he finally said. "Let me be clear. This isn't a game of Black versus white. This isn't white boys and Black boys getting in fights at the high school over the decisions adults have made." He leaned forward, put his fingertips on the counter as if balancing the weight of his body on their points. "We've already had us one murder; I don't want to have another one. We're sitting on a powder keg here, and I don't need anybody in this office playing with matches, Vicki, okay?"

She hesitated. Winston looked into her eyes, imagined her mind tossing around words and phrases she'd grown up hearing, long-held beliefs that she insisted on holding against Black men like Ed Bellamy and his dead son. Asking her to work against suspicions and beliefs so deeply held as to seem intrinsic to life was like asking Vicki to attempt the impossible task of separating her skin from her own skeleton.

"Yes, sir, Sheriff," she said.

"I need you," Winston said, "not to be on my side, but to be on the side of the law. I have to know that I can trust you, okay?"

"Okay," she said. She scooted her chair even closer to her desk and cast her eyes back down at her work. A storm had passed between them, destroying every structure in sight and ripping trees from the earth, but neither of them would ever acknowledge the carnage, choosing instead to live exposed to the elements in silence.

Winston watched her work for a moment, and then he asked, "Who answered Bellamy's call last night?"

Vicki stopped what she was doing and sat still for a moment, and then she turned and referenced a clipboard that sat on the edge of her desk.

"Deputy Englehart," she said, her voice escaping like a muttered admission that was outing a conspirator in the face of an authority who already knew the full scale of the operation.

"Can you give me his phone number?"

She looked through a few papers, grabbed a pen and scribbled the number on a yellow legal pad, and tore the sheet free. She passed it to Winston through the open window. He took it without saying a word, and then he turned and walked back to his office.

Winston found Bellamy with his back turned, his gaze fixed on the wall of framed photographs. Winston picked up the telephone receiver on his desk and dropped the paper with Englehart's number on it beside the cradle. "Excuse me," he said. "I have to make a call."

Bellamy did not turn around at the sound of Winston's voice. "Take your time," he said.

Winston dialed Englehart's number, and then he sat on the edge of the desk while the phone rang. It was just after noon, and he imagined Englehart still sleeping after being on call the night before, his closed eyes and his oily face lying in bed in a darkened too-hot room where a ceiling fan creaked above him, the closed blinds hot with the heat of the afternoon sun beating down on the windows. Englehart would stir when he heard the phone, perhaps snore himself awake at its ringing.

When Englehart's voice came on the line, Winston could not tell whether or not he'd been sleeping. It was the same syrupy, plaintive voice Englehart always used, and Winston imagined that voice speaking to Ed Bellamy the night before from the inside of a darkened patrol car while Bellamy stood on his porch with a rifle in the middle of the night. Winston looked over at Bellamy now where he still stood with his back turned. He knew Bellamy was listening, even if he wasn't watching.

"Englehart?" Winston said.

"Yeah?"

"This is Sheriff Barnes."

"Morning, Sheriff," he said.

Winston almost corrected him and said, "Afternoon," but he thought better of it. He resettled himself on the edge of his desk. His back was to Bellamy now, and he wondered if Bellamy had turned to watch him.

"I heard about what happened last night out in the Grove. You mind sharing with me what you saw?"

Englehart sighed. "Wasn't much to see, Sheriff."

"Wasn't much to see?" Winston repeated. "Even so, you need to write a report about each call you respond to. I wouldn't know a word about this if Ed Bellamy hadn't come up here—"

"That's the one that had him a gun last night," Englehart said. "He wanted me to arrest people who weren't doing nothing but driving around, and then he's out there waving a gun around in front of a cop. Sheriff, I ain't going to have them people holding guns on me and telling me how to do my job. That ain't going to happen again."

Winston heard the click of a lighter, and he knew Englehart was holding a flame to the tip of a cigarette.

"Well, you aren't going to be doing this job anymore anyway," Winston said. "Last night was your last night on duty. You come on up here and turn in your badge and your weapon."

"You firing me?"

"You're being relieved of your duty," Winston said. "It seems like you don't want to do your duty anyway, at least not the right way. Not on behalf of *all* the citizens of Brunswick County."

The phone was silent on Englehart's end for a moment. Then Winston heard him take a drag on his cigarette. Then the sound of him blowing smoke into the phone.

"I'm just going to consider this a vacation, Sheriff, because your ass is getting voted out next week, and as soon as that happens the first call I'll make will be to Bradley Frye to get my old job back."

"Well," Winston said, "tell him congratulations when you talk to him. In the meantime, bring your badge and your gun by. After that, stay the hell away from this office."

Winston hung up the phone and sat there for a moment, and then he turned his head and looked in Bellamy's direction. His back was still turned, and he'd crossed his arms.

"Well, that's that," Winston said.

Bellamy laughed to himself, just loud enough for Winston to hear it. "That wasn't *that*," he said. "That was nothing. That was taking a title from a thug who doesn't need one to do what he's going to do.

That's all that was. Now he doesn't need to wear a badge when he night rides in the Grove."

"Ed, I'm trying here," Winston said. "I'm doing my best."

"Yeah," Ed said. "Me too."

The two men were quiet for a moment. Then Bellamy turned toward Winston and pointed at the photograph of him as a young soldier in dress blues. "When'd you serve?"

"Nineteen fifty to fifty-three," Winston said.

"Korea?"

"Yeah," Winston said. "Army. I worked a supply station outside Busan."

Bellamy turned back to the wall of photographs. "Ever see combat?"

"No," Winston said. He paused for a moment, wondering about the track their conversation was taking. "You?"

"Oh, yeah," Bellamy said. "Oh, yeah."

"Vietnam?"

"Oh, yeah," Bellamy said again. "Marine sniper. Plenty of combat."

The room grew quiet again, but something had changed beneath the quiet; the air had become charged with something—tension or electricity or uncertainty. Winston looked at the carpet beneath his feet. He considered standing and facing Bellamy, asking him more questions about what had happened the night before, questions about what Rodney could have been doing on the runway in the middle of the night. But instead of doing those things, he decided to sit, and listen.

"They sent me to Marine Scout Sniper School because I knew how to handle a rifle," Bellamy said. "The rifles were Winchester 70s, 30.06. Scope was something I had to get used to, but I knew how to shoot. I knew how to hunt, so I had no problem hunting in the jungle. But I knew something else that my white buddies didn't know: I knew what it meant to be hunted." He turned and looked at Winston. "I still know what it means to be hunted. All these years later, we're still being hunted."

Winston pictured Bradley Frye's truck cruising through the streets of the Grove in the middle of the night, a man standing in the truck bed and operating a searchlight like a poacher looking for the glint of an animal's eye in the darkness.

Bellamy folded his arms and sat down on the other side of Winston's desk. "Back in 'Nam, I'd spend hours on my belly in the jungle, hunting. All of us would. Sometimes I'd be alone. Sometimes I'd have a partner with me. One of us aiming, one of us spotting, relieving each other while one slept and one kept lookout, a machine gunner in back of us, ready to cover." He laughed to himself. Then he sighed and shook his head. "So many hours, Winston—days and days, weeks probably—spent on my belly, crawling through mud and briars, pissing myself, shitting my pants if I had to. One position to the next, just waiting. No matter how long it took, I'd wait. But I was happy to wait, because at the end of all that waiting I knew I was going to get that one shot that would make it all worth it."

Bellamy stood from the desk and put his hands in his pockets. He walked toward Winston's door, and then he turned and faced him.

"That's what it feels like to be a Black man in America, Winston. I've been on my belly for years, looking up from the ground, getting stepped on while I keep on crawling forward. The only difference between then and now is that I don't have that one shot to look forward to."

Winston was uncertain of what to say, of what he could say. He stepped back behind his desk and set his hands on the back of his chair, thoughts careening through his head. "Ed," he finally said. "I need to tell you that I'm not going to win this reelection. I know that."

"I know that too," Bellamy said. "And I need to tell you there's still time for you to do the right thing."

"And what's that, Ed? I'm working to get to the bottom of what happened to Rodney. Aside from that, what can I do? Go after Bradley Frye? That's not going to make anything easier on anybody, especially you."

"You can get on your belly," Bellamy said. "Crawl through the jungle with me. I can do the firing, but I might need a spotter, and I might need some cover."

"I'm the sheriff, Ed, at least for now. I've got to follow the law."

The two men stood looking at one another for a moment, and then Bellamy put his hand on the knob and opened the office door. He paused before stepping through it.

"And I've got to protect myself, and that means I might have to go hunting, because I sure as hell am not going to allow myself to be hunted. Not anymore."

FOR THE FIRST time in the nearly twenty years they'd spent working together, Vickie left at 5:00 p.m. sharp without saying goodbye. Winston expected it, so he wasn't surprised, but it still troubled him. The whole afternoon—even the news of the bust down in South Carolina—had troubled him. Not long after she left, Winston locked up the office and climbed into the cruiser and headed back out to the airport. The light would be gone soon, and he was curious to know what Groom had been able to get done.

Once he'd arrived at the airport and trudged across the expanse of grassy field, he saw that the aircraft's tail had been jacked up and the broken landing gear removed. Agent Rountree stood by the plane, talking with one of Winston's deputies and a couple of mechanics that Winston didn't know. Glenn stood back, watching the scene. Groom was nowhere to be found. Glenn looked back at Winston and nodded at him as he approached.

"Looks like things are moving along," Winston said.

"I'd say so," Glenn said.

"I thought you weren't on airplane duty until after midnight," Winston said.

"I'm not," Glenn said. "I just wanted to watch them jack this thing up. I'll be back out here at two a.m."

Winston sighed. "Deputy Englehart isn't going to be working with us anymore," he said.

Glenn's eyes fell from the plane to the ground in front of him. He shook his head. "Does this have anything to do with what happened out at the Grove last night?"

"It does," Winston said. He sighed again. "I've got a bad feeling, Glenn."

Glenn looked at him, and then he looked back at the ground. "I wish I could tell you I got a good feeling," he said. "But I don't."

"Well, I'm on call tonight if you need anything," Winston said. "And tomorrow I'm going to take Englehart's spot out here on the runway. Hopefully we can get this plane out of here soon."

While Winston and Glenn stood talking, Agent Rountree wandered over.

"Your pilot seems to know what he's doing," Rountree said.

"He's not *my* pilot," Winston said, but Rountree ignored him.

"Said the aircraft is okay to fly. He plans on taking off day after tomorrow and setting her down in Wilmington. There's a hangar waiting for it. We'll take it from there."

"It looks like you've already taken it," Winston said.

"Yep," Rountree said. "I reckon so."

"Did you manage to find any prints?" Winston asked.

"We're on top of things, Sheriff," Rountree said. "Don't you worry."

"Did you hear about that bust outside Myrtle Beach?" Winston asked. "Rollins and I were thinking it might be related. Sheriff down there thinks it might be too."

"We're on top of things," Rountree said again.

Rountree walked past them and climbed into his car. Winston heard the engine start. He turned and watched Rountree back up and drive toward the parking lot.

Glenn broke the silence. "It'll be nice to have that airplane out of here, Sheriff," he said. "Regardless of where it goes next or what happens to it."

"We've still got a murder on our hands," Winston said. "I wish they cared half as much about that as they do about this damned plane or whatever was in it."

"I know," Glenn said. "We'll figure it out."

Winston didn't respond. "Where's Groom at?" he finally said.

Glenn looked over at Winston. "Marie came by here looking for you an hour or so ago. She'd been out picking up more campaign posters."

"Really?" Winston asked.

"I told her you were at the office. Groom asked her if he could catch a ride back to y'all's house." Glenn looked at Winston a moment longer as if trying to predict how he'd respond, and Winston didn't know quite what to make of it: neither Glenn's look nor the news he'd just shared.

"How's she doing?" Glenn asked.

"Pretty good, apparently."

"That's great," Glenn said. "Me and Elsie have been praying for her."

"I appreciate it," Winston said, looking away from Glenn's face and doing his best to conceal the warmth that crept up his neck and onto his cheeks. "Marie appreciates it too."

WINSTON'S FRIEND DAVID Worley's white Ford truck sat behind Marie's Buick in the driveway so Winston parked on the road in front of the house. worley's self-storage and equipment rental and the business's phone number were lettered on the truck's tailgate and both doors.

Inside, Winston found Marie, Groom, and David's wife, Dianne, standing around in the kitchen. Dianne's glasses were pushed up on her head and her purse was still slung over her shoulder as if she'd just arrived or was just about to leave.

"Dianne, I thought you'd be David," Winston said.

"Sorry to disappoint," Dianne said. "I've got the truck for a few days. David took the car up to Asheville to see about his mother. She's not doing well."

"I hope everything's okay," Winston said.

"She's just getting older," Dianne said. She sighed. "We all are, I guess."

When Dianne said that, Winston happened to notice the campaign posters that were lying on the counter beside her: the face of his younger self stared back at him with a stoic smile that was designed to evince calm and protection. Winston wondered whether or not he could feign that smile now.

"I had to go get more from the printer," Marie said. "Colleen and I ran out today. I called the office, but I couldn't get ahold of you, so I just went ahead and had them printed."

"Where's Colleen at?" Winston asked.

"Off somewhere with Danny Price," Marie said.

"I was hoping we could all go out," Winston said. "Take Agent Groom here for some shrimp and flounder. I wish she would've stayed home."

"Well, it's Halloween and she's out having fun," Marie said. "She needs to have a little fun."

Groom had stood listening as everyone spoke, and now he reached out and picked up one of Winston's campaign posters.

"You going another term, Sheriff?" Groom asked.

"I reckon so," Winston said. "We'll see what the voters decide."

"His opponent's just a nasty man," Marie said.

"Marie," Winston said. He raised his eyebrows to show her he didn't want her speaking that way in front of someone they didn't know.

"I'm sorry, Winston," she said. "I just can't help it."

"He is," Dianne said. "I have to agree with Marie."

Winston laughed. "That's enough now," he said. He looked at Groom. "You get settled in?"

"Yes, sir," Groom said.

Winston wanted to mention the drug bust and the arrests and evidence down in Myrtle Beach, but he didn't want to say a word of it in front of Marie, both because he was afraid she'd embarrass him in front of Groom with her own ideas of what it would mean, and because he wanted to appear professional, to make clear that he knew how to handle and protect sensitive information.

That night, over a dinner of grilled cheese sandwiches and tomato soup, Groom told Winston and Marie about flying missions in the C-47 in Vietnam, cruising so low over rice paddies and villages that he could see people's faces as they raised their hands to shade their eyes to look up at him.

"Were you scared?" Marie asked. She dipped a wedge of sandwich into her soup and took a bite, the melted cheese stretching out so that she caught it with her finger before it snapped free.

"Marie," Winston said, not quite scolding her for asking a question like that, but letting it be known that Groom didn't have to answer if he didn't feel comfortable.

"I wouldn't say I was *scared*," Groom said. "You're aware, sure, aware of what all could happen to you." He put a spoonful of soup into his mouth and looked across the table into the darkened living room as if he were looking into his past and studying it carefully. He swallowed. "In the C-47, the pilot was doing the flying and the aiming. They fit the window with a target, and the mini guns in back were aimed to hit on what you sighted. You know you're going to take fire. You just hope the guys in the back are giving it better than you're getting." He shook himself from his trance, turned back to his plate. "Every flight you take is an exercise in faith," he said, smiling. "Especially out there in the jungle. But that's what made it fun sometimes."

"Doesn't sound fun to me," Marie said.

Groom laughed. It was the first bit of good humor Winston had seen him express since he'd arrived. "It wasn't fun for the Viet Cong either," he said. "That particular aircraft scared them to death. They called them Ghost Planes."

"That sounds like what we've got on our hands out at the airport right now," Winston said. He took a sip of tea, and then he pushed himself back from the table and looked at Groom. "I couldn't find a single fingerprint in that damn plane."

"That would prove an unusual level of sophistication," Groom said. He picked up his napkin from his lap and wiped his mouth. He folded it and placed it back on his lap. "But guys like those will slip up. They always do."

AFTER DINNER, WHILE Marie cleaned up in the kitchen, Winston found Groom smoking on the front porch.

"Thanks for dinner," Groom said.

"You bet," Winston said. "It wasn't much."

"It was plenty," Groom said. "And thanks for letting me stay."

"Don't mention it." Winston put his hands in his pockets and rocked back on his heels, his mind turning over the best way to say what he was about to say. "We might have a little news on our airplane," he finally said.

Groom took a drag on his cigarette and then tapped it on the porch railing, knocking the ash into the damp pine needles below. He reached into his breast pocket and removed a pack of cigarettes. He held it out to Winston. "Marie said you quit years ago, but now might be a good time to start again."

Winston hesitated for a moment. He turned and looked back at the house, and then he reached out and took a cigarette that Groom had shaken loose from the pack. Groom struck his lighter, and

Winston leaned toward the flame. After its long absence, the feel of the smoke in his lungs shocked him at first, but the pleasant sweetness of the cigarette and the familiarity of it in his hand relaxed him. It all felt effortless and natural.

"What's the news?" Groom asked.

"Sheriff down in Horry County called today," Winston said. "That's Myrtle Beach. They made a huge bust."

"What was it?"

"Cocaine," Winston said. "About twenty kilos. Some weapons too."

"How far away is that?"

"Sixty-five miles or so."

Groom was quiet for a moment, as if he was thinking over what little bit of information Winston had given him. "That can't be all of it if it's tied to your aircraft," he said. "That aircraft is too large for that. If it is tied to it, more drugs will turn up."

"We're hoping they'll match something with what we've got, ballistics or something," Winston said.

Groom looked over at him. "I'd be hoping the same thing," he said. He took a long drag on his cigarette, and Winston did the same.

CHAPTER 10

Three garage-style doors opened out to the beach, and the breeze that ran through the bar was cool and humid. Colleen pulled her jacket tighter around her and took another sip of her beer. Although the voices of other people and the noise of the music weren't loud inside—not loud enough to drown out the sound of the distant waves at low tide—the buzz surrounding her met her ears like voices speaking in a dream. Everything seemed strange, even the weather, especially the weather. It was still summer in Dallas, at least it felt like summer, and thinking about this made Colleen feel that a fog had been lifted, and for the first time since returning home she felt the mystery of seasonal change in the air.

She and Danny had spent most of the evening at a restaurant/bar down by the Oak Island pier called Whale of a Time. They'd knocked back round after round of Budweisers, picked through a shared basket of fried flounder, coleslaw, and french fries, and even danced to the jukebox when one song or another spoke to them enough to leave their bar stools and wander out to the dance floor.

As usual, Danny was outspoken and funny, indifferent to the people who watched them dance or listened to the things they talked about. Unlike Colleen, Danny had dressed up for Halloween night, in black jeans and a black Izod shirt with the collar popped up around his face, a trail of blood on either side of his lips, and large, plastic vampire teeth that popped out of his mouth and landed on the bar or dance floor whenever he laughed. Colleen eventually wrapped the teeth in a napkin and slipped them into her purse without him noticing.

While he danced, Danny kept his eyes closed as if watching a movie of himself in his head, as if everything in the room were drawn toward him and his movement. Colleen, on the other hand, kept her eyes open; she watched Danny move, looked around at the costumed people in the bar, watched her own reflection in a narrow strip of mirror that hung behind the liquor bottles. Her hair was still pulled back in a ponytail that had spent the day working itself loose, and she wore a black tank top beneath her jean jacket and tight jeans with her Keds. Danny's dark brown hair brushed his collar where he wore it long in the back and spiked with gel in the front. A tiny gold hoop in his right ear caught the light. While they danced, Danny would open his eyes for a moment and wink at Colleen as if they were the only two people in the world. He made her feel that way, and she had never envied someone so much in her entire life.

Danny was a licensed realtor, and he worked in his father's real estate office, but Colleen knew he spent most of his time in Wilmington or Raleigh, places that could sometimes seem as far away as Mars. She couldn't imagine why Danny had remained in Oak Island after high school, but perhaps someone would ask the same question about why she had returned. Regardless, here they both were now on Halloween night, dancing to the Eurythmics, the Go-Go's, the Cure, and screaming over the music as if the bar were packed with people just like them.

Colleen lost count of how many beers she'd had, and the basket of fried fish sat in front of her, cold and congealed. She turned over a piece of flounder, found a french fry hiding beneath, and popped it into her mouth.

"Cheer up," Danny said. He leaned his body against hers, and she grabbed the bar to keep from toppling off her stool.

"I am cheery," she said. "I'm full of cheer."

"Bullshit," he said. "You look worn-out and angry."

"This is my 'I just lost my baby and my marriage is unraveling' Halloween costume," she said.

"Oh, honey," he said. He took a drag from his cigarette and put his arm around her and pulled her close to him. She felt him turn his head to blow smoke away from her.

"I just can't believe Myra Page told you about what happened at the grocery store," she said. "How embarrassing."

Danny took his arm from around her and sat up straight. He tapped his cigarette into the ashtray. "Myra didn't tell me," he said. He took a drag and blew more smoke. "Rebecca Henderson did. She's one of my daddy's agents, and Myra's the one who told *her*."

"Jesus," Colleen said. She dropped her forehead into her hands, the heaviness of her own head almost rocking her off the stool again. "That's even worse."

"Oh, come on," Danny said. "Who cares about those little tramps? Did you get a look at Myra's baby? If Pete thinks it's his then he's dumber than she is. If that girl had as many poking out as she's had poking in she'd be a damn porcupine."

Colleen raised her head to the ceiling and laughed. Danny smiled and took another drag.

"That's right," he said. "Keep your head up. You don't need to worry about what anyone on this damned island thinks. You're a Dallas girl now. Don't mess with Texas, bitches." He turned toward her so that his knees touched hers. He lifted his cigarette and pointed toward the beach outside. "And later, when you vomit on the beach out there, I'm going to be right beside you, holding your hair."

She leaned forward and rested her head on his shoulder. He dropped his cigarette in the ashtray on the bar and put his arms around her.

"Come on, now," he whispered. He rubbed her back. "Come on, now," he said again.

"You always make me feel better," she said. She sat up and looked at him. "Thank you for calling me. I wish I were more fun."

He gasped and widened his eyes as if gravely offended by what she'd just said. "You can beat me, tie me up, and make me write bad checks," he said. "But don't you dare bore me. Lord knows nothing about you has ever bored me."

"Well, thanks for listening to me bitch about my life," Colleen said.

She picked up her near-empty beer bottle and took the last swig. When she set it down, something caught the corner of her eye, and she turned to see a man looming behind Danny. He was dressed like Jason Voorhees from *Friday the 13th,* complete with the dirty hockey mask and tattered black union suit. Danny had no idea that the man was there until he saw the look on Colleen's face. Then he turned his head and peered over his shoulder. He gave a weak smile, and then he made a face at Colleen and laughed like he didn't know what else to do. The man wearing the hockey mask groaned and shuffled his feet as if he were trying to go through Danny to get to the bar. Danny tried to laugh it off, but when the man didn't stop leaning into him, Danny put his forearm against the man's chest. "All right," Danny said. "That's enough. You're going to spill my beer."

The man in the hockey mask lifted a machete that had remained hidden until that moment. It all happened so quickly that Colleen realized that the machete was made of plastic only when it grazed Danny's cheek without drawing blood. Danny slapped the machete away from his face and sprang from his bar stool. Colleen had never seen Danny fight—had never even imagined him in a fight—and she did not know what would happen if one broke out now.

But a fight didn't break out. The man with the machete laughed and lifted his hockey mask, revealing a handsome face and a blond haircut that reminded Colleen of nearly every guy she'd known in law school.

"Come on, Danny," the man said. "I'm just messing with you."

"Jesus, Brad," Danny said. He collapsed back onto his bar stool as if he were suddenly exhausted by the specter of an altercation. "I didn't know who the hell you were."

"I'm Jason Voorhees," the man said. He looked down at his costume as if checking to make sure he'd worn the right outfit. "Come on, I got the hockey mask and everything."

"That's not what I meant, Brad," Danny said. He shook out another cigarette and lit it.

Brad reached around Danny and set his machete and mask on the bar, and then he put his hands on Danny's shoulders and made a show of massaging them. "Relax, Danny," he said. "Relax and tell me what's up with the sales out in Plantation Cove. I thought you'd be slinging some more home sites for me."

"Market's been slow this fall," Danny said. "It'll pick up. It always does."

"Yeah," Brad said. He stopped his massage and patted Danny's shoulders with both hands. "Let's hope it does." He looked over at Colleen and smiled. "Is this your girlfriend?"

"This is Colleen," Danny said. He gave Colleen a quick look that was part apology and part cry for help.

"Colleen Barnes?" Brad said. He reached out his hand, and Colleen took it firmly in her own. It was soft and warm.

"Colleen Banks," she said.

"Shoot," Brad said. "I know who you are. Your daddy's a good man. It's a shame that he's going to lose next week."

"Okay," Colleen said, mostly because she didn't know what else to say.

Brad turned his attention back to Danny. "Danny's a good man too." He smiled, and then he reared back his hand and smacked Danny on the ass as if they were on a football field and Danny had just made a game-winning catch. "But he needs to get this sweet ass in gear and start selling some home sites." Danny didn't react, just took a drag from his cigarette and then knocked an ash into the empty bottle sitting in front of him. Brad leaned close to Danny's ear. "What did you dress as, Danny?"

"Dracula," Danny said, not turning around.

"What?" Brad asked.

Danny turned his head and spoke louder. "Dracula."

"Is that right?" Brad said. "You out sucking blood tonight?" He laughed, placed one hand on the back of Danny's neck, and squeezed.

Danny shrugged off his hand. "Just sucking down beers," he said.

"I bet you are," Brad said. He leaned forward again and picked up his mask and machete off the bar. "Well, y'all have a good night." He winked at Colleen. "Tell your daddy I said hello."

Brad left them and walked across the dance floor to a table on the other side of the bar where two other men sat. They were about his age, but they wore polo shirts and jeans. They looked like old college buddies who'd just left the golf course and had come to the bar to make a lot of noise and look for women to take home.

"What an asshole," Colleen said.

"Yep," Danny said. "Always has been. I hope your dad beats his ass."

"I thought you were about to try."

"Shoot," Danny said. "I should've." He looked at the bartender and raised his empty bottle, and a second later she came by and removed it and set down a fresh beer.

"What's Plantation Cove?" Colleen asked.

Danny took a long sip of his beer and set it down. "What *was* Plantation Cove, you mean."

"What *was* Plantation Cove?" she repeated.

"It's sinking," Danny said. He laughed. "In more ways than one." He picked up a napkin from the bar and wiped his mouth, and then he wiped the beads of cold sweat from the bottle.

"What do you mean 'it's sinking'?"

"Well, it's literally sinking," Danny said. "It's a new development off Long Beach Road. Brad came in and cleared swampland and decided to build huge houses on tiny lots. Some of the most expensive waterfront lots are literally under a foot of water, depending on the tide. And he can't sell the lots and build fast enough to keep it in the black." He looked over at Colleen, turned his head farther as if making sure Brad wasn't still looming behind him. "So," he said, "it is all, therefore, underwater."

"I thought he was some rich kid," Colleen said.

"He is," Danny said. "At least he was, anyway. He's still an asshole."

"I'm sorry that he was mean to you," she said.

Danny waved his hand. "Please," he said. "I can handle guys like Bradley Frye."

"I hope my father can handle him."

"Hell, the only reason Bradley Frye wants to be sheriff is so he can get a piece of whatever's out there."

"What does that mean?" she asked.

"He's going around telling everybody that that airplane was part of a drug-smuggling operation and that Rodney Bellamy was the ringleader." He took a drag off his cigarette. "Shit, if that's true, I bet Brad's jealous as hell. I bet he wishes he'd thought of it."

"You think that's why he wants to be sheriff?" she asked. "To make money illegally?"

"Aside from your daddy, I'd argue that's the only reason anybody in this damn county would want that job."

They sat in silence for a moment, and Colleen looked at Danny out of the corner of her eye. For some reason, at that moment, she saw him as the older man he would become, still handsome, still pretending to be as happy and reckless as he was before Bradley Frye had arrived and stolen whatever joy their evening together had conjured. Colleen knew that even as an older man Danny would be alone, at least alone in the way of those who live full lives while never sharing the breadth of their lives with certain people. And Colleen knew that she was one of those certain people with whom Danny had never shared his life. When she was younger, she'd had questions she wanted to ask Danny, but she didn't have the vocabulary to frame them. Now she had the vocabulary, but she no longer had the questions.

Finally, Danny stubbed out the remainder of his cigarette in the ashtray. Soft Cell's "Tainted Love" came over the speakers, and he grabbed Colleen's hands and pulled her off her stool toward the dance floor.

As they danced, Colleen couldn't help catching glimpses of Bradley Frye where he sat with his friends at a table in the corner. He wore his hockey mask pushed back on his forehead now, and she could feel his eyes on her, and that, along with his treatment of Danny and the things he'd said about her father, unnerved her. He was the kind of man who scared her, a man who acted like he had nothing to lose because he lived in a world without consequences.

Even though it was Halloween night, it was still a Wednesday, and at midnight the house lights had been brought up in the near-empty bar. Danny cupped his hands around his mouth and booed, and then he smacked his palms on top of the bar, trying to get the bartender's attention. She looked at him and rolled her eyes as if she were used to seeing him behave this way. "Fix your makeup, Danny," she said.

The streaks of blood he'd painted at the corners of his mouth were now nothing more than pink smears. Colleen laughed and reached for him, gently trying to get him to drop his hands. Unable to convince him to stop, she tried to get ahold of his hands to keep them off the bar.

"Stop it," she said. "She's going to call the police."

Danny stopped booing for a moment.

"Call the police, Becky!" Danny said. "Call them! And bring Sting! We need to dance."

"Night's over," Becky said.

"Not for the undead," Danny said. He swooped from his bar stool in a dramatic spin, swishing his arm upward as if lifting a cape to cover his face. Becky laughed and threw a bar towel at him. Colleen climbed off her bar stool, and she and Danny staggered across the now-lit dance floor toward the door. Colleen looked at the corner where Bradley Frye and the two men had been sitting, but while the two men were still there, Brad was gone. She looked around, hoping he wasn't outside, and then she spotted him on a pay phone, leaning against the wall in the hallway that led to the restrooms.

Outside, Colleen and Danny weaved through the parking lot on the way to his red Camaro T-top.

"Are you okay to drive?" she asked, already knowing what his answer would be.

"Are you okay to ride?" he asked. He had a cigarette in his mouth and was trying to line it up with his lighter's flame while he walked. He lit it and slipped the lighter into his pocket. He smiled, took a drag. "What a silly question," he said. "Colleen Barnes was born to ride."

She held up her ring finger, suddenly remembered that she had left her ring in her top drawer back at her parents' house along with the framed wedding photo.

"Colleen Banks," she said.

"Shit," Danny said. He unlocked his door and swung it open. "You'll always be Colleen Barnes to me." He climbed inside and reached across to unlock Colleen's door. She heard the click of the door unlocking and closed her hand around the door handle. She stared out toward the ocean that was apparent yet invisible in the dark night. She knew that she would always know herself as Colleen Barnes too.

THEY DROVE UP the street to a convenience store that was still open and selling beer. Danny parked by the gas pumps and went inside. Colleen settled back in the seat and allowed her head to drop against the headrest. The world spun when she closed her eyes. She opened them slowly, and she saw what looked like her mother's car parked across the street outside the closed Carolina Motel. The business was darkened, and there was little light, but Colleen could swear that she was staring at her mother's burgundy Regal.

She opened her door and stepped out, and then she walked across the dark, quiet street to the parking lot of the Carolina Motel. Her mother's car—at least the car that she thought was her mother's—was parked alongside the motel as if it had been left there, which didn't make sense to her. Her mother's car had been in the driveway when she'd left home, and there was no good reason for it to be parked here this late at night. She walked toward it to peer inside its windows, and then she heard a man's voice. Colleen turned to see a man on a pay phone at the other end of the lot. It was dark, and she was too far away to be certain, but perhaps it was her father. "Dad?" she called.

The man on the phone stopped speaking, and he turned to face her. She knew she had never seen his face before, and something about seeing it now in this dark parking lot after assuming he would be her father chilled her to her core. She stepped backward until she was in the middle of the street, and then she turned and walked to Danny's car. The man who'd been on the pay phone hung up and walked toward the burgundy Regal. He climbed inside, started the engine, and, with the lights off, pulled out and headed toward the west end of the island. She'd been mistaken. It wasn't her mother's car. The man hadn't been her father. She was drunk, and when Danny came back out with a six-pack of beer and set it down in her lap before climbing behind the wheel, she knew for certain that he was drunk too.

For Colleen, the night had changed, and along with feeling drunk she also felt the heavy regret of drinking too much and the acute knowledge that her regret would have grown by the time she woke up in the morning. She could feel Danny's eyes on her.

"Uh-oh," he said. "You're not going to throw up again, are you?"

"No," she said. "But I think it's time I get home."

NIGHT ON THE island was pitch black, but as Danny drove her home, the Camaro's windows down, the cool, humid midnight air wafting into the car's interior, Colleen looked to her right where the waterway rolled along on the other side of the trees, intermittently visible where the forest had been cut away for land to be claimed and squat houses stamped out or two-story vacation homes built.

Seated this way, her eyes fixed outside the passenger's window as the car hurtled forward, her head swimming with beer while the sound of the wind poured into the car, Colleen felt herself becoming dislocated, outside of time as if the car ride were carrying her somewhere mystical or spiritual instead of geographical. She wanted to explain this to Danny, but when she turned her head to look at him—her eyes sweeping across the glowing dash with its green numbers and buttons and dials—she saw that Danny's eyes were locked on the road, his index finger tapping out a silent beat on the steering wheel. He looked over at her and smiled. "You sure you're not going to throw up, Colleen Barnes?"

She smiled and shook her head, Danny's face blurring as she did.

"No," she said, "Colleen Banks will *not* throw up in this car or any other vehicle this evening."

Danny slowed and clicked on his blinker, the ticking sound filling the night like a clock that had suddenly been wound, the orange glow of its signal tossing light ahead and behind the Camaro in a way that illuminated the night with an unimpeded glow. Danny had turned off his headlights, just as he had done when dropping Colleen off late at night—both of them similarly wasted—when they were in high school and, later, when she was home from college.

As they slowed, darkness enveloped the car, folding over them as a solid thing. Danny's car crept into her parents' driveway, the soft light from the half-moon floating down in a way that seemed less like light and more like something physical that drifted on the air. Colleen could make out the dark lean of her parents' house, the soft edges of her mother's car parked in the driveway, her father's cruiser parked by the road, the clean slashes of trees.

Danny put the car into park and took his foot off the brake. "How long are you staying?" he asked.

"I don't know," she said. She let her head sag against the seat. "I haven't thought much about it. My mom needs my help, and my dad's got the election coming up, so—"

"Bullshit," Danny said.

Colleen lifted her head and looked over at Danny. She waited for him to say something else, but he didn't. "It's not bullshit," she finally said.

"It's bullshit if you think your mom needs your help," he said. "Your mom needs your help as much as your dad does, and I don't think your dad has ever needed anybody's help."

"He's probably going to lose this election, Danny."

"And you hanging campaign posters with your mom is going to change that? Please."

"What are you trying to tell me?"

"I'm not trying to tell you anything," he said. "But they don't need your help, Colleen. And you don't need their help either."

"I didn't say I needed their help."

He put his hand over hers. It felt warm and familiar. Colleen looked down at their hands. She turned hers over, palm up, and their fingers interlocked. "Look, honey," he said, "I'm about the worst and last person to be giving advice on relationships, but I think the only person who can help you and the only person who needs your help is back in Texas."

She let go of his hand and brought hers back into her lap. Out of nervous habit, she reached for her wedding ring to spin it on her finger, and again she remembered that she wasn't wearing it. She looked out at her parents' house. "Remember when we were in high school," she said, "and you'd drop me off late and wait for me to get to the front door, and then you'd lay on the horn?"

Danny laughed. "I do," he said. "I do remember that."

"Please don't do that tonight," Colleen said.

Danny put both palms on the center of the steering wheel as if preparing to honk the horn. He smiled.

"You bastard," Colleen whispered, trying not to smile herself. "Don't you dare."

"You'd better get back to Texas before my hands get heavy."

She gave him a playful slap. "I needed this tonight," she said.

"I know," Danny said. "Me too."

"I should've married you," she whispered. She smiled.

"Oh, honey," he said. He cocked his head and looked at her with mock sympathy. "There would've been a lot less screwing and a lot more drinking."

"There hasn't been that much screwing," she said, "but there's been plenty of drinking."

"Go home," he said. "To Texas."

She leaned over and kissed him on the cheek, and then she opened the door and climbed out. She leaned in the open door and put her fingers to her lips. "Keep your damn hands off that horn," she said, and then she shut the door and walked up the short driveway toward the front porch, her Keds crunching over the gravel and oyster shells that covered the walk.

She'd made it to the porch steps when she heard Danny drop the car into reverse and roll backward down the short incline of her parents' driveway. She stepped into the soft curve of yellow light where it cast a halo on the porch, and she felt as if someone's eyes were on her. She looked up at the second story, expecting to see her mother peeking through the aluminum blinds in the office's window. No one was there.

By the time she bent to retrieve the front door key from beneath her mother's planter—the one in the shape of a toad with red geraniums growing from its open back—the motor of Danny's Camaro was already too far down Yacht Drive to be heard. Colleen found the key and, as quietly as she could, lowered the corner of the planter back to the porch.

When she stood, she caught the scent of cigarette smoke, so overpowering that she could not believe that the near-empty bar in which they'd spent the evening had left such a strong smell clinging to her clothes and hair. It overwhelmed the damp odor of moss, the soggy wood on the porch, and the humid pungency of the dripping oak trees.

She inserted the key into the lock, and that was when she heard a man's voice lift from the dark at the far end of the porch. "Don't let me scare you," the voice said.

In what felt like one motion, Colleen turned the key in the already unlocked door, pushed it open, and nearly fell into the small foyer at the bottom of the stairs. She caught herself by holding on to the doorknob, and she gathered her breath before turning to look back outside. When she did, she saw that a man stood smoking at the other end of the porch, his presence so clear as to seem impossible to have overlooked. She was shocked to recognize him as the man she had seen on the pay phone just a few minutes before.

"I didn't want to scare you," the man said.

"I'm not scared," Colleen said. She slid the key out of the lock and slipped it into her back pocket. "You didn't scare me."

"Good," the man said. He took another drag on his cigarette, and then he tapped the ash over the railing and onto the pine straw bed below. "I'm Tom Groom," he said. "The pilot."

"Okay," Colleen said, mostly because her heart was still racing and she did not know what else to say.

"Your dad picked me up today," he said. He stubbed out his cigarette on the railing and took a step toward her. The halo of light coming from the fixture above the front door fell on him from only the chest down, but Colleen could still see his face. He was older than she had assumed after hearing his voice, perhaps in his early forties. He wore a dark polo shirt and what appeared to be slacks. The light shone on an old pair of well-cared-for leather boots.

"I think I saw you earlier," Groom said. He put his left hand on the railing and slipped his right hand, which held the cigarette lighter, into his pocket. Over the sounds of the night, Colleen could just barely make out the noise of him grinding the striker with his thumb from inside his pocket.

"Yeah," Colleen said. "I think so. At the motel. I saw my mother's car."

"Yeah," he said. "She asked me to get some things from the store, and I thought I'd make a call while I was out. I didn't want your parents getting charged the long-distance."

"They wouldn't mind," she said.

"Well, it's not even worth mentioning to them," he said. "Not worth worrying about."

Colleen nodded.

"Your mother said you're visiting from Texas?"

She nodded again.

He stopped speaking and turned to look out at the quiet, empty street. He looked back at Colleen.

"Was that your boyfriend?"

"What?"

He asked her again, but before he could finish the question a second time, she stopped him.

"No," she said, "no, that was a friend." Suddenly, she felt more exposed than when she'd first discovered that his eyes had been on her without her knowing it, and she stepped inside the doorway and began to close the front door.

"Sorry if I asked too many questions," Groom said. "And sorry again if I scared you."

"It's okay," she said, her hand still pushing the door closed even as she spoke.

"Nice to meet you," he said. She closed the door and left him on the porch.

She hadn't realized it before now, but she was nearly out of breath and her heart was racing. She was afraid that Groom would open the door and find her still standing there, so she slipped out of her shoes and, without turning on any lights, walked into the kitchen.

Standing at the sink, she stared through the window into the dark backyard for a moment, and then she ran water from the tap and took a glass from the cabinet and filled it. She sipped the water, tasting the Oak Island tinge, what they'd always described as beach water instead of tap water, and she swished it around her mouth and spit it into the sink, hoping it would take the aftertaste of beer with it.

She took another drink of water and swallowed it, and then she lowered her eyes from the window to the counter where her mother had left her rings by the sink in a small, handmade ceramic bowl the color of blue sky. She'd done this Colleen's whole life: slipped off her rings and left them in the bowl each evening after dinner before washing the dishes, cleaning the kitchen, and heading upstairs to read before going to bed. Colleen had never thought about her mother's ritual or the vulnerability of jewelry left so close to the sink and its drain. But now, with a stranger smoking cigarettes on their front porch in the middle of the night—a stranger who'd be sleeping down the hall from her with access to the entire house while no one was awake or watching—her mother's rings suddenly seemed under threat, as if leaving them out for the night guaranteed their disappearance by morning.

Colleen set her glass down on the counter and used her finger to sort through the rings in the bowl until she found her mother's engagement ring, at least what had served as her mother's engagement ring for nearly twenty years. Her mother's first ring, the one her father had proposed with when he got down on one knee alongside the banks of Lake Gaston back in 1954, had been replaced after the tiny solitaire diamond, what her father had since referred to as diamond dust, had fallen from its setting one day while her mother was cutting the grass in the front yard a few years after they'd moved to Oak Island.

After the diamond had gone missing, Colleen's father came home from work one afternoon and found Colleen playing in her room while her mother was busy vacuuming downstairs. Colleen's father stepped into her room and shut the door behind him, the sound of the vacuum now a muffled purr aside from the clacking sound the plastic wheels made as her mother pulled it across the floor in the foyer.

Her father had never closed her bedroom door upon entering before, and she feared that she was in trouble; her child's mind immediately flipped through a catalog of infractions that she could have committed in the recent past. But her fears were allayed when she saw her father's face. He wore his tan sheriff's deputy uniform, and he took something from his pocket and held it in his closed hand. He knelt in front of Colleen where she sat on her bed.

"You want to see something pretty?" he'd asked.

Colleen, suspecting that he'd gotten a present for her, nodded her head, afraid to speak for fear of ending a moment that felt like a dream. Her father opened his hand and revealed what rested in his palm: a simple platinum ring holding a solitaire diamond that Colleen would later learn was just over a carat, something she knew both thrilled and embarrassed her mother. Her parents were not fancy people. The nicest thing her father owned was the silver-faced Bulova watch her mother had given him just before Colleen was born. He still wore that watch, its nicks and scratches and the dozens of bands he'd gone through proving its age and wear.

Now, looking at her mother's ring, Colleen could remember her shock at its beauty and simplicity. When she'd held out her hand, her father had dropped the ring inside, and she'd immediately marveled at the weightlessness of such a gorgeous, delicate thing.

She still felt that way as she held the ring now in the soft light coming from the stars outside the kitchen window. She remembered what her father had said to her as she slipped the ring onto her tiny finger.

"Take it downstairs to your mother," he'd said. "Say, 'Look what I found out in the yard.'" And that became the joke. The original diamond chip had fallen into the grass years earlier and, over time, had grown into the diamond ring her mother had worn ever since her father brought it home.

But when Colleen had gone downstairs, the ring firmly clenched in her closed hand, her mother had not heard her calling for her over the sound of the vacuum. And by the time her mother turned around and used her foot to click off the vacuum's motor, she had seen Colleen standing in front of her holding the ring like a reward for the work her mother had just completed. Of the lines her father had fed her, Colleen had only been able to say the words "Look what I found" before her mother had dropped the vacuum to the floor and plucked the ring from Colleen's hand.

Now Colleen slipped the ring onto her finger and crept upstairs, still sensing Groom outside on the porch, and slipped into the bathroom, where she found what must have been his zipped-tight leather shaving kit sitting on the counter. She turned the light on and brushed her teeth, marveling at her drunkenness and the glimmer of the diamond solitaire, while she moved the toothbrush around inside her mouth and stared at her hand in the mirror.

She kept the ring on after she changed out of her clothes and climbed into her unmade bed, closing her eyes as the room began its now-familiar cycle of rotations. She rolled to her side, closed her eyes so tightly that she saw stars and pops of light, and spun her mother's ring on her finger, repeating, over and over, "Look what I found. Look what I found," still whispering it while she listened to Groom trudge up the stairs, go into the bathroom, and run the water and flush the toilet before closing the door to the office at the end of the hall, the final sound she heard before the night fell into silence.

THURSDAY,
NOVEMBER 1, 1984

CHAPTER 11

The sound of the phone ringing on the dresser on the other side of the bedroom ripped Winston from sleep just after 2:00 a.m. He leapt from bed and bounded across the room in two strides, snatching the phone from the cradle as if it were a bomb he hoped to defuse before one more ring detonated it. He was out of breath by the time he whispered into the receiver.

"Yeah," he said.

It was Rudy on dispatch, the same raspy, relaxed voice he'd heard on the kitchen phone two nights ago.

"There's a structure fire right off Beach Road," Rudy said. "Call just came. County fire's been dispatched, but I figured you'd want to know too."

Winston really didn't want to know about structure fires, at least not at this time of the night, but he was on call again because he was taking Englehart's place after firing him that afternoon.

"Where is it off Beach Road?" Winston asked.

Rudy described it; it was the new development where Bradley Frye was building houses. Winston didn't know if any of the homes were finished or occupied yet.

"The caller said this one's uninhabited," Rudy said.

"Who called it in?" Winston knew the development sat along the water at the mouth of the waterway, but it backed up to a forest that served as a border between it and the Grove. Winston imagined Bellamy standing on his back deck in his boxer shorts and white tank-top undershirt, squinting into the distance at a dark plume in the moonlight, convinced he smelled smoke.

"I'm not sure exactly who called it in," Rudy said. He read off the name and address, but Winston didn't recognize either one.

"Probably somebody living in the development," he said. "I guess I'll ride out there. It's Halloween night, after all. It's probably just some kids raising hell." He hung up and, as quietly as he could, dressed in his uniform in the darkness to which his eyes had finally adjusted.

When he was dressed, he stood by the bedroom door and waited, listening for Marie, but she didn't stir in her sleep or say a word to let him know she was awake.

"Marie," he whispered, but still nothing. He walked out into the hallway, but just before he stepped onto the stairs, he happened to look at the closed door at the end of the hall, and he suddenly remembered that Groom was staying with them. The thought of leaving Marie and Colleen home alone with a stranger, no matter who that stranger was, gave him pause.

He stepped back toward his and Marie's bedroom and reached around to push in the button that locked the bedroom from the inside. He pulled the door closed, pausing just before the latch clicked into the catch on the strike plate. He and Marie rarely closed their bedroom door, and he couldn't recall a time when they had ever locked it at night, even when Colleen was younger and living at home.

The door to Colleen's room sat opposite the landing at the top of the stairs, and when Winston placed his hand on the doorknob and tried to give it a gentle turn, he found that she had locked it before going to bed, and he felt a satisfied sense of her being his daughter, suspecting that she too had felt safer with her door locked while a virtual stranger was sleeping just down the hall.

Winston had never seen the new development he was en route to, but, following Rudy's directions, he found it easily. He took the bridge off the island and drove toward the airport, where he knew Kepler was out there on the runway, pulling his shift to keep an eye on the plane. None of the officers who'd been assigned a night watch were excited about it, but Winston knew it was something that had to be done. So much of the investigation had been taken from his office. He didn't want to lose what little bit of claim he still had.

Just before the airport, Winston turned right off Beach Road onto an unmarked blacktop road called, according to the street sign, Fishcamp Road. He'd driven past it probably a million times over the years, never having or feeling a reason to turn down it. He'd always assumed that eventually it would turn to gravel before winding down to the waterway, where, as the street name suggested, primitive camps sat on private land where families had fished for generations.

But that's not what Winston found when he clicked on his cruiser's high beams and drove toward the development. The road had been freshly paved, the grass mowed low and the woods cut back to reveal a five-foot strip on either side of the road. Ahead, his headlights fell on the entrance to the development, which comprised two cement signs encrusted with oyster shells that rose up from the manicured, landscaped beds on either side of the road. Dim lighting that had been hidden by clumps of variegated monkey grass that ringed the beds illuminated the gold, metal letters that spelled out the development's name: Plantation Cove.

Winston wasn't surprised by the name. All along Highways 87 and 133 leading into and out of the county, forests were slowly being clear-cut and reseeded with developments that were named with some take on the word or idea of *plantation*: Plantation Woods, Tara Oaks, Brunswick Plantation. The irony was not lost on Winston that nearly all these communities were developed with northern capital and that the majority of people who bought or built homes inside them were retired couples from New Jersey, New York, Pennsylvania, and Ohio who were in search of second homes where they could escape the snow and weather for the mild winters of the North Carolina coast. But he also wondered if it was more than that, especially given the seeming mania for the reanimation of the plantation past. Perhaps by accident of their regional births these seasonal transplants felt they were now reclaiming the power of a past that had left them out, a past that they, at least by virtue of wealth and neighborhood title, could now lay some claim to.

Plantation Cove had held on to its old, mossy oak trees while managing to bulldoze nearly every other tree in sight. Because of this, Winston had an easy time spotting the fire truck and the volunteer fire department vehicles that congregated in front of an under-construction two-story house just a few streets over from the entrance road.

Winston drove past a few completed homes with green, sodded yards and cars in the driveway, some with curious neighbors on their porches and lights burning in downstairs windows, others dark and seemingly empty. Several lots had been cleared, foundations dug, the stick-built frames rising from the sandy soil that would somehow, months from now, look like a yard.

After entering the neighborhood from Beach Road, Winston remembered what Bellamy had said about Bradley Frye wanting the land where the Grove sat, and, even in the dark of night, Winston could imagine the forest that divided the two communities being cleared, the tiny homes in the Grove being razed, a new, much grander entrance to Plantation Cove being erected right on 87 where locals and tourists alike would have to drive past it on their way in and out of downtown Southport. Night rides, shooting off guns, and flying the Confederate flag seemed like a bad way to induce a community to give up its roots, but Winston had seen this before a decade earlier when the schools desegregated, and he'd seen it work. All people, no matter their race, were motivated by fear and power more than they were motivated by money or pride, and he figured Bradley Frye's nighttime rides were just the opening shots in what would be a long, protracted war.

Winston came to a stop sign. In front of him, the land gave way to a marsh that then gave way to the bank of the waterway. He could see where more land had been cleared, and he imagined that a marina with boat slips, a clubhouse, and a swimming pool would be under construction soon. On his left he could see the faint streetlights of downtown Southport. On his right, the sweeping beam of the lighthouse at the far eastern end of the island. Ahead, on the other side of the bay, another island, a private island where the wealthy had built grand homes and a resort called Bald Head, sat in the unseeable darkness. It was part of the county, but the residents, most of them seasonal and only reachable by boat and then by golf cart as there were no cars on the island, wanted as much to do with the mainland as mainlanders wanted to do with them, and that was okay with Winston.

Down the darkened street to his left, Winston saw flashlights moving through the shell of a home that was under construction. A fire truck and two pickups that probably belonged to volunteer firefighters sat out front. He turned and drove toward them. He pulled the cruiser behind the fire truck, grabbed his own flashlight, and climbed out.

He didn't recognize the four men on the scene, but they recognized him and called him sheriff. Only one of them wore the full regalia of thick rubber boots, suspenders, and the heavy helmet with the plastic shield flipped up and away from his face. While the others loaded the hose back onto the truck, he stood in what looked to be the house's living room, where huge windows in the back of the room would reveal views of the marsh once the sun began to rise. The wall and floor in the corner of the room closest to the marsh were charred black. The fireman held the beam of his flashlight there and pointed with his free hand.

"It looks like an incendiary device, Sheriff," he said.

Winston stepped toward the burned area; the floor was wet, and shards of glass crunched beneath his feet.

"Somebody tossed a glass bottle full of accelerant," the fireman said.

"I see that," Winston said. He shone his flashlight around the room. The windows had not yet been installed. "Was it still burning when y'all got here?"

"Yes, sir," the fireman said. "Just barely. We doused it to make sure it was out."

Beneath the broken glass, the plywood floor was soaked through, and Winston could hear water dripping from the ceiling and the eaves outside the open gaps in the walls where the windows would go. He imagined the four firefighters spraying the house with water beginning with the exterior, snaking the hose through one of the open windows, and then doing the same inside.

"Looks like y'all might've saved the house," Winston said, "or what'll be a house one day."

"Thank you, sir," the fireman said, his body relaxing with a squeak of rubber as he shifted his weight to one leg.

"Let's hope he doesn't use more accelerant next time," Winston said, "or another incendiary device."

"Next time?" the fireman said. "You think he'll be back?"

"I would think so," Winston said. "Most people don't commit an arson like this one just to see a corner of a room get blacked up before the fire truck arrives. They learn something with each fire they set, and they usually don't quit until they're caught."

The fireman stood there another moment while Winston passed the beam of his light over the floor and ceiling, and then the man stepped outside to where the others had gathered in the dark around the fire truck. Winston could see the glowing end of a cigarette and hear snatches of conversation.

He walked to the window closest to where it appeared the fire had started, and he shone his flashlight on the dark gray, sandy ground outside, looking for fresh footprints. He climbed out the window and dropped the few feet down to the soft earth. Outside, there were countless divots in the ground that could have been the footprints of an arsonist or a construction worker or a firefighter or deer, or perhaps even spots where tools or planks had been dropped or where hard rain had come off the roof and fallen haphazardly without gutters to guide it.

He walked around the far side of the structure where a driveway had been scraped from the garage to the street but not yet filled with cement. He stepped down into the wide trough and looked out at the road, where a truck's headlights had just been extinguished. Winston raised his flashlight in the direction of the road and knew immediately that the truck belonged to Bradley Frye.

Frye walked around to the front of his truck and talked with the firefighters who were still gathered at the back of the engine. Winston could see that Frye wasn't dressed as if he'd just left bed in a hurry; instead, he wore a black union suit and boots. Once again, he had a pistol holstered on his belt. Winston couldn't hear what Frye and the other men were saying, but he chose to stay where he stood in the driveway instead of walking closer to where they were gathered in the street. Eventually the firefighter he'd spoken with inside the house looked up at Winston and gave him a wave.

"We're heading out, Sheriff," he said. "You need anything else from us?"

"Nothing right now," Winston said. "I may give y'all a call tomorrow if you don't mind putting together something about what you found when you got out here tonight."

"You got it, Sheriff," the man said.

Winston watched him climb into the fire engine as the other three men returned to their trucks. Bradley Frye stood on the edge of the yard, looking from the house to Winston. Winston watched him, not moving or saying a word until Frye set out across the yard toward the house.

"No, no, no," Winston said. He clicked off his flashlight and slid it through the loop on his belt, and then he stepped into the yard to intercept Frye before he could walk any farther.

"What do you mean 'no, no, no'?" Frye said. "That's my damn house right there."

"It's a crime scene now," Winston said. "I don't want anybody tampering with it."

"Tampering with it?" Frye said. "Tampering?" He turned and pointed to his left at the forest that separated the development from the Grove, which, this close to the water, was at least a mile away. "You need to talk to those thugs about tampering," he said. "We've lost tools, had homes and vehicles damaged, four-wheelers coming through and tearing up sod. And you're going to warn me, the owner, about tampering when you won't do nothing to stop them?"

"Maybe they'll stay out of your neighborhood if you stay out of theirs," Winston said. He walked past Frye without waiting for him to respond. He reached for his flashlight and clicked it on again, raised its beam once he was close enough to Frye's truck.

"What are you talking about?" Frye asked.

"Why are you even out here this time of night?" Winston asked. "You been out trick-or-treating?"

"Checking on my property," Frye said. "Somebody's got to keep it safe. Y'all ain't going to do it."

Winston shone the flashlight on Frye's truck, peered in its windows. "Where do you put them?" he asked.

"Put what?" Frye said, then, "Stay away from my truck. You don't have the right to look at it."

Winston laughed. "Oh, Brad, you've got a lot to learn about the law before they swear you in. You'd better start studying." He tapped the toolbox in the bed of Frye's truck with the end of his flashlight, heard the echo inside. "Is this where you keep your battle flags when you're not flying them?" Winston looked back at Frye, and then he continued moving the flashlight's beam around Frye's truck until he found what he was looking for: a bracket made to hold a flag had been fastened to the back of the truck's cab just below the back windshield. Winston looked at Frye where he still stood in the yard, his light steady on the bracket. "Is this where you put it?"

"Put what?"

"Your little rebel flag. The one you fly when you're trying to scare Black folks into believing you're a tough guy."

"Get away from my truck," Frye said, pounding down through the yard toward Winston. He grabbed Winston's arm that held the flashlight, causing it to clatter to the asphalt.

Winston took hold of Frye's left arm and spun his body so that his back slammed against the passenger's-side door. He splayed Frye's legs with his knee, and he threw his left forearm under Frye's chin to keep him pinned there. The men's faces were inches apart, and Winston could hear Frye's breathing and feel his pulse pounding in his neck and smell beer on his breath.

"Boy, *never* put your hands on an officer," Winston said. "Never."

He felt Frye's right hand flick toward the gun he had holstered on his hip, but Winston was faster, and before Frye was able to get ahold of his pistol Winston had his pressed against the soft skin below Frye's chin. He held it there, his mind thinking things that shocked him. Did he want to shoot Bradley Frye? Could he? How would he explain it, and could he get away with it? These thoughts passed through Winston's mind in the time it would've taken a bullet to leave his gun and enter Frye's head, which ended up being enough time for Winston to check himself. Instead of squeezing the trigger, he lowered his left hand and unholstered Frye's pistol and tossed it onto the dirt behind him. He wondered if drinking had made Frye braver and stupider than he otherwise was.

"I told you to leave that weapon at home," Winston said. He took a step back toward the house and lowered his pistol.

Frye stood up straight and ran his hands over his clothes like he was either grooming himself or checking his body for bullet holes.

"Do that in a couple of months and you'll be holding a gun on the high sheriff of Brunswick County."

"That'll be fine," Winston said. "I'll still be the faster draw."

"You going to shoot me now?" Frye asked. "First, you shot one in Gastonia and now a white boy down here. It'd be a hell of a way to end your career. Go from shooting criminals to shooting heroes."

"No," Winston said. He sighed, holstered his pistol. "I'm not going to shoot you. I'm not even going to kick your ass, especially not without an audience because you'd just lie about it anyway." Winston kept his eyes on Frye and walked backward in the yard until he stood over Frye's weapon. He bent down and picked up the gun and cracked the cylinder, turning it up so the bullets slipped out. He closed his hands around them, but he held the unloaded gun out to Frye, who took it and slid it back into his holster. "And you're not a hero, Brad. You're a soft-handed daddy's boy who grew up with money and mistook it for brains. If you become sheriff it won't make you any smarter or any braver than you were when you were a punk-ass kid ganging up on Black kids because you thought it would make your daddy proud."

"You keep my daddy's name out of your mouth."

"You keep out of the Grove, Brad, unless you're invited, and I can't imagine a soul there wanting to see your face. Those people have been through enough."

"Those people are drug dealers and vandals. You saw what happened to Rodney Bellamy. And now they're setting these houses on fire."

"We don't know what happened to Rodney Bellamy," Winston said. "And we don't know who set this fire. It could have been you. Stay out of the Grove, Brad." Winston, his fist still closed around the bullets, lifted his hand. "I'm going to hold on to these. Why don't you head home. My office will reach out to you tomorrow for a statement, maybe call you back out here to look around in the daylight."

"I've seen all I need to see to know what happened," Frye said.

"Then I reckon you can go."

Winston stood in the yard and watched Frye's truck drive around the cul-de-sac at the end of the road before turning and gunning his engine on the way past Winston. Winston stood there until the truck's taillights disappeared and he could no longer hear the noise of its engine. The sounds of the night—frogs, the lap of the water, crickets—lifted up around him like a television set that's volume was slowly being raised. He considered stopping by the address on Spoonbill where the call had come from, but the lights in the neighborhood had all gone off for the night and the fire had been put out, and whatever would need to happen next could wait until morning.

CHAPTER 12

Colleen woke to the sound of her father's voice outside her bedroom door, his knuckles tapping gently. She'd been dreaming—something about the water knocking through the pipes of an old European city, a place she'd never been. She opened her eyes now, slices of sunlight cutting into them like razor blades. Her wristwatch sat where she had left it on her bedside table, and she picked it up and examined it, but her vision was too fuzzed with sleep to read it, though she was able to see and feel that she still wore her mother's ring. She let her head fall back onto her pillow.

"Colleen," her father said. He knocked again. "I need you to wake up, honey."

She knew he was knocking because her mother had woken up and gone downstairs and had been unable to find her ring. She imagined the fear and panic that had probably shot through her upon discovering it gone. For a moment, Colleen wanted to feel that it served her mother right for leaving the ring exposed while a stranger spent the night in their home, and then she felt guilty for being the one who had taken it.

"Okay," Colleen said, just loud enough for her voice to escape her mouth. A headache thrummed on the edge of her temples, but she fought it with thoughts of a hot shower, Tylenol, and a glass of water.

"You up?" her dad asked, apparently not having moved from his spot outside in the hallway.

"Yes," she said, frustrated now, remembering what it was like to be woken up for school as a teenager or called by her parents to some other morning duty she didn't want to perform. Her mind confronted the possibility that perhaps Scott was on the phone, and her chest seized in an icy panic. She'd unplugged the jack from the back of the phone the night before just as she was falling asleep on the off chance that it would ring in the night for her father or in the early morning for her mother, and she had not considered that Scott might call her. But if it was early here it was even earlier there, and there was no way he would call unless it was an emergency. And Scott was alone in Dallas. There could be no emergency when Scott was alone because he was the most self-reliant person she'd ever met.

She stretched her arms above her head, her mind turning toward Danny and what he'd said the night before about her not having anything more in common with anyone in the world than she had in common with Scott, and she knew it was true and that Danny was right. At their wedding, Scott's parents' pastor had read the verses— she couldn't remember the name of the scripture—about love being patient and kind. But where were the verses about grief? Where were the verses about grief being selfish and cruel and solitary?

She sat up on the edge of the bed and put her elbows on her knees. She rubbed her eyes and ran her fingers over her face. She squeezed her mother's ring off her swollen finger and closed her hand around it. She checked her watch again, now fully awake. It was a little after 8:00 a.m. Her father knocked again.

"Jesus," she whispered to herself.

She stood and walked to the door, turned the lock on the knob, and opened it. Her father leaned against the door frame in the hallway. She opened her hand and showed him the ring. He was already wearing his uniform, but his eyes were red and rimmed with sleep-lessness, and his face had a look of confused exhaustion.

"Why are you showing me that?" he asked.

"I figured you were looking for it," she said. "I had it in my room."

He took it from her and held it in his hand. "I don't think your mother even noticed it was gone," he said.

Colleen leaned out into the hallway and saw that the door to Groom's room was open, but he was nowhere in sight. And then she heard the shower turn on in the bathroom across the hall.

"I need you to ride out to Rodney Bellamy's house with me," her father said.

"Why?"

"I need to question his widow," he said. "I know Rodney was probably just in the wrong place at the wrong time, but I need to at least ask about it now that she's had a day or two to recover from the shock of it." Her father stepped back and folded his arms. He raised his eyes to the ceiling. "And there's some other things."

"What other things?" she asked.

"Bradley Frye," her father said. "He's been driving through the Grove at night with some of his good ol' boys, flying rebel flags, shooting guns in the air, trying to scare people. I need to let her know I'm working on it."

"That doesn't surprise me," she said.

"I didn't figure it would."

"I saw him out last night with Danny. Danny said that he—" But she was interrupted by her mother's voice calling from downstairs.

"Y'all come on down here and eat," she said. "Tell Mr. Groom that food's on the table."

Her father had turned toward the stairs at the sound of her mother's voice. He looked back at Colleen, and his face had changed; he now looked annoyed, frustrated.

"You'll have to meet our FBI pilot," he said. "We're going to drop him at the airport on the way. Let him get back to work so he can get this damn plane out of here."

She considered telling her father that she'd met Groom only a few hours earlier, that she'd seen her mother's car parked outside the Carolina Motel and found him on the pay phone in the empty parking lot, that later she'd discovered him waiting for her when she returned home. But she didn't feel like explaining any of that to her father this early in the morning, didn't feel like admitting that she'd been drunk and confused and caught off guard. "What's he like?" she said instead.

Her father looked at the closed bathroom door across the hallway. He lowered his voice. "He's kind of uptight," he said. "Most of those FBI guys are."

"Yeah," she said. "That makes sense."

Her father went downstairs, and soon she could hear his and her mother's muffled voices coming from the kitchen. She knew he was probably teasing her mother about not knowing where her ring had been. Across the hall, the shower was still running.

Without thinking—at least without thinking clearly—Colleen crept down the hall past the bathroom toward the room where Groom had spent the night. She peered inside the open door. The bed was tightly made on the single mattress atop the simple frame that her parents had always kept pushed in the corner for guests who never came. Her mother's old sewing machine sat beside the bed on top of an old card table; several small chests with drawers full of ribbon, thread, and needles were stacked beside it. The boots that Groom had been wearing last night rested side by side beneath the bed. An army-green duffel bag sat beside them. Otherwise, there was nothing in the room that spoke to the fact that someone had spent the night there.

Colleen turned and looked down the hall behind her, made certain that she could hear the water continuing to run in the shower.

She walked into the bedroom and knelt on the floor, and then she unzipped the duffel bag and opened it just enough to see the contents. The shirt and pants that she'd seen Groom wearing on the front porch were folded on top. The first pocket she reached into held a money clip with Groom's Florida driver's license on top of what looked to be several folded twenty-dollar bills. In one of the back pockets, Colleen found a black wallet, and when she opened it she saw Groom's FBI identification, along with a gold badge. Her hands began to shake when she saw it, as if the gravity of what she'd just done had only now settled over her. She snapped the wallet closed and put it back, doing her best to fold the pants and shirt in the same manner she'd found them. Something crinkled inside the bag, and when she looked beneath the clothes, she found a shopping bag from Sears. Inside were a couple of polo shirts and a second pair of brown pants, the tags still fastened to them, along with a receipt from the store in Wilmington. At the bottom of the bag was a pack of black socks and an open package of men's briefs. Beneath the shopping bag was a holstered pistol and an open carton of a foreign brand of Asian cigarettes that Colleen had never seen before.

Colleen had grown up around guns, and seeing the weapon was not what bothered her about the luggage. After all, Tom Groom was an FBI agent. Of course he carried a gun and a badge. What gave her pause were the new, unworn clothes inside the shopping bag and the receipt from the store in Wilmington. She knew her father had picked up Groom at the airport, and she didn't remember him saying anything about taking Groom by the mall. She wanted to pause for a moment to parse the mystery in front of her—but in her pausing she realized that she hadn't been listening for the shower. She frantically stuffed the clothes back into the shopping bag, and then rearranged Groom's worn clothes on top of it before zipping the duffel bag closed and repositioning it where she'd found it beside his boots. She could now hear that Groom had turned the shower off, and she did her best to move silently down the hall. She walked into her bedroom and closed the door behind her. Her heart was racing, and she closed her hands into fists to keep them from shaking. Nothing had scared her except her reckless decision to snoop through Groom's room, but now that she'd gotten away with it, she found that something scared her still.

In the hallway, she heard Groom open the bathroom door and walk toward his room. He closed the door, and she wondered if the room felt like a different room than the room he'd spent the night in. Did something in his training or capability or character make it apparent to him that his belongings had been disturbed?

Colleen opened the top drawer in her dresser, grabbed socks and a pair of underwear, and then she found jeans and a shirt and opened her door and fled across the hallway to the bathroom.

WHEN SHE CAME downstairs, Colleen found her mother sitting at the table with Tom Groom, the two of them talking over country ham biscuits that her mother had made that morning. Her father stood watching them from the kitchen, his back leaning against the counter in front of the sink, his hands holding a coffee cup that was lifted and held to his lips as if he were considering blowing on it to cool it down.

From her seat at the table, Colleen's mother watched her come down the last few steps and make the turn toward the kitchen.

"Well, rise and shine," her mother said.

Colleen gave a halfhearted smile and walked past the table and into the kitchen. She took a glass down from the cabinet and filled it with ice and then, leaning behind her father, water from the sink. She took a sip and looked from one of her parents to the other.

"Do y'all have any Tylenol?" she asked.

"As a matter of fact, we do," her mother said. She pointed to the cabinet just inside the kitchen to Colleen's right. "Thanks to our guest. He ran out last night and got some."

"And coffee," Colleen's father said.

"Well, I need both," Colleen said. She opened the cabinet and found the pill bottle. She unscrewed the lid and popped two into her mouth. She took another sip of water and swallowed.

"Colleen," her mother said, her voice lilting in a way that told Colleen that she had done something moderately disappointing. Her mother gestured across the table. "This is Tom Groom. He's the pilot who's going to—"

Colleen opened her mouth to interrupt, to let her mother and father know that they'd already met. It seemed awkward to act otherwise in front of Groom, but he beat her to it.

"Nice to meet you, Colleen," he said. He smiled.

His greeting caught Colleen off guard, and, as she stood there, she understood that something secret had passed between them, but she didn't quite know what it was. Her discovering him at the pay phone? His smoking on the porch late at night? Her coming in drunk after her parents had gone to bed? Or maybe it was the first words he'd said to her—"Don't let me scare you"—which now seemed more ominous in her memory than they did when she'd heard them spoken.

"Nice to meet you," Colleen responded. She took another sip of her water, crunching bits of ice with her teeth. She imagined her headache already receding, the Tylenol dissolving in her stomach and passing into her bloodstream to do whatever it would do to ease the pain in her head and make everything seem clearer.

NOW THE THREE of them—Colleen, her father, and Groom—rode up Beach Road toward the airport after crossing the bridge. Colleen sat in the passenger's seat of her father's cruiser. Groom sat in the back.

Colleen and her father made small talk during the drive. He didn't ask her about Danny. He'd never asked her about Danny, and she knew it was because he viewed Danny as reckless and impulsive, and of course he sensed things about Danny that he didn't know how to broach.

Mostly, Colleen and her father's discussion focused, as usual, on her mother and her cancer. Does she seem tired to you? Has she been eating? What do her doctors say? Colleen would have forgotten that Groom was even in the car with them had his voice not finally broken the silence of the backseat.

"Sheriff Barnes, I want to thank you again for letting me stay with your family," Groom said. "For putting me up and driving me around. I really appreciate it."

"It's a pleasure," her father said. He looked into the rearview mirror and smiled at Groom. "We'd be eating, sleeping, and driving around anyway, whether you were here or not, so we might as well have you with us."

"I guess that's true," Groom said. The car grew quiet. The only sounds were the hiss and crackle of the CB radio. Her father had turned it down when they got in the car, and the voices coming across it sounded like whispers. "That reminds me," Groom said, "if anybody needs to come into my room for anything, just come on in."

Colleen's heart felt like a fist had been closed around it. She realized that she wasn't breathing. She waited for Groom to say something else, but her father spoke instead.

"No," Winston said, "it's all yours. There's nothing any of us need in there."

"Well, just come on in if you change your mind," Groom said.

"A phone," Colleen said. Her father looked over at her as if trying to make sense of the words she'd just spoken. She gathered herself, finding courage in her frustration that Groom seemed to be trying to pin her in. "I mean, there should be a phone in there," she said. "At least I think there is. If there's not, I can take the one out of my room and put it in there for you."

Colleen heard Groom shift in his seat.

"There's one in there," he said.

"I thought there might be," Colleen said. "Feel free to use it."

Winston turned the cruiser left off Beach Road and into the airport parking lot. Two cars were parked out in front of the office. He drove by the office, past small hangars. The doors of a few were open, revealing small, single-engine airplanes where men, presumably the planes' owners, seemed to be working on them or otherwise tinkering around inside the bays.

Past the hangars, they turned onto the runway, where crime scene tape was intertwined through sets of sawhorses. The airplane glinted beneath the sun at the far end. Colleen had only seen it from far away, but at this close distance it seemed enormous. A patrol car sat parked on the runway behind it. The way the sunlight fell, no one could be seen inside. The door to the patrol car opened, and a deputy stepped out and stretched his arms over his head.

"Has he been out here all night?" Colleen asked.

"Not all of it," her father said. "But most of it."

He parked and he and Groom got out. Her father spent a few minutes talking with the deputy. Groom walked past them toward the airplane where its tail sat jacked up off the ground. A mechanic appeared from one of the hangars, pushing a huge chest of what Colleen assumed were tools. Colleen watched Groom until her father got back in the car.

"He's an interesting guy," she said.

"Who, Groom?" her father asked.

"Yeah."

"That's one way of describing him."

"You don't like him?" she asked.

Her father drove through the parking lot and turned left onto

Long Beach Road. "I like him fine," he said. "About as much as I've ever liked an FBI agent."

"He seems weird," she said.

"This whole thing is weird."

"I saw him last night on the pay phone outside the Carolina Motel," Colleen said.

"Saw who?"

"Him," she said. "The pilot. Groom."

"Is that why you made that weird comment about the phone?" her father asked.

His seeing through what she'd thought was her cunning retort to Groom embarrassed her. "No," she said. "Yes, kind of. It just seemed weird that he was on a pay phone in the middle of the night. And he was driving Mom's car."

"That's because she let him drive it, Colleen. He went to the store. For aspirin and coffee." Winston clicked on his blinker and turned right and drove toward Southport.

"And to use the phone, which he could've done at our house," she said.

"Maybe he wanted privacy."

"There's a phone in his room," Colleen said. "He told me he didn't want to use your long-distance."

"Well, that was kind of him," her father said, and then he looked over at her. "When did he tell you that?"

Colleen felt her face reddening a bit. She should not be ashamed to have come in late, to have been drinking, to have been startled by Groom on the porch in the middle of the night, but something about neither her nor Groom acknowledging that in front of her parents made it feel like a shameful secret was now being unearthed.

"Danny thinks it's all drug related," she said. Her father looked over at her, his eyes lingering for a moment on her face before he turned back to the road.

"Oh, yeah? Is that what Danny thinks?"

"Yeah," she said. "And he thinks that's why Bradley Frye wants to become sheriff, so he can look the other way, like, maybe he'd get kickbacks or something."

"Huh," Winston said, acting as if he were amused. He drove in silence for a moment. "Well, I'll tell you what: between your friends and your mother and her friends, I think we might just have this case cracked. The sheriff down in Horry County might have a case connected to the airplane and Rodney's murder, but I'll tell him not to worry about it."

The intensity of her father's sarcasm pushed around Colleen's body like a physical thing that she could feel gathering around her face and shoulders. He was comparing her to her mother and her mother's friends, and although he had never directly said so, and Colleen had never directly asked, she had a good idea what her father thought about her mother and her mother's friends, largely because it was the same thing Colleen thought: her mother's curiosity was trivial and gossipy, her interests fleeting and presumptive, as if the rules of the world were fixed in such a way that she could easily un-ravel their complexities if she and her friends just spent enough time talking about it on the phone.

Colleen wanted to find a way to remind her father that she'd graduated from law school, that in law school she had studied and learned the rules of evidence and criminal procedure, had, in fact, studied them more closely and with more intensity than her father ever had despite his decades of experience in law enforcement. If she had opinions on this case—and, if she were being honest, she didn't—they would have been based on facts and education and ex-pertise, not on gut instinct or intuition or gossip. She didn't want to be like her mother, and she didn't think she was, but perhaps she wasn't much like her father either, a man she'd always held out as the epitome of fact-based rationality. She was more educated than either of them, had traveled more broadly than either of them, and, unlike them, was no longer living in the state of her birth. But the fact that she was not actually practicing law, that she had either postponed it or given it up altogether in favor of a child she did not have and a husband she was not with—a fact pattern that always hovered on the edge of her emotional periphery—shot through her heart with a cold bolt of self-realization. Maybe she wasn't like her parents—an older couple set in their ways and beliefs, operating on emotion and intuition. She was worldly, educated, and enlightened, and all these advantages had landed her here, back home, feeling very much like the same adolescent she was before law school, before traveling, before marrying Scott and moving to Texas and losing her baby.

No, she wasn't like her parents, but maybe she was worse.

Colleen couldn't remember if she had ever been in the Grove before. Had she ever had a reason? She'd had Black friends when she was young, playing softball and other sports, seeing them at a few birthday parties when they were little or at after-school events like plays or dances or club meetings. But she couldn't remember ever being inside one of the Black kids' homes. No playdates or sleepovers or things like that. And then she realized that none of the Black kids she'd grown up with had ever been inside her home either. And here she was, a grown woman of twenty-six who'd lost a child, going to visit a widow inside the home of a Black classmate who'd been shot and killed. The mysteries of life always seemed vague and inexplicable to Colleen, and as her father drove past the small brick and clapboard homes, their yards alive with flowers and ornaments and outdoor furniture or choked with weeds, she couldn't help but question the predestined vagaries of fate that had landed her here while also ending Rodney's life.

Her father drove into the Grove and slowed down, coming to a stop at the side of the street. He put the car in park. Colleen lifted her head from the passenger's-side window. They both sat without moving.

"I'm sorry," her father finally said.

She looked over at him. "For what?"

"For what I said. I shouldn't say things like that. I'd love to hear any ideas you've got. That lead down in Horry County probably isn't going to pan out."

"You don't have to apologize," she said.

"I've just got a lot on my mind," he said. "I had to fire a deputy yesterday because of this mess that Bradley Frye caused here in the Grove, and that's put me a man down, and I've had to keep somebody out at the airport. There's just a lot going on."

"I'm sorry," she said.

"Well, there's no need for *you* to say that to *me*," he said.

"What about Mom's?"

"Mom's what?" he asked.

"Mom's ideas about the case," she said. "You want to hear more of those?"

He laughed, nodded his head.

He dropped the car into drive and they continued on. "I think I'll hold off on hers if that's okay."

Winston turned into the driveway of a small, wooden-frame house. A burgundy sedan was parked on the road in front, and a white Datsun sat in the driveway with a pickup truck. A sheet of plywood had been nailed to the front of the house, apparently to cover a window that had been broken. By the time Colleen had taken off her seat belt, Rodney's father had stepped out onto the small porch. To Colleen he looked the same as he'd looked when she was in high school, despite the spots where his hair was graying around his temples. The same thick glasses, the same rigid demeanor. He wore a blue button-down shirt and khaki pants, and he stood with his hands in his pockets, watching Colleen and Winston as if he'd been waiting for them, uncertain whether to welcome them or ask them to leave.

"Mr. Bellamy," Colleen whispered to herself, obviously loud

enough for her father to hear from where he sat behind the steering wheel.

"Yeah," he said, his voice edged with resignation. He turned off the engine and opened his door. Colleen climbed out and followed her father down a short walkway to the porch.

"Morning, Ed," her father said.

"Sheriff," Bellamy said, nodding his head toward Winston, his voice portraying neither a warmth of welcome nor a coldness of indifference. Bellamy looked past Winston to where Colleen stood behind him. His face softened slightly, the way it would when a student would accidentally do or say something funny in class. "Colleen Barnes," he said.

She smiled and gave him a small wave. She suddenly felt very shy. "Hello, Mr. Bellamy," she said. "I am so sorry."

"Come on now, you're grown," he said. "Call me Ed." Colleen could never imagine calling him by his first name. "You're not in school anymore," he said, his face cracking into a slight, nearly imperceptible smile. "Y'all come on. Janelle's expecting you."

Colleen followed her father and Mr. Bellamy through the front door and into the living room of a home that was comfortably furnished. Immediately, Colleen got the sense of this being Rodney and his wife's first home, and although the house that she and Scott had purchased together in Dallas was very different, this home still carried with it the same luster of hope and possibility that she and Scott had invested in theirs. Colleen's chest seized with awful and terrifying grief, for both the loss she felt in her own life and the loss she knew Rodney's widow must be feeling, and she found herself desperate to see Scott, to touch him, to hear his voice.

But then Rodney's widow appeared, a beautiful young woman in a well-fitted purple dress with a made-up face and well-set hair, smiling, wiping her hands dry on a towel that she tossed on the counter, reaching for Colleen's hand and holding it and shaking it firmly, the woman's clothes or body or hair smelling faintly of something clean and soft, like vanilla or powder. Janelle introduced herself, and when she let go of Colleen's hand, a smile still on her face, Colleen placed the scent of what she had just smelled: baby. Janelle Bellamy smelled like her baby. She fought the urge to raise the hand that Janelle had just shaken and smell it to see if it too now smelled like a baby, but she knew there was no way to do that without looking strange and rude. But she was desperate for another whiff of that scent, which ran through her body like a drug she unknowingly had been craving and now knew she couldn't live without.

Colleen had known that Rodney and his wife had a baby—Winston had told her that just a few days ago—so of course she knew a baby would be in the house somewhere. But how had she forgotten? Her eyes quickly scanned the room for the child or any signs of it: a pacifier, toys, a blanket or a bottle; but there was nothing there.

Janelle looked from Colleen to Winston. "Can I get y'all something?" she asked. "Coffee or a glass of tea?"

"No, no," Winston said. "We don't want to take too much of your time." He paused and looked over at Colleen where she stood to his right. "I have a few questions I have to ask, just formalities really, and Colleen came along . . ." His voice trailed off, and it was clear that he was thinking about how best to frame her visit. "She was friends with Rodney."

"Rodney and I went to high school together," Colleen said. "Mr. Bellamy was my teacher." Janelle nodded her head and tried her best to smile at them both, and in that moment, Colleen felt like a child standing in her jeans and Keds in front of this put-together woman who had a child and who'd already lost a husband.

"Well, thank you for coming," Janelle said. She gestured toward the sofa.

Colleen and her father sat down, and Janelle sat in a blue armchair to Colleen's left. Bellamy sat in a matching chair to Colleen's father's right.

"Are you sure I can't get you anything?" Janelle asked.

"No," Winston said, "but thank you." He sat, leaning forward, his elbows on his knees and his hands clenched tight together. "Now, Mrs. Bellamy, I know—"

"Please," she said, "call me Janelle."

"Miss Janelle," he began.

"No, please," she said, "just Janelle. I prefer just Janelle."

"Okay," Winston said. He seemed flustered, embarrassed, and Colleen could not remember him ever coming across that way in front of her. It made her feel relaxed and in control, as if she might have to step in and manage or redirect any awkwardness Winston might reveal. Now she understood why he'd wanted to bring her with him. He needed her, and it felt good to play a role for someone, to be relied upon. She looked to the right across the small glass coffee table at Bellamy while Winston spoke with Janelle. Mr. Bellamy was no longer the gruff, demanding history teacher he'd been when she was a teenager. His eyes flicked to hers, and his mouth, which had been slack while he looked at Colleen's father, now flattened itself into a hard, straight line once his eyes met hers.

"Janelle," Winston said, "I've spoken with Ed about what happened out here at your home night before last, and I want to apologize to you as the sheriff of this county. No one deserves to go through something like that, especially after what you've all been through." He paused as if giving Janelle the room to say something, but she remained silent. "The deputy who answered the call without reporting it has been fired from the sheriff's office. I understand that Captain Glenn Haste has interviewed you and your brother, and I want you to know that my office will continue to look into—"

"It was Bradley Frye," Bellamy said.

Colleen's father turned to face him. "Ed, let me finish."

"There's nothing to look into, Winston."

Winston turned back to Janelle. "My office will continue to look into what happened, and if I find the person who broke that window, I will arrest that person. Until then, I can't do anything but warn people away from doing something like that again."

"That's not enough," Bellamy said.

"That's all I can do, Ed."

"That's not enough," Bellamy said again.

"No one could be identified, Ed."

"I saw Bradley Frye's truck flying through here in the middle of the night with that goddamned flag on the back of it."

"I can't arrest him for that."

Janelle spoke up as if attempting to break the impasse. "It's okay," she said. "I understand. Let's just—" She waved her hands in front of her as if signaling Colleen's father to continue.

"Janelle," Winston said, "I hate to have to ask you questions about what happened to Rodney, but I do. They're just going to be routine questions that should be easy to answer, but you take all the time you need."

Janelle inhaled as if she were preparing to do something physical. For the first time, Colleen noticed that Janelle had a tissue wadded up in her hand, and she figured Janelle must be carrying them in her pockets all the time now, having become adept at removing and using them discreetly.

"Can you tell me about the last time you saw Rodney?"

Janelle exhaled the breath she must have been holding, and she turned to look at her father-in-law. He nodded, his mouth even tighter and straighter than it had been before. She began.

"We'd been up late with the baby," she said. "He was colicky, a lot of crying, fussy." She looked down at her lap and paused for a moment. "Rodney was good with him when he was like that. Sometimes he could calm him down, get him settled." Her face drew in on itself in a way that pinched off whatever words she may have planned to say next. She lifted her hand that held the tissue and dabbed at one of her eyes and then her nose.

Janelle gathered herself and raised her face to Colleen's father, her countenance having taken on a look completely absent of the emotion they all knew she had just taken a moment or two to suppress, and Colleen found herself high on the realization that someone else's tragedy was not hers.

"I went back to bed," Janelle said, "but I could hear them across the hall, Rodney singing and talking to the baby. He finally got him down and came into the bedroom. I guess he could tell I was still awake. He told me he wouldn't be able to sleep so he was going to get diapers from the store."

"Did you need diapers?" Winston asked.

For a moment, Janelle appeared betrayed, as if Winston had not believed what she'd just said, but Colleen watched Janelle's face settle again, perhaps thinking, *This man has no idea how many diapers you need.* "Yes, we needed diapers," she finally said. "We always need diapers."

"Which store did he go to?" Winston asked.

"The Food Lion," she said. "Up on Beach Road."

"That's what I was thinking," Winston said.

"It's right up the road from the airport," Bellamy added. "He probably saw that plane come in."

"Did he seem strange or worried or upset when he left?" Colleen's father asked.

"No," Janelle said. "He seemed normal. He seemed like himself."

"Did he have any friends who were in trouble, or had he started to hang around with anybody who seemed like trouble to you?"

"Oh, come on," Bellamy said. He shook his head and looked at the front door for a moment.

"It's okay, Ed," Janelle said. She looked at Winston. "No," she said. "No new friends, no one who seemed like trouble."

"Did you get the sense that he was scared of anyone?"

Bellamy stood up from the armchair. "Excuse me," he said.

"It's okay, Ed," Janelle said again. "These are just questions."

Bellamy stepped around the coffee table, his back turned to the three of them. He had his hands in his pockets, and Colleen could see that he was clenching and unclenching them, the cotton fabric of his pants tightening and untightening around his thighs each time his fingers moved. He stared down at the carpet.

"Ed," Janelle said.

Without turning, Bellamy raised his head as if he were going to speak, but he must've decided against it. Instead he took one of his hands out of his pocket and opened the front door.

"I'll wait outside," he said before pulling the door closed behind him.

Colleen, her father, and Janelle all sat in silence for a moment.

"I'm sorry," Janelle said. "He's just—" But she stopped talking as if unsure of how to explain what her father-in-law was feeling and what had just happened.

"It's okay," Winston said. "I can't imagine what he's been through, what y'all have been through."

Janelle nodded her head as if she'd heard what Winston had said, but Colleen knew she wasn't really listening. Janelle had kept her eyes locked on the door after Bellamy closed it behind him, and Colleen knew what she was thinking: Ed Bellamy was now her only link to this place. Sure, Janelle had her baby, but the baby would keep her at home, anchored there, marooned away from the world. Colleen couldn't help but think about her own life back in Dallas, especially her life after they lost the baby: the long, interminable hours of daylight between the time when Scott left for work and the time he returned home, Colleen wandering the house that now seemed more like a fortress of solitude than a home, all the while feeling alternately enraged and forlorn at the idea that she and Scott could have ever made a life—much less had a family—there. Colleen shifted in her seat and shook her own life from her mind. Winston had returned to his questions, and Janelle's eyes had left the door and settled again on his face.

"Did you ever get the sense that Rodney was in debt, that maybe he owed people money?"

Janelle laughed a little, not at the absurdity of the question, but at the absurdity of what it seemed to imply.

"No," she said. "Absolutely not. Rodney had a great job with Brunswick Electric. They loved him, and he loved it. That job was what brought us back home." She stopped talking for a moment while her gaze took in the small living room around her as if she were making an inventory of the things inside it. "I wouldn't have let him take me out of Atlanta for just any job."

"Is that where y'all met?" Winston asked.

"Yes," Janelle said.

"At Morehouse? He went to Morehouse, right?"

"Morehouse is a men's university," she said.

"Oh," Winston said. "Is there a women's?"

"Yes," Janelle said. "Spelman. But I graduated from Emory."

Janelle kept her eyes on Winston as if the mention of the university might carry weight or mean something to him, but Colleen knew it wouldn't, not because he didn't believe in education or wasn't impressed by credentials, but because he didn't know enough about that world to extrapolate any differences between Morehouse and Spelman and Emory. Colleen knew that to people like her father college was a place where one went to learn something particular, perhaps peculiar, and one school was as good as another. But Colleen knew better. "What did you major in?" she asked, her voice coming out too clear, too bright.

"I double majored," Janelle said, "in journalism and communications. I was either going to write about the news or deliver it on television." She laughed and looked down at her hands, the tissue still clenched tight. "I got an internship at CNN, and I thought I was on my way. And then I met Rodney, got married, had the baby, and we moved here instead."

She raised her eyes to Colleen, and Colleen wondered what to read in her face. Irony? Sadness? Resignation? Colleen had the urge to tell her that it would all be okay, that she could go back to work in the career she had not yet begun, but she fought the urge because she knew how it felt to hear those things when people said them to her as if it were easy for women to start and stop, to have children or to lose them, to rely on a husband who might be out of the house for twelve hours a day or for the rest of your life. Janelle didn't need to hear any empty consolations from people like Colleen any more than Colleen needed to hear them.

Instead, Colleen offered an affirming nod at what Janelle had said, and her face slid into an apologetic smile as she asked Janelle if she could use the restroom.

"Of course," Janelle said. She turned in her seat and pointed at the hallway behind her. "It's the first door on the right, just down the hallway there."

Colleen stood and excused herself.

She heard Winston resume his questions as she closed the bathroom door. When she flipped the switch, the light over the sink came on, as did the exhaust fan, drowning out the sound of her father's voice.

Colleen ran a trickle of water in the sink and sat down on the closed lid of the toilet. She put her elbows on her knees, dropped her head into her hands. How did she get here? How had her life taken this turn? She heard something coming through the wall to her right, something low and muffled moving just beneath the purr of the exhaust fan in the ceiling above her. It was music.

She stood and turned off the water, and then she flushed the toilet and flipped the light switch so that the room was quiet and lit only by the glow of sunlight that came in through the closed blinds on the window behind the toilet. She recognized the song coming through the wall, although she couldn't place it. She wondered if Janelle had left the music on or if someone else was in the house.

She opened the door into the hallway, expecting to find the source of the music, but instead, directly across the hall, she saw a powder-blue wall peeking out from behind a cracked door. And then she heard the soft and unmistakable coo of a baby. She shuffled the three or so feet across the hallway, opened the cracked door a little farther, and peeked inside.

She found what she'd both wanted to find and feared finding. Pale blue walls; an old, weathered rocking chair in the corner; and a white, spindled crib with a swaddled baby boy inside. He was lying on his back with one hand worked free and a tiny fist inserted into his mouth, where his gums worked vigorously against his knuckles. Like all babies, his cheeks were full, and his eyes, even though they were dark, were glimmering with light. Black hair had begun to fill out across his small head, and his skin, which was the same tone as Janelle's, was smooth and crying out to be touched. Aside from her own son, who, strangely, had not crossed her mind in this moment yet was always on her mind, this child was the most beautiful thing Colleen had ever seen.

She found herself pulled across the room as if she were floating, until she stood by the crib in such proximity to the baby that she couldn't help but reach a finger down into the crib and allow his wet, warm fingers to wrap around it. It was as if she'd taken a hit of some powerful drug; her body felt alive and awake, perfectly attuned to life and all its attendant hopes and limitless possibilities. Which is why, later, when she would look back on this moment, Colleen would be shocked to realize that she had not heard her father open the front door to step outside to talk to Mr. Bellamy. Nor had she heard Janelle stand from her chair and walk down the hallway and into her son's room, where she would find a woman, a stranger she'd only just met, standing in the middle of the room and reaching down into the crib and taking her child's hand without permission.

Who did I think I was? Colleen would ask herself later. That question must have been similar to the one Janelle asked herself in that moment, but the words she chose—"Is he awake?"—were not a direct indictment of Colleen's trespass, but the tone Janelle wrapped around those words certainly was, and Colleen flinched when she heard the woman's voice.

She pulled her finger out of the baby's grip, her hand recoiling back toward her body as if the crib were a tank of murky water and an alligator had just emerged from its depths and snapped at her. The sudden movement scared the baby, and he began to cry. Colleen's body spun toward Janelle where she stood in the doorway, and Colleen saw that she had already set out across the room, her eyes locked on her baby. Colleen stepped away from the crib, and Janelle leaned over the side and scooped the baby from the mattress.

"I'm so sorry," Colleen said. *For all of it,* she wanted to add. For sneaking into the room, for touching Janelle's child, for making him cry.

"It's okay," Janelle whispered, but Colleen didn't know if Janelle was talking to her or the baby.

"I didn't mean to scare him," Colleen said. "I shouldn't even have come in here."

"It's okay," Janelle said again, this time clearly speaking to Colleen. Janelle bounced the baby in her arms and made her way toward the rocking chair, where she sat down and lowered the straps on her dress and bra and then raised the baby to her breast. He began to nurse.

The intimacy of the scene pained Colleen, and her own breasts began to ache as if remembering a sensation she had never experienced. She thought her heart was going to explode with grief. She was embarrassed to know that she had made the baby cry, and even more embarrassed to witness—aside from birth itself—the most private and maternal moment a woman can share with her child. She turned toward the door.

"I'm sorry," she said again. "I'll give you some privacy."

"Wait," Janelle said. "Stay. Your dad's talking to my father-in-law. It may be a while."

Colleen turned around, and Janelle gestured toward the matching wooden ottoman that sat in front of the rocker. It had a tan cushion resting on top of it. Colleen slid the ottoman away from the rocker to give herself more space to sit, and then she settled herself on it, her knees close together, her fingers interlocked in the middle of her thighs.

The baby continued to nurse, his eyes open and scanning what he could see of the room from his position, his left arm raised and grasping absentmindedly at the air. Colleen had never been this close to a woman who was breastfeeding a baby, and she tried to look at everything in the room aside from Janelle's exposed breast and the nipple the baby worked in his mouth.

"He's just absolutely beautiful," Colleen said.

"Thank you," Janelle said.

"What's his name?"

"R.J.," Janelle said. "Rodney James, or Rodney Junior. R.J."

Colleen nodded, not taking her eyes from the baby's face. "How old is he?"

"A little over five months," Janelle said.

Colleen was unable to control her mind as it flipped through the Brazelton book. She wanted to tell Janelle that by now R.J. knew her well enough to read her emotions, that he could understand the grief or hope or fear in her face. But the baby had closed his eyes while nursing, and Colleen watched him instead, wondering at the images and thoughts that flashed behind his eyelids. Was she the first person who'd ever scared him? Had anyone else ever made him cry?

The baby's arm continued to move through the air. Janelle touched it with her free hand, closed her fingers around it, and brought it close to her body. She kept her eyes on his face. "This one looks just like his daddy," she said. She sighed, and then she freed her hand from the baby's grip and wiped the tears from the baby's cheeks. "But he cries just like his mommy." Then, perhaps fearing that she'd said something too personal or given too much of herself away, Janelle looked up at Colleen and smiled as if to reset the moment. "Will you tell me something about him?" she asked. "You said you were friends with Rodney in high school."

"Yes," Colleen said.

"What was he like back then?"

"I'm sure he was the same as when you knew him," Colleen said. "It hasn't been *that* long since we were all in high school." But as she said it, she recalled the yearbook photo of Rodney she'd seen two nights earlier, and she combed back through her memories, searching for one that would reveal something about Rodney that Janelle did not already know.

Her mind settled on a face that was not Rodney's, and sharp, tactile memories and sensations of smell and sound washed over her as wholly as if the experiences had been lived just moments before. The face she recalled belonged to a boy named Billy O'Grady. They had all been in the tenth grade together and were probably only fifteen or sixteen years old, but when Colleen thought of Billy O'Grady's face in that moment she recalled the face of someone who looked like a middle-aged man, all sharp angles and sunken cheeks, tawny skin and a fluff of white-blond hair that seemed impossibly bright. She could not recall ever seeing Billy smile or speak, but somehow she knew his teeth had been crooked and misshapen, his accent thick, nearly unintelligible with its deep, twangy country resonance.

"There was a boy we were in school with in the tenth grade," Colleen said. She turned and gazed out the nursery's window as if the glass opened up to time itself, the dense trees lining the backyard less real than the memory she recalled. "Everyone made fun of him because he was poor and his clothes looked dirty, and we— Everyone called him a terrible name."

"What was the name?" Janelle asked.

Colleen kept her eyes on the window. "People called him Butt Munch," she said.

"Oh, my God," Janelle said. "That poor boy. Kids can be so mean." The baby stirred in her arms, and a near-silent moan came from his tiny body, continuing on until it ended in a sigh.

"It's awful to think about now, but we were kids, and no one really thought about it at the time."

"Did Rodney—?"

"No," Colleen said. "That's what I was going to say. I don't remember Rodney being mean to him. As a matter of fact, I can remember them shooting baskets before gym class." She looked from the baby back to the window. "Billy would take these really awkward, dramatic shots from half-court or the three-point line, and Rodney would rebound for him, chase the ball down, toss it back to him." She looked back at Janelle, who was smiling, her eyes wet. "I remember Rodney doing that."

"So that's what he was like in high school?" she asked.

"Yes," said Colleen. "That's what he was like."

"He was still that way," Janelle said. "He was just a really good person."

"That's how I remember him too," Colleen said.

The music that Colleen had first heard in the bathroom suddenly grew louder, and she was aware that a door had opened in the hallway. She turned to see a young Black boy standing in the doorway to the nursery. He wore black shorts and an Atlanta Hawks jersey. His hair was cut close and sharp, and his eyes were large, his body thin and long in the way that all teenage boys' bodies seem when they have not yet learned how to carry themselves.

"Jay," Janelle said, "this is Colleen."

"Hey," he said.

"Hello," Colleen said.

"She was one of Rodney's friends in high school," Janelle said.

"I'm so sorry about your brother-in-law," Colleen said.

Jay just stood there for a moment, his face portraying nothing. "Do we have any Coke?" he finally asked Janelle.

"I don't know, Jay," Janelle said. "I've got my hands full. You can check the refrigerator easier than I can at the moment."

With that, the boy was gone. Colleen could hear his heavy footfalls as he moved down the hallway, across the living room, and into the kitchen.

"I'm sorry about that," Janelle said. "That's my little brother. He moved up here from Atlanta for school, and he wasn't yet settled when all this happened."

"That's okay," Colleen said. "I'm sure it's nice to have him close."

"Not really," Janelle whispered, as if confessing a secret. "He was getting into some trouble, and my parents were just hoping—" She stopped as if searching for the right words or phrase, but she didn't finish. Instead, she looked down at her baby. He had stopped nursing, and he was threatening to close his eyes and drift off to sleep again. Janelle, perhaps sensing Colleen's awkwardness at the things Janelle had just said to her, looked up and smiled. "Do you want to hold him?" she asked.

"Me?" Colleen asked, as if someone else was in the room. "I mean, if that's okay. I'd love to."

"Do you mind burping him?" Janelle asked. She smiled as if knowing that she was offering Colleen the more undesirable half of the feeding process.

"No," Colleen said. "No, not at all."

Janelle lifted the baby toward Colleen. He had opened his eyes and was staring intently at her. She raised her hands and held him under his arms. She stared at him for a moment, making eyes at him, trying to get him to smile. He gurgled and smiled. Milk spilled from his mouth and landed on his shirt.

"Whoops," Colleen said. She turned the baby to face Janelle, and Janelle smiled and leaned forward and wiped the milk from the baby's mouth and shirt. She draped the towel over Colleen's shoulder, and Colleen held the baby so that his face rested there. She patted his back gently.

"It's not any of my business," Janelle said, "but your dad told me what happened to you and your husband, and, again, it's not my business, but I just want to say that I'm sorry."

Colleen stared at Janelle's face, her hand rhythmically patting the baby's back until his body heaved in a small burp. Even then she did not stop patting him. She was shocked, both by Janelle's condolences after her own recent tragedy, and that Winston had managed to mention it in the short time Colleen had been in the bathroom.

Colleen was crying before she realized it. Janelle cocked her head and whispered, "I'm sorry," and she reached out and touched Colleen's knee. Colleen nodded her head, but she didn't know why, and then Janelle reached out her arms for the baby, and Colleen passed him back to his mother. The burp cloth remained resting on Colleen's shoulder. Janelle passed her a tissue, and Colleen wiped her eyes.

"Thank you," she said.

"I hope I didn't say the wrong thing," Janelle said. "I just wanted you to know that I'm sorry."

Colleen thought of Scott in Dallas, all those miles and a time zone away. She didn't want to go back there, but she couldn't imagine living without him after what they had been through, even if it often felt as if they hadn't been through it together. She knew she had to go home, and she found herself wondering what Janelle would do.

"Do you think you'll stay here?" Colleen asked.

Janelle looked at the floor and shook her head. "Somebody killed my husband for no reason. And two nights ago we had the Klan or something show up at our door, shoot off guns, crash a log through my little brother's window. Will I stay?" Janelle said. She shook her head again. "Would you?"

IT WAS LATE afternoon, and Colleen was sitting on the bed in her bedroom, on the phone with Scott. After leaving Janelle Bellamy's house, Winston had driven her home before going back to work. As soon as she'd walked in the door, she'd gone upstairs to her bedroom and called Scott's office in Dallas. He hadn't answered when the receptionist patched her through to his desk, but Colleen had left a voice message, and she'd spent the day waiting for him to call back.

When he finally called back, Colleen had found herself in tears, recounting the visit with Janelle Bellamy, her memories of Rodney, and now the particular predicament Janelle found herself in with a new baby and a younger brother both living under her roof. Colleen had tried to imagine herself in that situation—the murder, the terror, the loneliness.

"I would leave too," Colleen said. "I don't blame her for wanting to."

"But who'd want to live in Atlanta?" Scott said. "It's hot and flat and traffic is terrible, and there's no water. It's totally landlocked."

Colleen laughed. "You just described Dallas to a T," she'd said. "T for Texas." Her mother's half-read magazines—*Southern Living, Ladies' Home Journal*—were open on the bed and scattered all around her.

"Yeah, I guess you're right," Scott said. He was quiet for a moment, but Colleen could feel him thinking on the other end of the line. "Is that why you left and went home? Are you thinking that she should go back to Atlanta because you went back to Oak Island?"

"I haven't come back to stay," Colleen said. "I think Janelle would go back to Atlanta to stay. That makes sense for her."

"That's good to hear," Scott said. "The part about you not being there to stay, I mean."

"I think Janelle should go back because it's not safe for her and her family here, and she doesn't have an anchor," Colleen said. "And she hasn't been here long enough for the place to get inside her, you know."

"Do you think Dallas could ever get inside you?" he asked.

"God, I hope not," Colleen said. She heard Scott laugh. She waited, wanting to say the right thing, the true thing. "But you're my anchor," she finally said.

"And you're mine."

After she hung up the phone, Colleen realized that her body was humming with contentment. She lay back on her pillow and stared at the ceiling, fighting the urge to call Scott back to fan the flame of what she now felt. She had not realized that she had spent the past few months hungering for this feeling until the very moment she felt it. And then she realized something else, something that both pained her and healed her: the conversation that she and Scott had just had was the first serious conversation they'd had without mentioning their son since the day they had lost him. That alone made her want to call him back, made her want to share this news with him, made her want to ask him what it meant. Had they healed? Had they forgotten him? Had they grown used to him being gone? Or had their lives—which is to say *life*, really—just moved on?

She recalled the feeling she'd had as she'd flown over the waterways before touching down in Wilmington, the feeling that her son's ghost or spirit had followed her from Texas. She thought of the nursery door she'd kept closed since coming home from the hospital, of the remnants of her child that she'd hoped to store there without them escaping. But he would be with her—was with her now—no matter where she went. She thought of Janelle and her baby and her brother, Jay, loading up the car for Atlanta, Rodney's spirit watching them leave and then trailing behind them as they headed south, flying alongside the car, peering through the back window at his child where he slept in his car seat.

Colleen dozed off and on, her mind never far from Scott or Janelle or her father or the feeling of holding Janelle's baby in her arms, the scent of powder that lifted from his body and clothes. From her bed, Colleen heard Winston come home, heard him speak to her mother, heard him refuse dinner on his way up the stairs. She opened her eyes. It had grown dark outside.

When she opened her door, she could hear Groom's voice downstairs, talking with her mother in the kitchen. The light was on in her parents' room, and she walked across the hallway and found her father sitting on their bed in his undershirt and pants. He looked exhausted.

"Hey," she said. She leaned against the door frame and crossed her arms.

"Hey," he said.

"You done for the day?"

"Done for the day," he said. "But not for the night. I'm on runway duty."

"I'm sorry," she said. With her father in his undershirt, she saw how thin his arms looked, how much older his body appeared now.

"But I've got some good news," he said. "Groom finished up with that rear landing gear today. We're cleared for takeoff, as they say."

"That is good news," Colleen said.

"One half of the puzzle solved," he said. He had his shoes off, and she could see his socked toes curling against the carpet. "Thanks for going out to Janelle's house with me today. That made it easier, I think. For me and for her. Hopefully, we can find out what happened to him."

"Any word on the bust down in Myrtle Beach?"

"No, no results back yet," Winston said. "But I'm hopeful we'll get a break."

"Me too," Colleen said. "I'm hopeful too.

FRIDAY,
NOVEMBER 2, 1984

CHAPTER 13

Maybe it was the strafing beam of the airport's beacon light that gave Winston the dream that he had, or perhaps it was his sitting up in the driver's seat, his head cocked back against the headrest, his mouth open, sucking damp night air through the cruiser's open windows. The light was in his dream, and so was his breathlessness, and so was the dampness. And so was the airplane.

In the dream it is dark, and Winston and Marie and Colleen are all floating in the ocean, the bright winking light of the Yaupon lighthouse hovering above the horizon in the inky, black distance. Winston knows the three of them are floating with the aid of something hard and buoyant, and as the lighthouse revolves and casts a weak beam like an arm reaching too far to touch you, Winston is able to make out the piece of the airplane's wing that he is clinging to. Colleen and Marie float within earshot, close enough for him to see that they too are clinging to pieces of the airplane, close enough to hear Marie's panicked cries, close enough to hear Colleen's terrifying silence. The ocean roars around them. Winston knows they are being pushed toward the shore, closer and closer to the breakers, where walls of water will soon crash down upon them. His clothes are soaked, and they are so heavy he fears they will either pull him down or be ripped from his body, exposing his skin to the sharp plane debris that floats around him. His fingers grip the wing as tightly as they can. He is terrified of letting go, going under and never seeing Colleen and Marie again. And then he thinks of them floating somewhere behind him. He looks back, sees that the ocean is on fire with the plane's wreckage, oil slicks burning like torches, Colleen's and Marie's faces lit in terror by the orange light.

"Hold on!" Winston screams.

When the radio blasted a voice into the quiet car, Winston lurched forward as if tossed by a wave, his feet kicking as if trying to swim to the surface. He was in the cruiser on the runway, the beacon light behind him, the airplane's silhouette lit by the moon.

"We just got another fire reported in Plantation Cove," Rudy's voice said over the CB.

"I can be there in ten," Glenn's voice responded.

Winston caught his breath, shook the image of the fiery ocean from his mind, and picked up the receiver.

"I can be there in two. I'm right out here at the airport."

"Meet you there," Glenn said.

Winston looked at his watch. It was a few minutes past midnight. He cranked the engine and threw the cruiser into reverse, cutting a wide semicircle before pulling it into drive and gunning it down the runway back toward the parking lot.

There was no traffic and he was already so close that there wasn't any need to turn on his siren or roof lights, but he drove as fast as he could down Beach Road before turning right into the development. He'd known the arsonist would keep setting fires, but he was surprised that he was back at it—especially back at it at the same place—so soon. It meant that, at least to the arsonist, the fires he was setting were personal.

Winston killed his headlights once he'd driven into the neighborhood, the cruiser's running lights giving him plenty to go by. He followed the road to where it ended in a T-bone at the marsh-front properties, and he looked to his left at the house he'd investigated the night before. It appeared quiet and vacant, but across the street from that house he caught the flicker of orange flames coming from another home that was under construction. He watched a truck pull into the muddy yard and turn its high beams on. Someone had beaten Winston there. He turned left and barreled down the road as fast as the cruiser could accelerate.

He slammed on his brakes in front of the house, and when he climbed out, he was surprised to hear someone yelling on the other side of the garage. He grabbed a flashlight and drew his pistol and kept it by his side as he ran up the yard, through the truck's headlights, and around the side of the house. There he found Englehart holding a rifle on someone standing at the edge of the woods. "Englehart?" he said. "What the hell are you doing here?"

"Don't move!" Englehart screamed at the person at the end of his barrel.

"Englehart," Winston said again.

"This is private property, Sheriff," Englehart said, then screamed at the person in the woods, "Get down on the ground!"

Winston clicked his flashlight on and pointed it toward the woods. A Black man was standing there, and Winston held his pistol on him. "Lower your weapon, Englehart."

"Hell, no," Englehart said. "I'm doing my job." He was wheezing, trying to catch his breath after running from his truck.

"You are no longer an officer," Winston said.

"Not for you."

The man at the edge of the yard must have seen an opportunity. He leapt out of the ring of light and disappeared into the darkness of the woods. "Stop!" Winston yelled. Englehart fired into the trees, and the crack of the shot deafened Winston for a moment. "Jesus, Englehart! Stop!" Winston holstered his pistol and ran after the fleeing man.

As he ran, he managed to work his walkie-talkie free of his belt.

"I've got a suspect on foot, heading east through the woods," he said. He ran at full speed. At each turn he took, the woods exploded with the bright light from his flashlight. He could hear the man's footfalls through the trees, and he could make out his movements as he crashed through the undergrowth.

"Stop!" he called. "Sheriff's office!"

The flashlight's beam bounced ahead of him, catching snatches of clothing as branches snapped and rebounded when the figure ahead of him shot past.

Before he knew it, Winston found himself out of the forest and running through backyards, his flashlight fixed on the man's back. He was out of breath, but he did his best to shout into his radio.

"Suspect is a Black male, approximately six feet tall, white T-shirt and jeans." He took a deep breath. "On foot in the Grove."

"Almost there," Glenn radioed back.

The man crashed through a wall of azaleas. Winston wasn't far behind him. Their foot chase had disturbed the quiet community. Dogs were barking and howling from inside fences. Porch lights and floodlights had come on, illuminating yards and driveways and carports.

Winston found himself in a backyard. The suspect raced toward the back of a house and tore through the tall hedges that separated the house from the yard. Winston saw the man's hands grab on to a window and try to raise it. Winston dropped the walkie-talkie and drew his pistol from its holster, aiming it and the flashlight beam at the center of the suspect's back.

"Brunswick County sheriff!" Winston screamed. "Do not make me shoot!" The man's hands dropped from the window and disappeared into the tall shrub. Winston could see nothing except snatches of the man's white T-shirt and his tennis shoes beneath the bushes. "Come out," Winston said. "You're cornered. There's nowhere else to go."

A light came on in the window the man stood outside of, and inside the house someone tore back the curtain. It surprised Winston, and for a moment he raised his gun and pointed it at the person standing behind the glass. It was Janelle Bellamy.

Janelle and Winston locked eyes for a long moment. She squinted against the bright light of his flashlight, his weapon pointed squarely at her chest. He lowered his gun slowly, bringing it down to aim once again at the figure in the bushes, a person whose identity he was pretty sure he now knew.

Winston kept his eyes locked on the area beneath the window that was bathed in light, but he could hear Janelle unlocking and then opening the window.

"Jay," she called out. "Jay, what did you do?"

"Come out of those bushes, Jay," Winston said. "This isn't a big deal. Nobody got hurt. Nobody has to. Just show me that your hands are empty."

The boy lifted his hands above his head over the top of the shrubs.

"Keep them up, and come on out," Winston said. He could hear the siren from Glenn's cruiser growing closer. The bushes began to move, and then the boy stepped out into the open. Winston was surprised at how young he looked, at what a kid he actually was, and he couldn't understand how he'd mistaken his fleeing figure for a man's.

"Jay, I want you to keep your hands in the air," Winston said, "and I want you to turn around and walk backward toward me."

The kid did as he was told. Over the kid's shoulder, Winston could see Janelle watching the scene from the window.

"What did he do?" she asked. "He lives here, Sheriff. That's my little brother. He wasn't breaking in. He's only fourteen."

"Keep coming," Winston said, doing his best to block out Janelle's face and her voice coming from the open window.

"What did he do?" she asked again, but by that time Jay had walked backward all the way to Winston, and Winston had holstered his gun and flashlight and removed his handcuffs from his belt. He closed his fingers around Jay's narrow wrists and clasped the handcuffs around them. He picked up his radio where he'd tossed it on the ground. "Suspect in custody," he said.

Winston turned Jay around so they were facing one another.

"You're under arrest on suspicion of arson," he said. "You have the right to remain silent—"

"I'm calling Ed," Janelle hollered from the window. More porch lights and floodlights had come on in the houses around them, and the yards were suddenly lit up as if it were early morning.

Winston finished reciting Jay's rights, and then he led him around through a little gate to the front yard, where Glenn was waiting for them, his cruiser parked out by the road.

"I didn't do anything," Jay whispered when he saw Glenn's cruiser, the lights still spinning in reds and blues atop it.

"Okay, Jay," Winston said. "Let's just get ahold of Mr. Bellamy. And then we'll find a lawyer for you."

"He wants to ride through here at night and scare my sister? He'll see."

"Okay, Jay," Winston said again. "Please don't say anything else until we get ahold of Ed." Winston led Jay toward the top of the yard, where Glenn stood, the back door of his cruiser open and waiting.

In the distance, Winston heard the sound of another automobile coming toward them, and he listened as it grew closer. All the adrenaline that had abated once he'd handcuffed Jay now flooded back into his bloodstream. He could feel his body reactivating to a threat he feared was on the way.

Bradley Frye's truck careened down the dark, quiet street and screeched to a stop in front of Glenn's cruiser about thirty yards away. The truck Englehart had been driving pulled in behind him. Frye burst from behind the wheel, his gun already in his hand. Englehart climbed out of his truck too, and Winston could see that he was still holding the rifle he'd fired earlier. He left the driver's-side door open and took up a position behind it. Frye pounded across the yard toward Winston and Jay. He stopped ten feet from them and raised his pistol, pointing it at the boy. At the top of the yard, Winston saw Glenn draw his pistol and point it at Frye's back.

"Give him to me," Frye said.

Winston held on to Jay's forearm. With his free hand, he laid his fingers on his .38 where it sat holstered on his belt. "Put that weapon away, Brad. And go home. There's no reason for you to be here."

"I told you," Frye said. "I told you they're wild. And you ain't doing a damn thing about it."

Through the woods behind them, Winston heard the curl of a fire truck's siren as it pulled into Plantation Cove. At the sound, Frye turned his head while keeping his eyes on Jay. He hollered over his shoulder to Englehart, "Get back over there, Billy. You get that under control." Englehart scrambled back into his truck and turned it around and drove back up the road.

"You get out of here too, Brad," Winston said. The tips of his fingers remained on his pistol. Winston saw that Frye's eyes were wild with anger and nerves, and Winston feared that Frye was capable of doing just about anything.

"Give him to me," Frye said again. He moved his pistol from Jay to Winston. Winston drew his weapon and pointed it at Frye.

The only sounds Winston could hear were his own breathing and the rumble of Frye's truck where it idled in the road. Behind him, Winston heard the door to Janelle's house open, and then he felt Jay tear loose from his grasp. He didn't turn to see where Jay was running; instead, he watched Frye swing his pistol around and draw a bead on Jay as he sprinted toward Janelle and the open front door.

A shot rang out, and Winston flinched as a warm spray of blood hit his face. He blinked and opened his eyes to see Frye staggering toward him, the front of his shirt dark and heavy with blood. Frye's eyes stared wildly at Winston, and his lips moved as if he were trying to say something important but couldn't find the words. The pistol slipped from Frye's grip, and he looked down at his chest, gently placing both hands on his shirt. His fingers touched the bloody fabric as if searching for something, and Winston knew that he was watching a man die before his eyes, the force of life slowly leaving him. Frye collapsed to his knees at Winston's feet, and Winston stepped back just as he fell facedown on the grass.

It had all happened with such speed that Winston had not had time to consider the danger he might be in, but now he raised his eyes and scanned all he could see of the street. Someone had taken the shot that killed Frye from a pretty good distance, and they had either disappeared into the night or remained hidden and still. At the top of the road, Glenn had hunkered down inside his cruiser's half-closed back door. He peered around it and looked at Winston. "Where'd that shot come from?" he yelled.

Winston signaled for Glenn to stay low, and then he bent at the waist and crept across the yard toward the cruiser. Winston knelt beside Glenn, his back against the rear fender. "It came from the other side of the road," Winston said.

"Is Frye—"

"Yeah," Winston said. "I think so." He looked down into the yard, and he could see the bottoms of Frye's boots where he'd fallen.

"Shit," Glenn said.

Both of them stayed like that, their breath coming short and fast, the night otherwise resettling itself. A few dogs barked. Winston could hear voices in a few of the nearby houses. He knew people were looking out their windows, trying to figure out what they'd heard, what they could see without putting themselves in danger.

"Whoever it is isn't shooting at us," Glenn said, but Winston didn't want to take any chances.

"We don't know that for sure."

He looked over the top of the trunk toward the other side of the road, and then he rose and raised his pistol, making a long, slow sweep from his left to his right, his eyes scanning darkened windows, roofs, the tree line, front porches, and the shadows cast by cars, bushes, and houses. There was nothing to see, but Winston kept looking. The shot could have come from anywhere, but not just anyone could have made a shot like that in the dead of night.

Glenn crept to the front fender and assumed the same position as Winston. They stayed that way as the thrum of crickets and frogs returned to a low roar, as dogs in backyards settled in for the night, as lights in living rooms and on front porches began to shut off one by one. Soon the only lights left burning were behind them in Janelle's windows and on her front porch, and the only sound was the idling of Bradley Frye's engine where his truck still sat parked in the road.

AN HOUR LATER, Winston sat at the table in the small conference room at the sheriff's office. Jay, freshly out of handcuffs, sat on his right, Ed Bellamy beside him. The boy was a minor, and because Janelle didn't want to bring the baby and because she couldn't leave him at home, she'd asked Bellamy to accompany him, and Winston had agreed. But he'd kept Jay handcuffed and made him ride in the back of Glenn's cruiser in order to scare him as much as possible.

And Jay seemed scared. He sat, his uncuffed hands in his lap, either staring at the flecks of Frye's dried blood on Winston's shirt or turning his head to look at Bellamy for guidance after each question Winston asked.

Jay had told them everything, from hanging out with some white kid in the neighborhood to taking Rodney's rifle out of his closet. He told them about meeting Frye in the woods, about him showing up outside Janelle's house with a posse of men on the night after Rodney's body had been discovered. The kid was scared and angry and hurt, and Winston didn't blame him for what he'd done. He'd wanted to do much worse to Bradley Frye, but now someone had gone and done it for him. It made it hard for him to want to bring charges against Jay, especially with all he and Janelle and Bellamy had been through.

Once Winston and Glenn felt comfortable leaving their spots by the road, they'd gone into Janelle's house, weapons still drawn, to retrieve Jay. Janelle had been in the baby's room, holding the sleeping boy with the light off and the door open. She hadn't spoken or even acknowledged Winston's presence in the doorway when he tried to explain to her what had happened and what they were now doing inside her house.

They'd found Jay, his hands still cuffed behind his back, hiding in his closet, tears streaking his cheeks, his chest heaving in choked-back sobs.

"They tried to kill me," he kept saying.

"That shot wasn't meant for you, son," Winston had said in return. He waited inside the house until the ambulance arrived and the paramedics covered Frye's body. After that, he led Jay out of the house to the backseat of Glenn's cruiser.

Winston left Glenn behind to secure the crime scene and deal with the coroner's office, and he and Jay rode in silence to the office, where they waited for Bellamy to arrive. In the meantime, Winston had already heard from the fire department. The fire in Plantation Cove had essentially burned itself out before they'd arrived. Englehart had been right behind the fire department, none of whom had known he'd been fired from the sheriff's office. They'd left him there, thinking he'd be securing the scene, and that had pissed Winston off. He'd had about all he could stand of Billy Englehart.

Now Winston and Bellamy sat alone at the conference table. Once the questioning had ended, Winston had allowed Jay to leave the conference room and disappear into the restroom.

Winston hadn't said a word to Bellamy about what had happened to Frye, and Bellamy hadn't asked him a thing about the blood spatters on his shirt. Bellamy sat, his fingertips on the edge of the table, his eyes looking down at his hands from behind his thick glasses. Winston watched him for a moment. The room was quiet.

"It's a mess, isn't it?" Winston finally said.

Bellamy spoke without raising his head. "Turn this boy loose, Winston."

"Ed, I can't just—"

"Yes you can, Winston," Bellamy said. "You're the sheriff. You know you don't have to charge him if you don't want to."

"People know what he did, Ed."

"Who?" Bellamy asked. He looked at Winston. "You? That dead boy laying in Janelle's yard? That cracker you already fired? Who knows, Winston?" Bellamy put his elbows on the table and leaned forward. "Jay's parents are coming up here tomorrow for Rodney's funeral. And they're planning to take him back to Atlanta. What his daddy's going to do to him is much worse than anything you can think of doing. I promise you that."

"Is Janelle leaving too?" Winston asked.

"You bet your ass she's leaving," Bellamy said. The force of his words and the anger behind them caught Winston off guard.

A toilet flushed across the hall, and Winston pictured Jay now standing at the sink, washing his hands and staring at himself in the mirror, wondering how he'd come all the way from Atlanta to set houses on fire while people were being shot left and right. Winston figured it must've been a hell of a thing for a kid that age to think about. His own mind flashed back to those moments he'd spent at the barrel end of Frye's gun. Had Winston finally felt what he'd made James Dixon feel all those years ago in the pharmacy back in Gastonia? There'd been no one there to protect Dixon at the last second before Winston took his life, but tonight had gone differently for Winston. He looked at Bellamy where he still sat with his elbows on the table. "You still have that Winchester?" he asked.

Bellamy was still for a moment, and then he leaned back in his chair and interlocked his fingers in his lap. "I'm not sure what you're talking about," he said.

"That sniper rifle you were telling me about."

"I haven't shot that thing in years," Bellamy said.

"Well, I might need to take a look at it."

Bellamy shook his head. "I don't know that I could even find it."

Winston smiled, shook his head too. "I thought Bradley Frye was going to blow my brains out tonight," he said.

Bellamy removed his glasses and rubbed his eyes. "He could have," he said. "But he didn't." He put his glasses back on and looked at Winston. "Now turn this boy loose."

The bathroom door opened out in the hall and Winston heard Jay's footsteps as he walked toward the conference room. Jay stopped in the doorway and leaned against the door frame, his hands stuffed deep inside his pockets. He seemed diminished now, even smaller than when they'd arrived, even younger than when Winston and Glenn had found him, crying in his bedroom closet after Frye had been shot. Winston wondered how he had ever mistaken this terrified boy for a grown man. Bellamy turned his head just enough to see Jay over his shoulder. He looked back at Winston. "Turn him loose," he said.

"I'd really be sticking my neck out, Ed," Winston said.

"I know," Bellamy said. "I know all about sticking your neck out. I know all about that."

Winston sat quietly for a moment, his mind trying to parse the difference between the right thing and the legal thing, and somewhere just beyond his grasp was an answer that wrapped together everything that had happened so far—Rodney's murder, the mystery surrounding the airplane, the fires, Frye's having been shot before his eyes—in a way that made it all, if not palatable, then at least easier to look at without causing anyone more pain. But Winston couldn't find the words, so instead he gestured with his head toward Jay, and Bellamy stood up from the table and walked toward the door. "Come on, son," he said.

Winston stood and walked toward the door too, and he watched as Bellamy and Jay made their way down the hall to the reception area. "No more fires, Jay, okay?"

Jay stopped walking and turned to face Winston. "Yes, sir," he said.

"Come on, son," Bellamy said again.

WHEN WINSTON PARKED Glenn's cruiser in front of Janelle's house, he found Glenn standing out by the road. The ambulance was gone, and with it Frye's body. The Grove had reclaimed its quiet stillness. Aside from the porch light, Janelle's house was dark. Winston knew that by now Bellamy had returned Jay and gone back to his own home, which sat just a few streets away. Winston imagined Jay inside the house now, lying in his bed, staring at the ceiling, replaying the night's events in his head just as Winston himself had done during the drive and would continue to do in the few hours he would lie beside Marie before he would have to rise from bed and drive Groom to the airport for the final time.

Winston got out and walked around to the passenger's side of the cruiser, and Glenn got in behind the wheel. They drove back to Plantation Cove for Winston's car where he'd left it parked at the scene of the fire. Winston looked at his watch; it was after 3:00 a.m.

"Hell of a night," Glenn said.

"Hell of a night," Winston repeated.

On the drive, Glenn told Winston that Janelle had not come

outside after Jay had been arrested, nor had anyone else in the Grove. Glenn had taken a flashlight and searched the street and yards around Janelle's for any signs of the person who'd shot Bradley Frye, but there seemed to be nothing to find. The paramedics had told him that Frye had been shot in the center of his back, that his heart had probably been punctured, and Glenn knew that only a high-powered rifle and a shooter of considerable skill could've done that much damage from that far away.

After they drove into Plantation Cove, Glenn slowed and came to a stop behind Winston's cruiser. He put his car in park and looked over at Winston. "I think we should go back to the Grove, set up a perimeter. Call in patrol. Maybe even knock on doors to see if anybody saw anything."

"I don't know," Winston said. "There's just no way to know where that shot came from. I don't even know where we'd start, especially getting people up out of bed."

"That whole neighborhood was awake when it happened," Glenn said. "No way anybody could've slept through all that commotion."

"Better to wait until morning," Winston said. "Get a team out there."

"Sheriff," Glenn said, "with all due respect, your challenger was shot dead tonight right in front of you. It's in the county's best interest and yours too to make sure we investigate this the right way. There's a vigilante out there who knows how to use a rifle, and he might not be done killing."

"Whoever took that shot saved that kid's life," Winston said. "Probably saved mine too."

"That's not the point," Glenn said. Winston could feel Glenn's eyes probing the side of his face as if trying to uncover something he did not want to reveal. "Is there something you're not telling me, Sheriff?"

Winston clenched his teeth as if conscious that his mouth could open and he could speak and tell the truth at any moment. He and Glenn had worked together for years, and during that time Glenn had been his most trusted deputy, and Winston hoped that one day Glenn would become sheriff because he was honest and consistent and fair. As far as he knew, they had never misled each other or withheld anything, and they'd certainly never lied to one another. But Winston knew that he was lying now; if not lying, then what was he doing? If he were being honest, he would admit that he wasn't sad that Bradley Frye had been shot and killed—and perhaps he would even admit to Glenn that he, if only for a moment, had considered doing the same thing just the night before—but he also wished that Frye were still alive because his being murdered made the way forward more complicated for everybody. But regardless of what Winston wanted or didn't want, in that moment, he knew that he could be either a good man and keep his mouth shut, or a good sheriff and tell Glenn all that he knew. He hoped that if Glenn ever became sheriff, he would somehow find a way to be both a good man and a good sheriff all the time. Winston had always assumed that would be true of himself, but now he knew differently. "Tomorrow morning," he said, "we'll knock on doors in the Grove. Get the coroner's report, see what can be learned about the weapon."

"It's a mistake to wait until tomorrow," Glenn said.

"It might be."

"It is." Glenn sighed and shook his head. He turned and looked up at the house that Jay had set fire to just a few hours earlier. From where they sat, it was too dark to see much aside from the white construction plastic that covered the structure's exterior. "What do you think Englehart was doing out here?"

"Playing security guard," Winston said. "It's pretty clear that Frye hired him to keep an eye on things. I reckon Englehart was trying to get in good with the new sheriff."

"Maybe he was already in with him," Glenn said.

"What do you mean?"

"I don't know," Glenn said. "It just strikes me as strange that Frye sent Englehart back out here after the fire." The mention of the fire seemed to remind Glenn who'd set it, and he looked over at Winston. "What did you do with that kid?"

"Turned him loose," Winston said.

"No charges?"

"No."

"That's what I figured you'd do."

"Yeah," Winston said. "It seemed like the right thing."

"Hard to say," Glenn said.

"It always is."

The two men sat there for a moment as if waiting for the other to either confess something or ask a question that would lead to a confession, but neither of them spoke.

"Well, I'm going to get," Winston finally said. He put his hand on the door handle. "We've got liftoff tomorrow morning."

"Yep," Glenn said.

"All right," Winston said.

Glenn nodded in the direction of the house. "I might nose around up there," he said.

"What are you hoping to find?" Winston asked.

"I don't know," Glenn said. "I'm just not ready to go home yet."

"All right," Winston said. He opened the door and stepped out.

"Sheriff," Glenn said. Winston turned and looked back into the car. "Get some sleep."

"Yeah," Winston said. "You too." He closed the door and walked to his cruiser and climbed inside. He turned around in the cul-de-sac, and as he passed the scene he could see the light from Glenn's flashlight searching the ground around the house.

Winston had only made it out to the development's entrance when Glenn's voice called to him over his walkie-talkie. Winston stopped the car and took the radio from his belt. "Go ahead," he said.

"Sheriff," Glenn said, "you might want to turn around."

WINSTON PARKED IN front of the house and walked up through the muddy yard where Glenn waited at the corner of the garage. Around the corner, the driveway ended at an aluminum door, large enough to accommodate two cars. Here, the side of the house was burned black and charred, except for the spot where Glenn held his flashlight beam on a sheet of bright, new construction plastic that had clearly been placed on the house after the fire.

"What do you make of that?" Glenn asked.

"I didn't think Englehart was in the construction business," Winston said.

Glenn raised his flashlight and shone it along the expanse of the garage. "No windows," he said. "All the other garages in these houses have windows." Winston turned to look at the houses in the distance to see if Glenn was right, but it was too dark, and the other houses were too far away.

"You try raising the garage door?" Winston asked.

"It's locked," Glenn said. "Front and back doors are too. So are all the windows on the first floor."

"A big gust of wind could tear that plastic loose," Winston said. "We might've found it that way."

"I think that is how we found it," Glenn said. He stepped forward, and without speaking, he reached out and tore the plastic off the corner of the house. The staples popped free, and the sheet came down easily. Glenn kept tearing it, backing up as he pulled the whole sheet free. Beneath the plastic, the flames had burned a hole through the plywood and the insulation beneath, revealing charred wall studs and damaged drywall. Winston used his flashlight to knock some of the drywall loose, and he found that it left behind a hole large enough to stick his head and shoulders through. He and Glenn looked at each other, both of them thinking the same thing: they had done something together that they probably shouldn't have done; but Winston was also thinking something that he knew Glenn could not possibly have been thinking: they had come back to one another in this moment of complicity.

Glenn held the flashlight while Winston bent at the waist and braced his hands against the house's exterior and poked his head through the wall. There wasn't enough light, and he'd been able to see only a little of what was inside the garage, but what he saw was enough for Glenn to take a crowbar from one of the home sites and pry open the garage door. Only then, standing at the entrance to the garage, did they have a full appreciation of exactly what they'd found. In the garage's back left corner, their flashlight beams passed over four pallets loaded with brown-paper-wrapped squares that had been shrink-wrapped and stacked waist-high. One of the pallets had been unwrapped, and it was clear that packages had been removed. In the middle of the garage sat a folding table, piled with scales, baggies, ties, and various items. Whoever had been at work here had been comfortable; they'd left behind empty beer bottles, cigarette butts, wadded-up bags of potato chips.

"I'll be damned," Glenn whispered.

For Winston, it all came into focus: the comments Englehart had made about Bellamy on the runway the morning after the plane came in; Bradley Frye's showing up at the crime scene and asking about the FBI; his insistence that Winston keep people out of Plantation Cove; and his willingness to employ Englehart to serve as the night watchman. He'd wanted Jay turned over to him because he was afraid of what the boy might have seen, which was the scene that Winston was taking in at that very moment, the scene Englehart had tried to keep anyone from seeing.

"We'd better find Englehart," Winston said. He called in to Rudy and had him pull everyone off patrol to head for Plantation Cove except for one deputy tasked with locating Englehart. But he was nowhere to be found.

In the hours remaining before dawn, Winston and Glenn set up a perimeter around the scene, and, along with a few fresh deputies, they began the process of cataloging every shred of evidence inside the garage, beginning with those shrink-wrapped pallets.

CHAPTER 14

Winston arrived home as the sun was rising, three boxes packed away in his trunk, each item in each box cataloged and filed. The pallets of drugs had been moved and locked away in the evidence room at the station, waiting for the FBI to claim them, but Winston wanted to hand-deliver the evidence in his possession to Rollins and Rountree up in Wilmington. He and his men had cracked this case wide open, and he wanted that to be clear. The knowledge of what they'd found, how it implicated Bradley Frye, and the high it gave him all coalesced to push his exhaustion aside.

He set the coffeepot in the kitchen, and while it was brewing, he snuck upstairs and peeled off his clothes in the bathroom and took the hottest shower his skin could stand. His mind swirled with ideas and possibilities, some of them hard to decipher through the haze of the past several hours. While they'd worked, Winston, Glenn, and the deputies on the scene had parsed everything that had happened, from Rodney Bellamy's murder to Frye's to the discovery of the drugs there and down in Myrtle Beach. So much of it had come together, and while Winston didn't know exactly who had killed Rodney, he felt certain that he knew why Rodney had been killed: he'd stumbled upon something he wasn't supposed to see, and he may have even recognized people like Bradley Frye. Questions remained about who had murdered Frye, but Winston hoped those questions would wane with time. Bradley Frye had been exposed as a drug dealer—and if the bullet that killed Rodney ended up matching Frye's weapon, probably a murderer too. It was fine with Winston if people in the county believed that the same unseen hand that had landed the airplane was the same one that had shot and killed Frye to keep him quiet.

The shower made him feel fresher, but he suddenly found himself very tired despite his adrenaline. He did his best to be quiet, but Marie woke up while he was getting dressed, and she opened her eyes into the weak morning light coming through the closed blinds and frowned at him. "What in the world kept you out all night?" she asked.

He stood at the foot of their bed in his dark slacks and undershirt. He buttoned up his uniform while he talked. "Marie," he said, "I can't begin to explain all of it." But of course there were things she needed to know. He told her about Bradley Frye's death, and then he told her about finding the drugs.

"That's terrible," she said, and it was. But Winston could read in her face the recognition that it meant that, at least for a while, he'd remain sheriff and the thing they'd both been dreading would not happen. There was a lot left to untangle, but at least Winston would be the one untangling it, not Bradley Frye. He could attend Rodney Bellamy's funeral service that afternoon with the assurance that progress was being made on the investigation and the promise that, hopefully, justice would be served.

In the kitchen, Winston found Groom sitting at the table, a cup of coffee in front of him, his duffel bag at his feet. "Morning, Sheriff," Groom said.

"Morning," Winston said. He picked up the coffeepot and poured a cup, and then he looked out the back window. A gentle breeze came off the waterway and stirred the tops of the pine trees. It seemed like the perfect day for flying. Winston found himself smiling. He looked at Groom. "You're going to hear about it when you touch down in Wilmington," he said, "so you may as well hear it from me. We had us a major break last night."

Groom's relaxed demeanor became serious. He cocked his head. "How major?" he asked.

"It's still early, but it looks like we found about twenty million dollars' worth of cocaine packed up and sitting in a spec house about a mile from the airport. And it looks like we now know who the local was."

Groom's face took on a look of disbelief. He smiled, and then he laughed. He put his hands on the edge of the table and sat back in the chair. "I'll be, Sheriff," he said. "I'll be. Congratulations."

MAYBE IT WAS the news of the bust or the fact that he'd fixed the aircraft and would be in the air soon, perhaps even back home in Florida by that evening, but whatever the reason, the drive to the airport was the most relaxed and talkative Winston had seen Groom since he'd arrived. He asked Winston about who Bradley Frye was and the crime scene and the string of events that had caused the previous night to take such unpredictable turns. Winston told him what they'd discovered, about his plan to deliver the evidence to the Wilmington field office.

"I can't believe they didn't make it any farther than across the street," Groom said. "These guys must've been serious amateurs."

"Well, there's also the bust down in Myrtle Beach," Winston said. "So they at least moved some of it that far, but who knows? We might not ever know. Maybe we can match the prints from that scene to this one. We'll see."

"Good stuff at the scene?" Groom asked.

"Yeah," Winston said. "Lot of fingerprints, which is funny because we didn't find a single one in our aircraft. Maybe they got reckless once they thought it was safe."

"They always slip up," Groom said. "Somebody always gets reckless."

"Other stuff too," Winston said. "Scales, food, handwriting, a pistol, cigarette butts."

They came to a stop at the one stoplight on the island. A newspaper carrier in an old pickup truck rumbled past them toward the beach. Groom followed the truck with his eyes, and he watched it pass until it disappeared around the bend toward Caswell Beach. Then he turned to Winston. "You want to fly with me?" he asked.

"What?" Winston said. He looked over at Groom, expecting him to have been joking, but it was clear that he wasn't.

"Fly with me," Groom said. "You're planning to drive the evidence up to Wilmington anyway to hand it off to the office. You might as well give it to them at the airport instead."

Winston laughed because he didn't know what else to do. The stoplight changed to green, and he made the turn toward the bridge. "In that airplane?" Winston asked. "The one you just fixed?"

"Hell," Groom said. "You're never going to take a safer flight than this one. And think about it, you climbing out of that plane and delivering this evidence on the runway in Wilmington? It'll be like a movie."

It would be like a movie, Winston thought. They'd managed to keep the fact of Groom's departure a secret from the media, but Winston knew word would spread once the aircraft took off for Wilmington. He imagined the news stations would be there, cameras rolling, when Groom came in to land. It would mean something, especially after what had happened last night to Bradley Frye, if Winston had a hand in delivering to the FBI both the airplane and the evidence that implicated Frye. After all, the election was in four days, and while he was now running unopposed, maybe he should consider it. He could call home from Sweetney's office, ask Colleen to pick him up in Wilmington. They could be back in plenty of time for Rodney's funeral.

He and Groom were crossing the bridge now. Winston pictured Colleen as a child in the backseat, asking over and over about the bridge collapsing, about their car plummeting to the water below. As he considered Groom's offer, Winston did not feel the accustomed dread he sometimes felt crossing the bridge—dread at the possibility of descending toward something that may have no bottom. Instead, as the car climbed higher, he felt a lifting, as if—at any moment—he could take to the sky.

CHAPTER 15

Colleen had set her alarm for 8:00 a.m., which would give her plenty of time to wake up and get dressed, have a cup of coffee, and then drive her mother to the beauty shop to have her hair done before Rodney's funeral. She woke up thinking about Rodney, but she also woke up thinking about Tom Groom. He was set to take his miraculous flight that morning, and as she lay in bed, Colleen could feel that his presence was gone from the house. She could also feel the absence of her father, which was something she'd grown accustomed to as a little girl, and that feeling had only grown more familiar as she'd gotten older.

She was in the bathroom brushing her teeth when the phone rang. She stuck her head into the hallway, heard the shower running in her parents' bathroom. She finished brushing and spit into the sink and walked into her bedroom and picked up the phone. She sat down on the edge of the bed.

"Colleen," Winston said.

"Hey," she said.

"Listen, honey." The line went quiet for a moment.

"Dad?" she said.

"Yeah," he said. "I'm here. Listen, honey, I need you to do something for me."

"What?" she asked. "I have to take Mom to get her hair done."

"What time is her appointment?"

"Eleven a.m.," Colleen said. "What's going on?"

"That's plenty of time," he said.

"For what?"

"I'm going to fly up to Wilmington," Winston said.

"You?" she finally said. She laughed. "You're going to fly in that plane?"

"Yeah," he said. "I think it'll be fun. And I have to drive up there anyway to drop some stuff off."

"What stuff?"

"I'll tell you about it later," he said. "Listen, I need you to come pick me up at the airport. We're going to leave here soon, so if you don't mind, go ahead and leave. I'll be waiting for you when you get there. Same spot I picked you up."

"You're going to fly?" she asked again. "You?"

"Yeah," Winston said. "I'll see you in a bit. Tell your mother you'll be home in time for her appointment."

"Okay," Colleen said. "This is crazy, Dad, but I guess I'll see you in Wilmington."

"Okay," her father said. "See you in a bit."

She walked into her parents' bedroom and poked her head into their bathroom, where her mother was still in the shower, steam pouring from behind the curtain, the mirror fogged over.

"Change of plans, Mom," she said.

COLLEEN DROVE HER mother's Buick Regal down Oak Island Drive with her eyes scanning the sky, the clouds, the tops of the trees for any signs of the airplane.

By the time she reached the bridge stretching over the waterway, she'd given up hope of spotting it, knowing that she'd missed the takeoff, or at least, she thought, she'd missed the scene of it not being able to get off the ground after all. She'd missed it because of those few moments she'd sat on her bed, thinking about her father's sudden willingness to get on an airplane, those few moments of talking to her mother before getting into the car. As she drew closer to the top of the bridge, she looked to her left down the waterway in the direction of her parents' house.

And that was when she saw it in the water's reflection as it emerged low over the trees across the waterway. Colleen's eyes followed the silvery glint of the airplane as it rose sharply into the sky, its metallic shell so close it seemed that she could have rolled her window down and reached out and run her fingers over its shiny belly, the huge black propellers on either wing so close that she almost felt their power buffeting the side of her mother's car. She watched the plane through her driver's-side window as it rose slowly, nearly hovering in the air, and she followed it in her mirrors as it passed. She slowed her car to a stop at the top of the bridge, and she climbed out in time to see the wings wobble as the plane leveled off over the ocean and then banked left. It circled back toward land in a magnificent sweep and headed north along the coast toward Wilmington.

As she watched the plane go, relief washed over her body that Groom and her father had made it off the ground, that she had not seen the airplane plow through the trees on its course toward the waterway or nosedive into the ocean after climbing into the sky.

When she arrived at the Wilmington airport, she cruised slowly through the pickup area. She expected to find her father there, standing on the curb, but she didn't see him. She parked near the same spot where her father had when he'd come to pick her up only a few days before. Outside, she could hear and see airplanes taxiing, landing, and taking off, and although Colleen knew her father and Groom would've arrived before her, she could not help but search the skies for the silvery plane she had seen take off in Oak Island. Taxis were lined up at the arrival doors just as they'd been lined up when she'd arrived from Dallas. Although she did not see him, Colleen wondered if the taxi driver she'd spoken to when she'd first arrived was watching her now. What would he have to say about her? A few days ago she had been a woman waiting for her father to come get her after she'd done something unpredictable. Now she could not help but think of the irony in the fact that she was a woman coming to get a father who'd done something even more unpredictable.

Inside, the small airport was alive with people standing in line at the handful of ticket counters, checking luggage and making their way toward the airport's single terminal. Colleen didn't know where her father's airplane would have landed, so she walked toward the huge windows at the terminal's mouth that looked out on the runway, expecting to see something—police cars or FBI vehicles or the DEA or some other sign that people had been waiting to meet her father's plane. But nothing outside the windows appeared any different than when Colleen had arrived days ago.

A small information desk sat in the middle of the airport, and an older woman, probably a volunteer from the community, sat behind it. The woman smiled when Colleen approached.

"My father just landed," Colleen said, but she stopped. She tried to think of what to say next, how to explain what she needed to know in order to find him. "He's with the FBI."

"Oh," the woman said, as if it were the most surprising thing she'd heard all day. "Okay. Well, what airline did he fly in on?"

"He wasn't on an airline," Colleen said. "They flew in from Oak Island. They should've landed maybe half an hour ago. I just don't know where to meet him."

"Okay," the woman said again with a slowness that Colleen thought might cause her to scream. "Let me check on that." The woman picked up the phone on the desk and then searched a piece of paper for the correct number she wanted to call. She lifted the phone to her ear and waited.

Colleen looked back out toward the runway, but she was too far away from the windows to see anything. She turned and looked down the expanse of the terminal, expecting to see her father walking toward her, smiling with relief at having landed safely. But there was no one there that she knew.

"Yes," the woman said into the phone. Colleen turned back around and looked down at the woman. She smiled at Colleen as if getting someone to answer on the other end had accomplished half of what she'd set out to do. "Do we have any flights in from Oak Island today?" she asked. She kept her eyes on Colleen's, nodding as if she was learning important information. "Uh-huh," she said. "Okay." She hung up the phone. "I'm sorry," she said. "There are no flights scheduled from Oak Island today."

"This isn't a *scheduled* flight," Colleen said. "I mean, like, this isn't an airline. I need to know where a plane would land if the police or the FBI were flying it."

"I'm not sure I understand," the woman said. "We don't have any flights today from—"

"Jesus," Colleen said. She turned away from the woman, and then she walked back toward the windows and looked out. She walked halfway down the terminal, and she looked out the windows there. She still did not see the airplane, and she still did not see her father or Groom or the police or the FBI. She could feel her heart in her chest, and she knew her vision was narrowing as if she were looking at the world through a periscope. She walked back to the information desk. The woman saw her coming. She smiled hesitantly.

"I need to use your phone," Colleen said.

"I'm sorry," the woman said. "We just don't have any flights—"

"I know that," Colleen said, louder than she'd intended. "I understand that. I still need to use your phone."

The woman kept her eyes on Colleen and lifted the phone from her desk and set it on the counter between them.

"I need a phone book," Collen said.

The woman nodded, and she bent at the waist and opened a couple of cabinets at her knees. She found a phone book and handed it to Colleen. Colleen flipped through the pages and found what she was looking for. She dialed the number. It was Saturday, well past 9:00 a.m. The office would be open. That's where her father would be. That's where they had taken him instead of leaving him at the airport to wait for her.

A woman's voice answered on the other end. "FBI Resident Agency, Wilmington," the woman said. "How may I direct your call?"

"I'm looking for my father," Colleen said. The woman behind the desk stared at her intently, and Colleen turned her back and spoke quietly into the receiver. "His name is Winston Barnes. He's the sheriff in Brunswick County."

"Okay," the woman said. "Okay, let me—" Colleen could hear the sounds of something—papers rustling, static. She could hear the woman speaking to someone else in the room, her voice muddled as if her hand had been placed over the phone's receiver. Colleen closed her eyes and tried to recall the names of the agents her father had mentioned.

The woman's voice came back on the line. "I'm sorry," she said, "can you hold—"

"Rollins," Colleen said, the agent's name suddenly popping into her mind. "Agent Rollins."

"Okay," the woman said again.

"Is something wrong?" Colleen asked. "I'm at the airport to pick up my father."

"Give me one more moment," the woman said.

Colleen held the phone against her ear with her left shoulder, and she folded her arms across her chest. She closed her eyes tight, realized she was holding her breath while the line remained silent on the other end. And then a man's voice came on.

"Agent Rollins," the man said. "Is this—?"

"Colleen Banks," she said. "Sheriff Barnes's daughter. I'm look-ing for him. He was supposed to meet me—"

"And you said your name is—"

"Colleen Barnes," she said. "Jesus, Colleen Barnes. My dad is Winston Barnes."

"Ma'am," Rollins said, "I understand that you're frustrated. I know your father. I've worked with him. We're trying to figure out what happened."

"What do you mean 'what happened'?" she asked. "What hap-pened? What are you saying?"

"Miss Barnes," he said, "that aircraft hasn't landed. At this mo-ment, we can't confirm—"

"No. That's not right," Colleen said. She felt her knees grow soft and begin to buckle. She straightened her body. She held the phone with her left hand and reached back to the counter with her right to steady herself. "No, no, no," she said. "I saw it take off."

"We know it took off, Miss Barnes. We've been in contact with the airport down in Oak Island. The plane should've landed forty-five minutes ago. We're working to locate it right now."

"Honey," the woman behind her said. Colleen realized she was leaning against the counter, and she turned and saw that the woman at the desk was standing now, reaching her arms out to Colleen as if to steady her. "Are you okay?" the woman whispered.

Colleen looked at the phone in her hand. The agent's voice was still coming from it. She wanted to hang up and call someone who could give her answers, but who? Scott? Her mother? Her father's office? She knew no one would be able to tell her anything because there was nothing to tell. She hung up the phone.

SHE WAS CRYING by the time she made it back to the windows at the mouth of the terminal. She lifted her hands to her face and held her fingers together as if she were praying, but she wasn't praying.

She was scanning the runway for anyone or anything that looked like her father or Groom or the airplane. She tried to control her breathing, and she wiped tears from her eyes so that if there was something to see, she would see it.

Colleen did not know it then, could not have known it, but by May she would be pregnant with her second child, and she and Scott would have moved back to North Carolina, buying a home in Wilmington with plenty of room for the new baby and for her mother should she ever decide to join them. Scott would take a job as a prosecutor at the federal courthouse downtown, and she would spend the summer before the baby was born in September studying for the North Carolina bar exam.

She would be sitting at her desk, her study guide open, pages and pages of multiple-choice questions spread out in front of her, when she received the phone call from Agent Avery Rollins, informing her that her father's body had been discovered by hunters in the woods a few miles north of Burlington, Vermont, near the border. He had been stripped of everything—his badge, his belt, his weapon, the boxes of evidence he'd planned to hand-deliver—but they had identified him by the patches on the sleeves of his uniform and the watch that Colleen's mother had bought for him just before Colleen was born. The bullet that killed him would later match the bullet that had killed Rodney Bellamy, but the weapon would never be found. A few days later, the FBI's Miami field office would finally release a statement saying that Agent Tom Groom had taken a vacation on the same day the DC-3 landed on the coast of North Carolina; they'd had no idea that he was even in the state, and they certainly had not sent him to fix and fly an airplane. The aircraft had disappeared, and so had he.

But Colleen was months away from learning those things. For now, she stood at the windows inside the airport, for how long she did not know, unaware that she was waiting for a plane that would never land. The certainty of her father's death and the possibility of new life were still months away. She saw a passenger jet lift from the runway and soar out over the trees. She watched the airplane flash in the sunlight as it ascended, and she imagined all the passengers aboard it looking out their windows at the receding earth below, while the ghosts of the people they'd left behind floated alongside them, staring into the windows, tapping on the glass, begging not to be forgotten.

Acknowledgments

Writing a book is an incredibly long and solitary process, but I am fortunate to have had so many people encourage me and assist me along the way. I especially want to thank my editor, David Highfill, for helping me find the story, as well as Nat Sobel and Judith Weber for the love and attention they give everything, from my books to my family. I also want to thank Sharyn Rosenblum for bringing her energy and heart to the finish line, and Tessa James for bringing order to the chaos.

Thank you to my incredible students and my colleagues in the English Department at the University of North Carolina Asheville, where writing and literature are not only taught, but valued and sustained. I also want to thank Chancellor Nancy Cable, Vice Chancellor Garikai Campbell, Vice Chancellor Kirk Swenson, and David and Dianne Worley.

My endless gratitude to the Weymouth Center for the Arts and Humanities in Southern Pines, North Carolina, and the Doubletree Hotel at Biltmore Village in Asheville, North Carolina, where so much of this novel was written and revised.

I am fortunate to have an incredible community of family, friends, creatives, musicians, and writers who pushed this book forward in so many ways, and I am so lucky that there are simply too many of them to mention by name. I hope a heartfelt thank-you will suffice.

The best thing about me, as both a writer and a human, is my family. To Mallory, Early, and Juniper, there are no words to express how you sustain my heart and my soul. During the years I worked on this book, we called it "The Mysterious Airplane" because that was how Early and Juniper referred to it. Eventually, they began asking me who flew the airplane, and I did not yet have an answer, so they decided for me: a ghost flew it. That simple supposition changed the course of this novel in profound ways. When it came time to title the book, one day Early sat on my lap and pecked away at the keyboard as I spelled out the titles the girls had in mind:

The Mystery of the Man from the Air Station
The Mystery of the Stormy Coast
The Mystery of the Cat in the Volcano

And finally:

Long Ago People Who Lived Before Us Left a Little Bit of Themselves Behind

and

Many Decades Have Passed and the Human World Is Still Dangerous

Dear Early and Juniper, nothing I have written in these pages is as true as those last two titles. Your mom and I hope to leave something of ourselves behind for you, and we hope to leave it behind in a less dangerous world.